TIME STARTS NOW

MICHAEL WALSH

DIVERTIR
PUBLISHING
Salem, NH

Time Starts Now

Michael Walsh

Copyright © 2020 Michael Walsh

Cover design by Kenneth Tupper

Published by
Divertir Publishing LLC
PO Box 232
North Salem, NH 03073
http://www.divertirpublishing.com/

ISBN-13: 978-1-938888-28-1
ISBN-10: 1-938888-28-6

Library of Congress Control Number: 2020947917

Printed in the United States of America

Dedication

Dedicated to Tiffany, Henry, and Anne.

Table of Contents

CHAPTER 1

Sunday September 18, 2016

L ATER, EVEN I wondered how I could arrive home without immediately noticing the black smoke coming from the house next door.

I had a lot on my mind, which is to say I had descended the proverbial rabbit hole. What led me there wasn't the potential consequences of some foreign diplomatic crisis, or the terminal disease one of my parents was in the throes of—actually, they're both in good health. Rather, it was a cocktail party, although that was a fanciful description of the thing. 'Cocktail party' usually meant a smoky parlor with floral carpet and heavy drapes, men in double-breasted suits, and women more clever than they let on.

Tonight hadn't been that.

What tonight *had* been was the annual faculty party for the Spalding University Philosophy Department. My colleagues always arrived at these shindigs fully prepared. Each of them brought an arsenal of anecdotes about professional conferences conquered, forthcoming publications, and a litany of the slight, but grandiose-sounding ways they were about to upend some traditional philosophical viewpoint. They were always sure to relay these tales with a dizzying array of –ists and –isms, many of which even I had to look up. I, on the other hand, arrived with eyes for a stiff drink—not that it usually helped much—a set of real-time calculations for the first opportunity to make a discrete exit, and a cache of forced smiles and vague expressions like, "yeah, I can understand that."

Now that I was on my way home, and on the wrong side of a three martini high, random scenes from the party buzzed across my mind. I recalled Margo Leslie, the party's host and department chair, showing me into her living room when I arrived as most of my colleagues pretended I wasn't there. My left shoulder still ached after I'd been leaning against a corner bookcase for too long, hoping no one would notice that I wasn't involved in a conversation. Those displays of social agility were nothing to be proud of, but something else had started all this joyless reminiscing. I'd been drifting along the periphery of party conversations when I thought I heard a snide comment about me and my "philosophy of time business."

Had I *really* heard that? Maybe whoever said it merely mentioned it and the sneering tone was something I cooked up in my imagination. And who exactly was it that—

"Damn it!" I said aloud, slapping the steering wheel. *What are you going to do*, I asked myself, *lose sleep because someone you don't even like takes a dim view of your research*? Not so deep down, I knew the answer was probably 'yes.' However, before my self-loathing became truly weaponized, Spalding U's radio station, WSPL, played the first few notes of *When The Sun Hits*, which I hadn't heard in a while. It was a tune by Slowdive, a band I'd grown up with and arguably the preeminent Shoegaze band of the early 90s. The traffic light turned green, and my mind fell into a natural groove with the dreamy lyrics about losing sight of a lover who grows distant as time passes.

Many songs just go from verse to chorus and back again, but this song's chorus actually *blooms*. A collage of memories from the early 90s, activated by the swooning guitars and haunting vocals, replaced the half-seen images from a faculty party gone sour.

The song ended just as I pulled up near my apartment, located in a renovated Victorian house. The edge of my vision was foggy, 'fishbowl-head' as I'd taken to calling it in graduate school. Nothing to do now but get inside, brush my teeth, and settle under the covers.

I started up the front steps to my apartment, thinking mostly about getting into bed, when I thought I heard someone say the address of the house next door. All at once, I noticed four or five college-aged people standing on the sidewalk in front of the house. One of them held a phone to his ear, while two others stared uneasily at my neighbor's house.

I started walking over to them, about to ask what was going on, when I saw black smoke coming from an open window in the front of the house. "Oh, God. There's a fire!" I exclaimed, feeling foolish at stating the obvious.

"Yeah. I just called 911," the young man with the phone said.

My martini buzz evaporated instantly. An older woman named Miriam I occasionally said 'hello' to lived in that house. She was probably still inside. "Did they say how long until the fire truck gets here?" I asked, speaking rapidly.

The young man shrugged and stared at the house. "I don't know. They said they were gonna come, like, right away."

That didn't inspire much confidence. I looked up the street, listening for sirens, but heard nothing. "Did any of you try to get in there?" I asked, getting a response of head shakes and slightly guilty looks. A series of actions unfolded in my mind, all of them starring yours truly, Cal Sutherland. I was no firefighter, yet I couldn't just stand around with these kids.

"Shit," I said aloud as I bounded up to the front door, armed with the cockeyed confidence borne from a total lack of forethought. Naturally, the door was locked. I ran around the side of the house as one of those kids said, half-laughing, "Dude. Just wait for the fire department." I reached the back door and found it locked too. The door had a window. There was a small garden with a brick border next to the back patio. I hesitated.

My life seemed to be a series of situations just like this: If I didn't act, I'd regret it for weeks afterward; if I did act, it would turn out to be a rash decision that I would also regret, probably more so. I pictured breaking the window only to have Miriam come walking along, find me here, and laugh about burning some toast.

Then again, the smoke at the front of the house wasn't from burnt toast.

I wrested a brick from the ground, grimaced for a moment at the window, and then easily smashed it with the edge of the brick. Smoke didn't pour out and choke me, which I saw as a good sign. I felt a deadbolt inside and unlocked it. Once inside, I pictured Robert Redford at the end of *The Candidate* looking into the camera and saying as if to me, "What do we do now?"

If Miriam was here, she was probably upstairs in bed. I galloped through the kitchen to a small hallway and stopped in the doorway to the living room. The room was rapidly filling with smoke. It was surreal to see Miriam's furniture—a small love seat, oval coffee table, and wing-back chair—sitting there as if nothing was amiss, just as she'd left them before going up to bed.

Fire spread along the front wall toward the bottom of the stairs, as black smoke filled the opening to the second floor. I crawled toward the foot of the stairs but had to stop because I couldn't breathe. I stumbled back to the far side of the room, coughing violently as I collapsed on all fours. My eyes stung with tears, and the whole scene momentarily faded.

When I finally stopped coughing, I felt disjointed. The light beige carpet went in and out of focus. All at once it seemed as if this was happening to someone else, like being in a dream with a complete set of your own memories, yet convinced you're seeing the world through another's eyes.

People in movies sometimes wet down blankets before running through a fire. I had passed what was probably a guest bedroom off the hallway that led from the kitchen. Maybe there were some bed sheets or heavy curtains I could soak. As I turned toward the bedroom, I genuinely believed I was in an off-kilter dream world.

A man stood in the bedroom doorway.

Neither of us moved, which made his presence even more unsettling. I just stared at him, wondering for a moment whether the fire had somehow taken physical form so it could finish me off. That was silly, of course, but his sudden presence—where the hell did he come from—unnerved me in a way the fire hadn't. He was a couple of inches shorter than me, with white hair that matched his white shirt. He also wore one of those yellow air tanks like firefighters wore. He held something in his left hand. It might have been a book, but it was hard to focus on anything specific, his mere presence here being so unnerving.

He looked right at me, but he hadn't reacted to me otherwise. Strange, as my presence must have been as surprising to him as his was to me. There was an odd expression on his face, too. Was he trying to hide a smile?

Maybe he was a firefighter. Why else would he being wearing that yellow air tank? I finally recovered enough to shout hoarsely, "I think there's a woman trapped upstairs. We need to get her out of here!" I could hear the desperation in my voice. Yet he just stood there without so much as a glance toward the stairs. I shouted, "Didn't you hear me! There's a woman trapped upstairs!" My growing aggravation dampened my fear and sharpened my mind. It was absurd having to spell this out to a firefighter. It was like the end of *Dr. Strangelove*, where Peter Sellers actually has to convince Keenan Wynn that it's okay to damage a Coke machine because it would help avert a nuclear holocaust. *That* was a funny thought.

"I know," the man said flatly, which wasn't funny at all. He still hadn't moved from the doorway.

"Well, come on! I can't make it up there because of the smoke, but maybe you can." The smoke was getting to me again. Was I speaking incoherently? Maybe that was the problem. The man looked over to the stairs for a moment, then back down at me.

"You know we can't save her," he replied. I barely knew Miriam beyond a few 'hellos' and idle pleasantries, but saving her suddenly became a matter of principle. I resisted the urge to grab this guy by the collar and shake him.

"We *have* to try!" I shouted, trying to get to my feet.

"I'm sorry, but I'm afraid it won't work," he said in an oddly sympathetic way before turning away toward the bedroom. He paused and said to me over his shoulder, "Perhaps you ought to be going as well."

I swore at him and tried returning to the living room. I ducked down as low as I could to draw a breath, but it was no use. If I had the air tank he was wearing, I might be able to make it to the stairs. He wasn't too large. Maybe I could tackle him and get the thing off him. What the hell kind of firefighter acted like this anyway?

I crawled back toward the empty bedroom just in time to see this strange man step into a closet and shut the door behind him. My outrage ebbed as I crawled over and yanked open the door.

The closet was empty.

Part of me must have expected this, because his sudden disappearance didn't feel nearly as surprising as his appearance in the bedroom doorway. I stared into the closet, willing him to materialize out of thin air. *Had he been there in the first place,* I wondered.

Finally, I got to my feet and stumbled into the hallway. It was so smoky that I immediately fell to my knees again and had to crawl through the kitchen. I tumbled out the back door and into the yard, coughing and hacking the whole time.

"Hey buddy," I heard a muffled voice say nearby. It seemed real in a way that nothing during the last couple of minutes did. I turned to see a yellow boot tip a foot or so from my face. A firefighter looked down at me. When I saw his breathing mask my eyes must have grown in alarm because he bent down and asked me, "You okay, man?" I nodded weakly. "Is anyone else inside?"

I struggled for breath and spoke hoarsely. "I think there's a lady trapped upstairs." I heard him shout something down the alleyway about needing rescue and an inch and three-quarter line. What he said seemed so banal that I was convinced it was really happening—at least the part where Miriam's house was on fire.

The firefighter helped me to my feet and walked me to the front of the house. The formerly small crowd of young people had moved to the grassy median on the other side of the road. A dozen more onlookers had joined them. There were now three red trucks of varying sizes parked out front and beige hoses running everywhere. Flames enveloped the entire front of the house, lighting up half the block, overwhelming the artificial glow of the fluorescent lights from the fire trucks. I didn't want to look, but I did. It was an impressive sight, even beautiful in a strange way.

The firefighter walked me to a smaller rescue truck and left me with a paramedic. The paramedic asked if I was having any difficulty breathing or wanted oxygen, but I turned him down. He smirked when I blew a wad of ebony-colored mucus into my handkerchief. A moment later, another firefighter walked over to us. A police officer accompanied him.

"Could I get your name?" the firefighter asked.

"Cal Sutherland," I replied.

"What the hell made you run in there, man?" he asked with a trace of condescension that I didn't appreciate.

"It wasn't something I spent weeks deliberating over."

"Well, go ahead and leave it to us in—"

"What about Miriam? Did you get her out of the house?" I interrupted.

The police officer eyed me suspiciously. "How did you know someone was in the house?" he asked. He reminded me of the grim-looking highway patrol officer from *Psycho* who discovered Marion Crane sleeping in her car.

"I didn't *know* for sure. I live next door and figured she might be inside."

"You live next door," he repeated. "You have any ID on you?" I reached into my back pocket for my wallet and handed him my driver's license. He looked at it without smiling before handing it back.

"You know her well?" he asked.

"Not really. Just to say 'hello.'"

He seemed to consider this for a moment. "Where were you tonight?"

"A party," I said. He asked me for the names of people who had attended the party, claiming it was just routine.

"What about Miriam?" I asked again.

"We were the first engine on the scene," the firefighter said. "But the guys in the rescue didn't pull anyone out as of a couple minutes ago. If anyone was still in there..." his voice trailed off.

"Well, what about the other fireman that was in there?" I blurted out, as if accusing them of playing a trick on me.

He hesitated. "Uh. Which...which one?"

"The one in the house with me." All three men exchanged confused looks.

"The first unit on scene was Rescue 33," the firefighter said.

"One of their guys brought you up here," the paramedic added.

"Why the hell didn't he go upstairs for Miriam when he had the chance?" The three of them exchanged looks again, which was becoming aggravating. "What?" I asked harshly.

The paramedic bit his lower lip. "Well, Dave—that was the guy who brought you up here—he said he found you in the backyard."

"Okay," I said.

"He saw you come *out* of the house. He hadn't been inside yet."

"And we rolled up right when you got here," the firefighter added. The police officer looked at me in a way I didn't like.

"It wasn't him," I said angrily. "There was another guy, another *fireman* in the house."

"What makes you think he was a fireman?" the cop asked.

"He had on one of those air tanks." The three men continued looking at me with a mixture of confusion and disbelief. I felt like I was pleading with them now. "He had on a white shirt. I'm not making this up. I *talked* to him!"

Had I talked to him, though?

"Our lieutenant wears a white shirt," the firefighter said, "but he was in the engine with us. Plus, he'd never go into a structure fire without the rest of his turnout gear."

"And no one else came out of that house but you," the police officer added without smiling, as if it was supposed to be some dramatic coda to a soliloquy.

I felt like I should be angry and indignant. He as much as called me a liar. Instead I felt embarrassed and foolish for charging into a house fire totally unprepared. Even worse, I told them what I'd seen inside when I didn't fully believe it myself.

The three of them moved a few feet away. They talked in low voices, and occasionally glanced my way. I stood up and walked a few paces towards Miriam's house, staring at the hive of activity.

What on Earth had happened tonight?

CHAPTER 2

Monday September 19, 2016

I HADN'T SLEPT well the previous night, so I overslept this morning and got to my office later than usual. I put forth a less than heroic effort to avoid dwelling on the fire. In my defense, living next door to the burned out house didn't help. Getting to my office at Spalding U was a relief. I had a graduate seminar this afternoon that I hoped would take my mind off things.

I settled in at my desk to make some notes on a journal article for an upcoming class. After a while I glanced up at the black and white poster of Orson Welles smiling knowingly during a key moment in *The Third Man*. It felt like he was mocking me. I heard a light tapping at my office door and looked up to see Margo Leslie, Chair of the Philosophy Department, standing in the doorway.

"Morning Cal. Mind if I sit down?" She sat down before I could answer.

"I guess I'll get over it," I said.

"So what's new?" she asked brightly.

"Not much," I replied, trying to sound noncommittal. In contrast to the rest of my colleagues, Margo and I got on easily. She was an iconoclast, often about intellectual matters, which rubbed some other faculty members the wrong way. They didn't always appreciate her good-natured ribbing and what could best be described as locker-room talk. Margo could fill a room, but she wasn't full of herself. She sometimes came by to chat me up, even though she knew how small talk made me ill at ease. That was the thing with Margo— small talk with her didn't feel like small talk.

"Good weekend?" she asked. I thought I saw her look at me a little longer than necessary when she asked.

"Eh, uneventful."

"Was it now?" she said eagerly. "And don't try to tell me the faculty party I gave was the highlight, because I know what an anti-social stiff you are."

"If you wanted to thank me for making your party such a smashing success, you could have just sent a card."

"I could've." She shrugged. "But then I wouldn't get to ask you why the police were checking up on your whereabouts for Saturday night."

"Damn it," I spat.

"Oooo," she said with glee. "So there is something more to this!"

"No," I said, trying to make it sound final.

"Oh, c'mon Cal, it's just us girls. You're not on the lam, are you?"

I paused for a moment, trying to think of how and what to explain. "The house next door to me caught fire."

"My goodness," she said, genuinely concerned. "The fire didn't damage your place, did it?"

"No, no. Nothing like that. They got it out relatively quickly. In fact, the fire had just started as I was pulling up."

She seemed to consider this for a moment. "Well, other than being the house next door, what does this have to do with you? More to the point, what does it have to do with me?"

I'd been hoping the next part of the story wouldn't come up. I rolled my eyes as I answered. "Well, I went into the house and—"

"You mean while it was on fire?"

"Yeah. I kind of knew the woman who lived there, and these kids were just standing around out front when I pulled up. The next thing I knew I was breaking a window and going in through the back door."

"Well, I'll be damned," she said, clearly impressed. I felt the color rise in my face. The more I reviewed it in my mind, the more foolish I felt for going into that burning house. I hadn't come close to saving Miriam. Plus, there was the 'other thing' after I got inside. "So Jack *was* right," she said.

"About what?" Jack was her husband, an insurance broker. A nice enough guy, but I didn't like that he and Margo were talking about me.

"That the police figured you set the fire."

"Wonderful," I grumbled.

"Arsonists are often attention-seekers. Jack's heard of dozens of cases where an arsonist will turn up at the scene of a fire that he himself set, even trying to quote-unquote help out the firefighters. Or, in your case, set a fire to have the opportunity to show off."

"I hope you weren't that forthcoming with the police."

"Certainly not," she snapped. "I just mentioned that you were an attention whore, and that I felt sorry for you, what with all the money problems and legal woes you're having at the moment."

"Thank you," I smiled.

"Anyway, I wouldn't worry about it. You have an airtight alibi that three-fourths of the Philosophy Department can confirm. I'm just glad you turned up here today, safe and sound." She paused for a moment. "Talking of which, you have your, uh, seminar today?"

"Yes. My 'uh' seminar is today," I said.

"It's going all right then?"

"Fine," I said, waiting for her to work up to whatever was on her mind.

"How many students are enrolled again?"

"You're the department chair, Margo. You already know the answer to questions like that. What are you trying to tip-toe around?"

She sighed and smoothed out her pant legs. "I think I'd like you to offer something more…let's say, traditional next time around."

"What's wrong with what I'm teaching?"

"Well, nothing per se. It's just…"

"Just what?" I asked, sounding more indignant than I'd intended.

"Now hold on, Cal. I'm on your side. But you have to remember there are other points of view I have to consider."

"Such as?"

"Our department is developing a reputation for biomedical ethics."

"Which I don't have much taste for," I interjected.

"Nor do I Cal, but that isn't the point. You've got all of seven students in your seminar, and we could easily get four times that many if Hardwick taught a biomedical ethics class."

Bruce Hardwick had been in the department about ten years longer than I had, although 'in the department' was a relative term. He'd become a sacred cow in the field of biomedical ethics and rarely condescended to actually teach a class—and even when he did, 'preening' would probably be a better description for it. He spent most of his time padding his already lengthy CV by jetting off to conferences on the university dime. As far as I could tell, he'd been publishing the same two or three articles for the last eight years, making only minor revisions to them and changing the titles.

My mind flashed back to Saturday's faculty party. As I'd made my way around the party—mingling without really mingling—I briefly joined in on a conversation he and some others were having. The conversation centered on Hardwick, of course. When I casually inquired what they were discussing, Hardwick seemed to think it was a chore to have to explain it to me. The rest of the group was mildly amused, which I didn't appreciate.

"So Hardwick is pissed I'm teaching a seminar this fall while he's pulling a Jerry Hathaway and using his newfound grant money to renovate his house?"

Margo looked around uncomfortably hoping no one walked by and overheard that. I'd gone a bit too far with that remark. "Sorry, Margo. I know you've got plenty of people around here to try and keep happy."

She nodded. "It isn't entirely a numbers game, Cal, but the plain fact is that enrollment *does* figure into my decisions about teaching assignments. Therefore, so does subject matter."

"Ah," I said, catching on.

"It's what you teach, Cal. I mean…philosophy of time and time travel?" She said this as though she herself were trying to understand it.

"It's a legitimate area of study within metaphysics," I said. "It may not be that popular, but it isn't any more far out than some other areas of philosophy. Just because biomedical ethics is the flavor of the moment doesn't mean—"

"Hold it a moment, Cal. Physicians *actually* practice medicine. They *actually* deal with many of the issues discussed in biomedical ethics. Now, when was the last time you bumped into a time traveler?" I stared hard at her for a moment before looking away. After a while Margo continued. "Look, you know there was some opposition to offering your philosophy of time course as a graduate seminar. I was the one that helped push it through. I didn't mind doing it, either, but I can't do it again any time soon. Not when there's greater interest in other subjects."

"Okay," I said flatly.

"We all go through these infatuations with unusual areas of study," she said. I caught her glancing surreptitiously at the classic film posters I had hanging on the walls. "So, you've had your fun, you've enjoyed it, and you're working on a journal article too, right?"

I had written an article on time travel and ethics following a colloquium this past April. It was already turned down for publication twice, but Margo didn't know that. "The best thing to do, Cal, is focus on getting tenure during the next academic year. You could use another article under your belt before the penultimate tenure review meeting next spring. After that, your turn at a graduate seminar will come up again, and who knows what you'll find yourself interested in."

We chatted for another minute or two, even though my mind was elsewhere. This must have been how people who worked regular jobs felt when the boss sat them down for a talk about a lack of productivity. The trouble was I enjoyed what I studied. I enjoyed it very much, and maybe for purely personal reasons. Couldn't I just be left alone to pursue it?

Being left alone, however, didn't seem to be a possibility any more.

§ § §

I got back to my apartment around 5:30, following my seminar. I made some spaghetti and garlic bread but didn't feel like eating all of it. By the time I finished the dishes the sun was setting. I rolled up a skinny joint and cracked the side window of my bedroom, which faced Miriam's burned-out house. Most of its front was either badly charred or missing, and there were gaping holes in the roof. Yellow caution tape hung limply around the front porch, and someone had boarded up the window I'd broken on the back door.

I took my time hitting the joint and stared at the house as day turned into twilight. As often happened when I smoked up, my mind bounced along in many different directions at once. Inevitably, they turned back to my conversation with Margo earlier today.

Philosophers—who never tire of drawing distinctions—sort those who study the nature of time into roughly two camps: the presentists and eternalists. As the name suggests, presentists argue that only the present moment is real. The past was formerly real, while we were experiencing it, but no longer exists. The future has yet to occur, so it will become real at some point, but is not yet real. Eternalists, on the other hand, take the position that the past, present, and future are equally real. Yes, it may no longer be the year 1951, but 1951 is just as real as the present moment even if we aren't experiencing 1951 in the same way we experience the present moment.

I was solidly in the eternalist camp. While that didn't have the same cachet as being an impressionist painter or a libertarian, being an eternalist did have one very important implication: it meant I believed in the possibility of time travel. After all, in order for one to travel back in time, the past has to be a real "place" one could actually arrive at.

This belief in time travel put me at odds with much of the philosophical community. Those who bothered to think about it didn't believe that time travel was even possible. Among other reasons, travel to the past opens the door to closed causal loops, or as they are usually misnamed, paradoxes.

Ordinarily, one event causing another isn't problematic. The sun emerges from behind a cloud and *causes* the air temperature to rise and flowers to bloom. The sun came out first and the other events occurred later in time. Nothing extraordinary there. Introduce the possibility of time travel, however, and matters quickly go off the rails.

Off and on during my life, I dreamed of writing a screenplay for a great film. If I had a time machine, one would think I'd be in an awful hurry to travel back in time so that I could "write" a screenplay that had already been written and take the credit for it. Seems straightforward enough, and haven't there been dozens of movies where something like this happens?

So let's say I settle on 1950's classic *All About Eve*. I travel back to late 1948, presumably just before Joseph Mankiewicz has started work on the screenplay I revere so much. I arrive in 1948 and turn in my own copy of the screenplay to the poohbahs at Zanuck Studios. Voila! *All About Eve* premieres to wide acclaim in 1950, and we see 'Written for the Screen by Cal Sutherland' during the opening credits.

At first glance, this seems like a perfectly coherent plan. Now take a closer look: the hall of fame screenplay for *All About Eve* is what caused me—in 2016—to travel back in time in order to turn in the screenplay for the very film that caused me to write the screenplay. Put another way, I would have caused a film to exist which *later* caused me to undertake the action that caused the film to exist in the first place! It's a bit like claiming that my being wet at 1:00 pm caused it to start raining a half hour earlier at 12:30 just so my hair would be dripping at one o'clock. This is an example of a closed causal loop. If it sounds incoherent, it most certainly should. Future events can't cause past events that bring about the future events that led to the existence of those past events in the first place.

Knowing all this may not ruin the plot of *Terminator 2*, but to most philosophers it makes the prospect of time travel impossible. Any trip back in time, they reason, would necessarily involve a closed causal loop of some kind. I, however, didn't believe that. Rather, I figured there was a great deal that a person *could* do if he traveled back in time. That, for better or worse, was my primary area of research. However, as Margo had correctly pointed out, there were no time machines and time travelers. I wasn't just barking up the wrong tree, I was barking up a tree that didn't even exist.

I tried not to let that bother me, but it did. I was coming up for tenure soon. If I got it, I'd have a job for life. If I didn't get it, I'd be lucky to find a job where I spent forty hours a week in a cubicle, or running around town chasing after someone else's shit. I didn't have any other serious philosophical research interests, so I didn't know what I'd do for the next couple of years.

I stubbed out my joint and watched Miriam's house fade into the darkness.

Tuesday September 20, 2016

It was another one of those weekday evenings where I'd run out of things to do around six o'clock. I decided to walk up the street to get a coffee. As I left my building, a car pulled into Miriam's driveway. I didn't pay much attention to it. There had been cars and trucks coming and going from there since Sunday afternoon. I continued down the front steps and started up the street.

"Excuse me," a female voice called out. I turned to see a man and woman walking toward me. "Do you live here?" she asked.

"Mm-hmm," I answered warily.

She gave a sad smile. "Then it was you the other night?"

"Sorry?"

"During the fire. One of the firefighters told us a neighbor went into the house to try and save my mother. We only caught a glimpse of you that night. There was a lot going on."

"Oh," I replied blankly. It was all I could think to say.

"I'm Nancy. This is my husband Eric," she said, pointing to the man behind her. We nodded at each other. She stopped for a moment, apparently trying to compose herself as her husband looked on sympathetically. "I was hoping to run into you, because I wanted to say how much we appreciated…"

"Forget it," I said before she could finish. "I just wish I could've…well, you know." A moment of quiet lingered. "I knew your mom a little bit. You know, just to say 'hello.' She seemed like a very nice person. I'm sorry this happened." Nancy nodded and pressed her lips tightly together.

Eric put his hands on her shoulders to comfort her. "We just stopped by to go through what's left of the place one last time before they tear it down next week," he said. "Technically we're not allowed inside, but I think we've got a right."

"No argument there," I said. "Is there much left?"

"A little," Nancy said. "A lot of my mom's things were burned up."

"Or water-logged," Eric grumbled.

"I'm glad you were able to recover a few things," I said, beginning to feel uncomfortable. I genuinely felt bad for them, but I had no idea what to say to these people other than the usual bromides.

"There was one thing we weren't able to find the other day when we were here," Nancy said.

"Oh?"

"My brother's old Bible."

"Well, I guess that would be a tough thing to find after a fire. Especially with the thin paper they use in Bibles."

Nancy shook her head in frustration. I hoped I hadn't said something insensitive. "It wasn't where my mom left it. It should've been in the back bedroom downstairs, but when we were here on Sunday we couldn't find it."

That piqued my curiosity, though I couldn't say why. "If you don't mind me asking, how do you know it would've been there?"

Nancy sighed. "That was my brother's old bedroom. The Bible was a First Communion present."

"Have you asked your brother about it? Maybe he has it and doesn't realize it," I said, trying to be helpful. As I said this both of them flinched.

"My brother was killed in a car accident," Nancy said solemnly.

"Shit," I hissed, wanting to disappear. "I'm sorry, I didn't know that."

"It's all right," she said, waving her hand dismissively. "Mom kept the Bible in his old room. Every night, before she went up to bed, she would go into his room and pray for him on that Bible. I know how it sounds, but she felt like she was talking to him. She used to say that she didn't want him to think she'd forgotten about him just because he died." This time I was smart enough to keep quiet. I was an atheist myself, but I could hardly fault Miriam for mourning her late son this way.

"Anyway," Nancy continued, "I know Mom would've wanted to be buried with his Bible. I just can't imagine what happened to it."

"Probably a firefighter got sticky fingers," Eric said.

"Oh Eric. A firefighter wouldn't take a Bible. It's not as if it was worth any money. We'll find it somewhere."

I wished them luck with their search, but I knew that Bible was long gone. It was a victim of the fire, just like Miriam.

Wednesday September 21, 2016

And...Done!

My undergraduate metaphysics students had a paper due in two weeks, and I'd just finished writing up a list of topics to hand out in class tomorrow. As the list of topics rolled off the printer, I heard a faint chime amidst the Doves album that was playing. I clicked over to the tab with my email and stopped breathing for a moment. I had a new email with 'editor@namphilreview' in the 'from' column. The title of my latest manuscript was in the subject column.

I'd been dying to hear back about my article, so naturally the first thing I did was sit there staring at the screen, idly wondering what the message said. This was the third journal where I'd submitted the manuscript. The previous two journals seemed wholly uninterested in the article and hadn't even given me suggestions for revisions. I sometimes wondered whether manuscripts were truly blind reviewed.

My latest attempt was with the *North American Philosophical Review*. It was a second-tier journal, but still perfectly respectable. I took a deep breath and clicked on the email. 'Dear Prof. Sutherland:' it began. I got halfway through the first sentence when my heart sank.

Thank you for submitting your manuscript entitled "Time Travel and the Ethical Safeguards of Closed-Causal Loops," which we regret we must decline on editorial grounds.

The rest of the letter was boilerplate about how many perfectly good articles are rejected and how they hoped I'd find some success elsewhere—as though they were sitting around holding their collective breath for poor Cal Sutherland to catch a break.

"Fuck!" I slammed the keyboard drawer closed.

CHAPTER 3

Thursday September 22, 2016

A NIGHT'S SLEEP must have done me some good, because I didn't wake up with yesterday's rejection foremost in my mind. There were other journals, after all, or so I told myself. I showered, shaved, and walked to the nearby corner store for a newspaper. It was mid-morning, always my favorite time of the day, especially on a weekday. Today was sunny and just cool enough to remind everyone that it was becoming autumn.

The Beechtree Avenue section of town—dubbed the Beechtree Village by the zipper vest and Subaru crowd or the Beechtree Strip by everyone else—was an older neighborhood that had become "urban chic" during the last few years. It was a bustling commercial district lined with prideful independent businesses and teeming with self-satisfied hipsters. I don't always care for that vibe, but I love the look of the neighborhood. I often pictured this neighborhood in some past era, with porch swings, men in fedoras, and pig-tailed girls jumping rope on the sidewalk as the sun set on an April evening.

I noticed the rhythm of people in passing cars going to work, caught up in a stream of mundane tasks. I felt bad for them. I had an enviable work schedule and made it a point to notice the shops along Beechtree Avenue opening for the day while everyone else just passed them by. It sometimes seemed as if it were all happening just for me.

As I returned to my apartment, I noticed a white-haired man in Miriam's front yard looking up at her house. I figured he was from the insurance company or something. I nodded 'hello' to him as I walked up my front steps. He answered with what sounded like a British accent. I went inside, closed the front door behind me, and froze.

Was that the man I saw inside Miriam's house during the fire?

Of course it wasn't. That was as paranoid as it was ridiculous. Then again, the man in the fire had white hair, too, and he was about the same height. I thought about going back outside to talk with him, in the light of day this time.

Then I realized why it couldn't have been him: whoever was in the house with me that night got a good look at me. The man outside Miriam's house just now had clearly seen my face, yet he hadn't given me a second glance.

I continued up the stairs and into my apartment. I dropped the newspaper on the couch and just stood there. My heart beat more rapidly than it should. I crept into my bedroom as if someone was watching and listening to everything I was doing. I went to the side window and cautiously looked out just in time to see the man walk up the driveway and into the backyard. I fully expected him to look up at me and give a sinister nod, but he kept his eyes on the house the whole time. He looked the house up and down and stopped at the back door. I saw him touch the wood that covered the window I'd broken. He frowned and appeared unusually curious about it. He wore an olive-colored suit jacket and took a small notebook out of his breast pocket to write something.

My mind was an utter tangle. I felt just as powerless to continue standing here as I did to go out and talk with him. Then another thought occurred to me.

I could follow him.

That seemed like my most ridiculous idea yet. Following him would either end with me learning nothing—very likely—or with him catching me and my having to brush it off with some half-baked excuse—somewhat likely. Then again...

"Aw fuck it," I said aloud. There was no telling how long this would take, so I threw my lecture notes into my shoulder bag in case I had to drive straight to Spalding for my afternoon class. I flew out the door and down the stairs. When I got outside, I casually looked over toward Miriam's house but didn't see the man there. My car was parked two houses away, so I sat in the driver's seat waiting for him to leave. I wished I had a straw hat to throw onto the shelf below the back window like the undercover detectives in *The French Connection*.

A minute after I got into my car, the man walked down the driveway. I instinctively hunched down in my seat, but he never looked my way. He got into a small black sedan and pulled away from the curb.

"Here we go," I said, allowing a moment to go by so that he would stay far enough ahead of me. At the next intersection I held back to let another car get between the two of us. He drove down a few other residential streets. He didn't seem familiar with the neighborhood, because he backtracked a little and nearly turned the wrong way down a one-way street. Finally, we turned left onto Beechtree Avenue. I had to smile when I guessed correctly that he was turning onto the expressway. It was a shame I hadn't grabbed my *Vertigo* soundtrack when I left. It was a bright day, just like the first time Scottie followed Madeline around San Francisco.

I stayed a few cars back from him on the highway. I usually took the same route to Spalding. There were a number of commercial office parks near the campus. I pictured myself following him into one of the nondescript glass office buildings and cooking up a cover story so that the receptionist would let me in. I even imagined being especially daring and following him into an elevator, standing just behind him with a knowing look on my face. But I could never pull that off. I wasn't that smooth.

Worse still, even if I tracked this guy to where he worked and found out his name and title, how would that begin to explain why he was in Miriam's house during the fire? What's more, he'd done a pretty good job disappearing that night. He probably didn't want to be discovered. How might he react if he knew he was being followed?

I put it out of my mind as his right turn signal came on. He was taking the same exit I usually took to Spalding. I went extra slow around the ramp as we merged onto Marenda Boulevard. I could see the top of the red brick clock tower at the center of Spalding's campus. I was two cars behind him in the right lane as we came to the last intersection before the entrance to campus. I prepared to turn right.

He kept going toward campus.

I threw my hands up in a futile gesture of confusion. What the hell was he doing at Spalding? Did he know I was following him? If he saw me that night and knew I lived next door, he could've found out all about me. He probably even knew my class schedule; it was online after all. Maybe he led me here today just to have it out with me.

I started to sweat as he continued through the campus. The school's three and four-story red brick buildings were usually a pleasant sight, but right now I barely noticed them. What could I say to this guy if he confronted me? Then again, what did I need to say? I worked here, didn't I? I even had my notes with me for my afternoon class. I had a perfect right to be here. So what if the two of us happened to arrive at the same time?

He turned toward a section of the campus that I was only vaguely familiar with, some distance away from the Philosophy Department. Spalding dated back to the late 19th century. Noll Hall, the cathedral-esque home of the Philosophy Department, was built during the 1920s. The man I was following pulled into a small parking lot outside a newer-looking building. It was a charmless square structure made of brown bricks that reflected a total lack of effort to blend in with the surrounding campus. It was probably built during the style-bereft 1960s or early 70s.

The parking lot was too small for me to enter without being noticed, so I rolled past and made a U-turn a little farther down the road. I watched him get out of his car and turn away from me toward the building. I stared open-mouthed as he walked up the front steps and disappeared inside, just like he seemed to disappear into that closet the other night.

My mind was a sea of doubt. Had he really been in the house that night?

Had *anyone* been in the house? Who was I following just now? I rolled slowly past the parking lot. The name of the building was Dancy Hall. Then I noticed something else.

His sedan had a faculty parking tag hanging from the rear view mirror.

Friday September 23, 2016

Finding out who I'd been following turned out to be easy. A quick search of Spalding University's website yielded a list of departments in Dancy Hall, along with photos and CVs of the faculty. The man I followed was a member of the Physics Department.

Lionel Bradshaw.

As I now sat outside Dancy Hall, I pictured his photo in my mind. His white hair and small brown eyes made him look like any one of a hundred-thousand grandfathers. He also appeared to be hiding a smile, as if he knew something none of the rest of us did. That sent a chill up my spine. He gave me the same half-smile in the fire that night—a strange mixture of amusement and sympathy—just before he disappeared into Miriam's closet.

From his CV I learned he was originally from England but had been teaching at Spalding for a little over 20 years. He was a full professor who specialized in quantum engineering, whatever that was. Some of his published articles contained words in the title like 'polarization and magnetization,' 'temporal waves,' and 'electro-deposited multilayered wires.' He didn't seem to pad his CV like most academics. For someone who'd been around as long as Bradshaw was, you'd expect a CV of at least 20 pages consisting of the same few publications and presentations with slightly altered titles. Bradshaw's CV was well under 10 pages. So what had he been doing all this time?

I'd been sitting outside the entrance to Dancy Hall for about fifteen minutes, hoping Bradshaw might walk out and I'd overhear part of a conversation. Yesterday I sat here for over a half hour. Finally, I decided to do what was either the smartest or the foolhardiest thing yet: go inside the building and poke around a little.

§§§

"Are you sure this job is worth the trouble?" he asked the man in the suit.

"No turning back now," the man in the suit replied cheerfully.

The first man pursed his lips. "Even so, there's a bit more danger in this one."

"I don't know that 'danger' is the word, but I am taking more than the usual precautions." He nodded toward a yellow air tank leaning against a wall in the far corner.

"Including visiting what's left of the house in broad daylight?"

The man in the suit frowned. "Yes. Including that."

"You know he followed you again," the first man said gravely.

"He was rather hard to miss the other day, wasn't he?"

"Do you know who he is?"

The man in the suit chuckled. "As a matter of fact I do, though you may want to sit down for this, Roger." He reached behind him and picked up a folder, opening it so the first page of its contents was visible. "I managed to attend a colloquium he spoke at last April. That's a copy of the paper he delivered."

"Jesus Christ!" the first man exclaimed as he flipped through the paper.

"Indeed."

The first man spent a few minutes skimming through the folder as his companion looked on. "So this is why he's been following you?"

The man in the suit shook his head. "I don't think it is at present."

"But how can you say that? I mean, look at this," he said, waving the folder in front of him.

The man in the suit put his hand out to calm his companion. "I'm not saying this bloke's field of study isn't rather an amazing coincidence, but I believe there's another reason he's so interested in me."

"Which is?"

The man in the suit turned serious. "Think it through a moment, Roger."

Roger put down the folder and stared intently at the floor. Suddenly he looked up in alarm. "God, no!"

"It would appear he's seen me somewhere before."

"And this is the next door neighbor? I warned you this isn't worth the trouble."

"Call me a soft touch, if you like. I know how much it would mean to that poor woman's family."

"Do you think he'll figure out what we're doing? If he hasn't already, that is."

"He might, actually."

"What should we do about him then?"

The man in the suit chuckled again. "Well, we're not going to assassinate him, if that's what you're asking."

"Do I need to remind you he's been following you? He's been inside this building."

"I know."

Roger threw up his hands. "What, and that's it?"

The man in the suit shrugged. "Warning a fellow off isn't really our style. Perhaps we should just let him be. Despite who he is, there's a very good chance he'll never figure out what we're really up to."

"And what if he does figure it out?"

The man in the suit smiled. "Then we tell him everything."

CHAPTER 4

Saturday September 24, 2016

I T RAINED OVERNIGHT as a cold front passed through. There was now a noticeable bite in the air, but the front dried everything out and left a clear, sunny weekend day in its wake. My students were between assignments, so I didn't have any grading. I spent the day alone, as I often did on the weekends, cleaning my apartment and going for walks around the Beechtree Strip. My parents, which is to say my mother, often chastised me for not getting out more and "making a few friends." Maybe she had a point, but if there were any existential problems in my life, they weren't due to a paucity of friends.

Last night I'd gone out for a while to a nearby bar, The Green Friar. It was a relatively new species of bar known as a 'Gastropub.' That meant it featured "gourmet" pub food, a selection of three dozen or so hard-to-find craft beers on tap, and a growing number of insufferable hipsters from the surrounding neighborhood. Their pseudo-intellectualism sometimes dampened the vibe of the place, but I guess they didn't do any real harm.

I'd gone there last night for a beer—which turned out to be a very good English brown ale—and to meet with Jimmy, my weed connection. He was a visual arts student at nearby Vizenor College. He was a nice kid and didn't seem put off because he was an undergraduate and I was a professor. Jimmy was a good example of the kind of people in my life these days: not bad people, but not close friends, either. I had a steady girlfriend for a while last year, but we called it quits around the holidays. I can't remember whose idea it had been.

When I returned from my after-dinner walk, I saw a copy of the manuscript for my recently rejected article sitting on my desk. I resolved yesterday to send it out for publication again, this time to the *Quarterly Journal of Metaphysics*. I stared at the manuscript for a moment. Sure, I'd send the damned thing off again, but even if they published it, would it make any difference?

"Eh," I growled, shaking myself out of the gloom. It was Saturday night and I had no other plans, so I decided to smoke up and watch a movie. I opened the middle desk drawer and took out my stash and a glass pipe. Jimmy told me this strain of weed was called 'White Widow.' He claimed it gave a nice mellow high and was good for creativity. Out of the corner of my eye, I noticed the shade covering the side window. I was sick of looking at Miriam's burnt out house.

Strangers on a Train had been in and out of my mind lately, so I decided to watch Hitchcock's 1951 classic about two men who discuss the idea of "exchanging murders." They figure, or rather the villain figures, that if each man kills someone associated with the other man, there will be nothing to connect the murderer to the victim, and hence no way to be caught. "Criss-cross," as Bruno Anthony, the villain, delightfully puts it. I had to admit, it was a pretty good plan. What's more, Robert Walker is spectacular as Bruno Anthony. He's Hitchcock's second best villain after Norman Bates.

I took a couple hits from my bowl and started the movie. The weed took effect quickly, and the film swallowed up my attention as the opening credits finished and Hitchcock made his cameo, trying to force a double bass on to a train. The film took my mind off the last week or so, at least until just past the halfway point when the police start following the main character, Guy Haines, because they suspect he murdered his wife.

My mind returned to following around this Lionel Bradshaw. Maybe it was the weed-induced social paranoia, but I realized I could've gotten into a ton of trouble for following him, especially at a place like Spalding. Professors are often touchy and very insecure; it does a lot to explain our choice of profession. What if my following him came to the attention of the university administration? Would I lose my job?

Meanwhile, the film had flown by. I fired up my bowl again during the tense scene where Bruno reaches through a sewer grate, straining to grab the cigarette lighter with Guy Haines's initials engraved on it. Bruno plans to frame Guy by dropping the lighter where Bruno earlier murdered Guy's wife. It always struck me as funny that a cigarette lighter was the key to unraveling this carefully planned murder. The police find Bruno clutching it in his hand at the end of the film.

I almost laughed aloud as I realized something else: the name of the murder victim in the film is Miriam, just like my late next-door neighbor. Far out. As I hit the bowl, the night of the fire flashed through my mind again. I didn't want to picture Lionel Bradshaw standing there looking down at me, but I couldn't help it. I'd still swear he had a sympathetic look on his face and a small black object in his hand. Maybe it was a book. It didn't matter anyway. So what if he had a book that looked like...

I started coughing violently as smoke billowed out of me. I set the bowl down and got up to walk a few paces to stanch the coughing fit. The film played in the background but seemed very far away. I had hold of something in my mind's eye, like the flash of a solution to a problem. I pictured the night of the fire again, only this time I tried not to focus on Bradshaw's face but what had been in his hand.

"That looked like a fucking Bible!" I gushed aloud. Miriam's daughter told me they couldn't find her late brother's old Bible. Did Bradshaw have it? That was idiotic. Bradshaw having the Bible didn't make any sense. Why would someone break into a house to steal a Bible that only had sentimental value to the old woman who lived there?

Maybe Bradshaw set the fire—that would explain why he knew to wear that air tank—but even then, grabbing the family Bible on the way out didn't fit. He might have guessed that Miriam's family would be anxious to get it back, but even if they offered a reward, it couldn't be that much. Even worse, there was no way he could have known they would be looking for it until *after* the fire. My spine turned to ice.

"*After* the fire," I gasped, falling to my knees.

I suddenly had a coherent explanation. In fact, it explained everything perfectly: why Bradshaw wasn't in a rush to save Miriam, why he looked at me the way he did, and how he ended up in that burning house in the first place. Yet I felt like a complete ass for even considering it.

I didn't know whether to try and put this out of my mind or not. I had hold of an idea too ridiculous to believe and yet too plausible to ignore. I only half heard the music playing over the closing credits to *Strangers on a Train*.

It figured to be another sleepless night.

Tuesday September 27, 2016

Yesterday I'd chickened out. I watched Lionel Bradshaw come out of Dancy Hall and suddenly decided I had no idea what to say to him. I cut and ran before he even got to his car. I might as well have been sixteen again, picking up and putting down the phone half a dozen times before calling up a girl for a date.

I had good reason to lack confidence beyond my usual neuroses. Consider how this grandiloquent solution of mine came about: while getting stoned and watching a classic film, I somehow unraveled why a man was in a burning house wearing an air mask and refusing to save a woman's life. To top it off, the conclusion I reached was even more ridiculous than how I arrived at it.

I looked back at the entrance to Dancy Hall. No one had come out for almost ten minutes. Maybe I could find out a little more about Bradshaw before I started asking him questions. He must have a publication that would shed some light on this situation. I got up and started down the steps, away from the building.

I nearly bumped into Lionel Bradshaw.

My heart hammered inside my chest, and my mouth went dry. For a moment I couldn't remember why I'd even come here, let alone what I might say to him. He looked at me with an oddly amused expression.

"Hullo," he said evenly, with an unmistakable British accent. I just stood there like an idiot. "Uh, are you waiting for someone?" he finally asked. For a moment, I felt like he was playing games with me.

"No...well, yeah. Uh, she should be here any minute." He looked me up and down and seemed to consider this for a moment.

"I see. I'll be on my way then," he said, starting toward the entrance.

"Oh, you work here?" I said louder than I intended. I saw him stiffen at this question and expected him to wheel around, angrily demanding to know just who I was and what I was really doing here. Instead, he smiled at me.

"You know perfectly well I do."

"What're you talking about?" I said, laughing unconvincingly.

"Mmm. Perhaps it was my mistake. Nevertheless, I'm glad we're meeting *today*. Had I run into you a couple of days ago, you might have had me at a disadvantage." I stood there with my mouth open, trying to work out what he meant by that. Finally, he said, "I fancy a cup of tea. Would you like one?" I looked nervously from side to side. "Just inside," he said, motioning toward the building.

"In there?" I asked stupidly.

"It's only a campus building. You've surely been inside one before." As I mulled over whether to go along, I pictured Virgil Sollozzo in *The Godfather* telling Tom Hagen 'Relax Consigliere. If I wanted to kill you, you'd be dead already.' His face didn't look menacing at all. In fact, it seemed like he'd be hurt if I didn't go with him.

"Okay," I shrugged, following him.

"Excellent."

There seemed to be a slight spring in his step as he led me down the hallway. He stopped in front of an office door. He was on the verge of opening it when he suddenly snapped his fingers. "Why don't we go to the lab instead? A bit more room there." We walked down the hallway to a door marked 'Lab 7.' Lionel swiped his card and the door unlocked. "After you, old man," he said, holding the door open.

I entered into an expansive space that was about a story and a half tall with small rectangular windows near the ceiling. There was what looked to be unused equipment scattered along the walls. The lab seemed a little cluttered, but hardly in disarray. In the far corner, I saw what looked like a paint-booth. It was a couple of steps above the ground and surrounded by transparent plastic paneling. I couldn't make out whether there was anything inside because the booth was dark. There was a table in front of the booth that had two flat-screen monitors, dozens of switches, and a keyboard interface. Off to my right was a glassed-in office with the door open. Lionel walked over to the office and set his briefcase down on the desk. "Why don't you have a seat, and I'll put the kettle on. Is Darjeeling all right?"

"Uh, sure," I said, assuming Darjeeling was a brand of tea. It was difficult to process the situation. Not five minutes ago, I was working up the fortitude to speak to Lionel Bradshaw. Now here I was inside his lab while he fetched me a cup of tea. Why the hell had he invited me here? If he was going to warn me off, this was a needlessly elaborate way to go about it. I pulled out a swivel chair from under the table and sat down. As I did, I noticed something I hadn't seen before. Near the entrance to Lionel's office, unobtrusively leaning against the wall, was a yellow air tank. My pulse quickened again.

It was the first piece of direct evidence that corroborated my memory of seeing him in the fire. Before I had time to reflect on this apparent victory, Lionel emerged from his office. I must have jerked my head too abruptly, because he turned around to follow where I'd been looking. He seemed to consider the air tank for moment before casually sitting at the worktable opposite me. He nodded behind him, towards the air tank.

"I suppose that allows us to cut through some of the preliminaries, doesn't it? However, we ought to be *properly* introduced. It's Calvin Sutherland, I believe." He held out his hand and I shook it. "I'm Lionel Bradshaw."

"Call me Cal," I said.

"All right, Cal. I'll come straight to the point. What exactly do you believe is going on here?" He asked it without a trace of animosity or irony, just as I'd ask a student a question, hoping they'd give the correct answer.

"Uh…well. I don't actually *know* what's going on here," I stammered.

"Perhaps, but you must have something you want to get off your chest. After all, you've been following me around for the better part of a week."

He may have been right, but I hated being called out on it. "What were you doing in Miriam's house during the fire?" I asked reflexively.

"Ah! You mean how did I end up there?" His eyes brightened. "That's for you to figure out, old man. Now if I were to guess, you have a pretty well worked out theory on what I was doing there. But you're afraid of how ridiculous it would sound in the light of day." He paused for a moment before adding, "Try me."

I felt my ears get hot. The son of a bitch was right. No matter how many times the night of the fire replayed in my mind, or how much I told myself I believed my interpretation of events, I couldn't bear to utter it aloud. In fact, there was a very good chance he was trying to bait me into making a fool of myself.

"Forget it," I said, standing up to leave.

"Now you're just being disingenuous."

"Huh?"

"You're not forgetting anything, especially this. You want too badly for it to be true."

I pursed my lips. "You don't even know what I'm going to say yet."

Lionel shrugged. "Allow me to make a deal with you. You tell me *how* you believe I ended up in that house, and in return I'll tell you *why* I was there."

I took a deep breath before speaking, even though I couldn't look Lionel in the eye while I said this. "You traveled back in time." My heart beat quickly, and I felt embarrassed. Lionel looked at me sympathetically. He leaned forward and rested his head on his hands.

"Go on. What led you to that conclusion?"

I imagined myself in front of a class being challenged to explain the reasoning behind some position. It no longer seemed that he was leading me up the garden path, but I needed to make sure of something first. "It *was* you I saw in the fire, right?"

"It most certainly was."

I relaxed. "It's funny. Until I noticed the air tank just now, part of me still didn't believe it was you." Lionel nodded understandingly. "Well, for starters, you just disappeared into thin air that night. No one saw you leave. In fact, other than me, no one saw you there at all. So how did you just vanish like that, let alone enter the house in the first place? Hell, even I had to break in through the back door."

"But all by itself that doesn't add up to time travel," Lionel said.

"Not even close," I said. "Last week I ran into Miriam's family. Miriam was the woman who lived in the house, but you probably knew that already." Lionel nodded. "Anyway, they were looking for an old Bible that belonged to Miriam's late son. They were sure it was in a part of the house undamaged by the fire, but they couldn't find it. Then, over the weekend, I remembered you were holding something that looked like a small black book. I assumed it was the Bible, but that didn't make any sense. For one thing, why would you steal an old family Bible?"

"If I may interject," Lionel said, "I didn't steal it."

"No," I said, looking at him for a long moment, "I don't believe you did. At any rate, it all seemed like an amazing coincidence. Miriam's family comes in search of a missing Bible that wasn't where it should have been. I see you holding a Bible, in a burning house of all places, on the night Miriam died. Then I realized why it seemed like such a coincidence: you couldn't have known they'd be looking for the Bible, because they wouldn't be looking for it until *after the fire*. I don't claim to know exactly how you became aware of it, but you must have found out about the Bible after the fire and traveled back in time to get it."

It felt like I hadn't talked that much in years. I was so absorbed in my explanation I'd forgotten Lionel was even there. "That's rather a remarkable account of things," he finally said.

"What's more, you're not a firefighter, but there you were wearing an air tank in the middle of a neighborhood house fire. How else would you have known to do that? I doubt you drive around with an air tank strapped to your back, looking for burning houses that are about to swallow obscure family heirlooms."

Lionel chuckled. "No, I can't say that I do."

"You had to have known about the fire in advance. Maybe you set the fire yourself, but that wouldn't explain how you ended up with the very Bible Miriam's family would only *later* be unable to find." I was surprised to see Lionel sitting up straight and looking at me with an approving expression.

"I suppose it's time for my end of the bargain," he said cheerfully as he walked back to his office. As he returned, I could see he was carrying something. I knew what it was without having to ask. "Here you are."

My hands trembled a little as I looked at the Bible. I opened the front cover and saw an inscription:

To Andy
on the day of your First Communion
May 2, 1988

"Jesus," I finally said after staring at the Bible for a while.

"Quite," Lionel said as I handed it back to him. "You more than likely have some questions of you own."

"That's understating things a bit."

"I guess we can start with the reason I have this Bible, though if you're a little disappointed I'll understand. During the week after the fire, probably around the time Miriam's daughter Nancy spoke to you, I was hired to find it."

"*Hired?*" I don't know what I expected Lionel to say, but it wasn't that.

"Yes. You see we—my colleagues and I—have what you might call a historical research and recovery firm. People hire us to find things, things they otherwise believe are lost to history. Like that Bible for instance."

"You mean Miriam's daughter knows that you're..." I started to say.

"Oh, certainly not. We don't explain to our clients *how* we're able to re-cover their valuables. We invent cover stories for that end of things. Take this

Bible," he said, holding it up. "Naturally, when there's a house fire, some bloke has to investigate the cause. During the course of the investigation, while he was collecting evidence, perhaps this Bible fell into his possession. It was purely an accident, of course, but being that I have connections with various government agencies, it was no problem for me to track it down."

"And you think they'll believe that?" I asked skeptically.

"They always do. I grant it sounds implausible to you, but then again you know the truth of the matter. Time travel isn't a possibility that would occur to most people. Plus, our clients are so happy when we recover their treasured items, they likely wouldn't care if we robbed someone to obtain them."

I couldn't believe what I was hearing. In all the years I'd spent research-ing and pondering the possibilities of time travel, this never occurred to me. Yet now that Lionel brought it to my attention, it made perfect sense. "Yeah," I said aloud, "with a time machine you could do that. In fact, you'd be in an unusually good position to do just that. If you knew exactly when some object disappeared, you could travel back to that very moment and recover the item immediately *after* it disappeared. Because, unlike the person who lost it, you'd know just when to look for it. You could even observe a conversation at a critical moment, because you not only know when it takes place, you know the future events to which it pertains."

"My word, Cal. You are a quick study."

"Well, I've been preoccupied with the philosophical side of this for a while now."

Lionel seemed to consider this for moment. "Yes. I rather enjoyed your presentation at the university colloquium this past April. I never would've considered the past as a, how did you put it? 'A garden of ethical safeguards.'"

I stared at Lionel wide-eyed for a moment. I was about to remark on the unearthly coincidence that he happened to attend a philosophy colloquium nearly six months ago, but I couldn't help smiling as I thought about it in a different way. "So, did you travel to the colloquium just before or just after you encountered me in the fire?"

Lionel grinned. "Just before, as a matter of fact. It seems all out sequence, I know. My colleague and I noticed you following me. When we did a little digging and found out you lived next door, we guessed that you'd turn up during the house fire, which was probably why you were following me in the first place. Once we learned that you were on the faculty here, I figured I'd try to learn a little more about your research interests. I suppose I could've read something you'd published, but…"

"Since you happen to have a working time machine, you traveled back and attended the colloquium in person," I said.

"Indeed."

I pictured the colloquium in my mind. "I'm trying to remember whether I saw you there or not."

"It's doubtful. You wouldn't have known to look for me."

"True."

"For what it's worth, I found your paper fascinating. Is a publication forthcoming?"

I frowned. "Not so far. In fact, it was rejected again the other day. That makes the third rejection."

"Oh, dear," Lionel said. "I am sorry to hear that."

"It's not a total surprise. Even around the Philosophy Department, what I do isn't considered an emerging area of research."

"Good thing, too," Lionel said. I looked up at him sharply. "Oh, don't misunderstand. I think what you're doing is wonderful, in and of itself. In fact, the way you responded to some of the questions people threw at you back in April showed a remarkably keen understanding of the ways of time travel.

"No, what I meant was…well, I don't think I need to impress upon you the need to keep secret what we do here. If the fat arses of the university administration, let alone the general public, ever learned of what we're up to…I don't even want to think about the consequences."

I nodded affirmatively. "I understand, believe me."

Lionel patted my shoulder as he stood up. "I knew you would, Cal. Best to have them thinking you're a doddering eccentric. It's some of the best camouflage there is, and you still get the last laugh. You know I…"

A low sound of machinery interrupted him. He turned abruptly toward the enclosed area that resembled a paint booth. The lights inside the booth were now on and cast a dull yellow glow. Both monitors at the desk in front of the booth suddenly displayed data and graphics I couldn't make out from where I sat. Lionel looked back and forth between the instrument desk and me.

"Stay right there. I just have to attend to this. Oh, and for the time being, leave the explanations to me. Shan't be a moment." He hurried off toward the instrument desk. As he did, I bolted up from my chair.

"Holy shit! Is that the time machine?" I yelled, thunderstruck.

"Of course it is, Cal. You didn't think I was making all of this up, did you?"

I shuffled over to where Lionel was standing. "It just seemed too good to be true." He was fast at work at the instrument desk, clicking through graphical menus and occasionally adjusting some of the nearby switches. He seemed to know what he was doing.

The whirring sound grew louder, and the lights inside the enclosed booth were brighter. For a moment, I felt like Roy Neary standing on the landing pad at Devil's Tower at the end of *Close Encounters of the Third Kind* as the alien ships swooped in. I didn't know precisely what was going to happen next, but you would have needed a crane to move me from where I stood.

Just then, I noticed two cylinders—one lowering from the ceiling, the other rising from the floor—enclosing an area inside the booth. They met about four feet off the ground with an audible click as the mechanical whirring reached a crescendo. Then the cylinders slowly began to part.

"Oh my God," I drawled.

"Sometimes the proverbial picture is a worth a thousand words," Lionel said with a smirk. As the cylinders moved apart, they revealed a man.

He looked very unhappy with me.

CHAPTER 5

THE MAN INSIDE the booth had thinning black hair and stood half a foot taller than Lionel, closer to my height. His attire was striking. He wore a black suit that seemed cut a little longer than one would usually see. Underneath was a matching black vest with a pocket-watch fob attached. He also wore a dress shirt with a detachable collar. He held a bowler hat under one arm and a small attaché case in the other hand.

He looked back and forth from Lionel to me and sauntered out of the booth, fixing me with a displeased look. Lionel hurried over to him.

"Ah, Roger. Good to have you back. How did everything go?"

"Well enough, I suppose," Roger said with a noticeable British accent.

"Excellent," Lionel replied. His joviality now seemed forced. "There's someone I'd like you to meet." He turned back to me. "This is Cal Sutherland. Cal, this is my colleague, Roger Blanchard." I extended my hand. He just looked at it without offering his own hand. He turned back to Lionel.

"Lionel. A word," he said harshly, walking past me to the far corner of the lab. Lionel gave me an embarrassed look.

"Not to worry, Cal. Just stay right here. I'll be back momentarily."

Lionel hurried over to meet Roger on the far side of the lab. From Roger's body language, I could tell he was very upset. He shook his head at Lionel and even angrily pointed in my direction once. I turned away from them, looking toward where I'd just seen Roger materialize—materialize from some past time! I shook my head at that. Would any of this ever seem completely real?

At that moment, the door to the lab opened. A younger man with tousled dirty blonde hair entered. He wore a faded green backpack and looked to be in his early twenties. He had a pair of white earbuds in each ear. When he saw me, he froze for a moment and plucked out the earbuds. He looked over at Lionel, who gave a disarming wave. The young man looked back at me and shrugged. He set his backpack down on the table.

"Uh, hi," he said, more unsure of himself than unfriendly.

"Good afternoon." I replied.

"I'm Jack. Jack Greenwood," he said, extending his hand.

"Good to meet you," I said, shaking his hand. "My name's Cal."

He drew back surprised. "Cal Sutherland?"

33

"Uh, yeah."

"Oh cool," he said. "I started reading that paper you wrote. It was really interesting."

"Really?" I asked, incredulously. If three people outside of my department had read that colloquium paper, I would've considered it an unprecedented success. Now here was the second person to have mentioned it this afternoon.

"Oh yeah," he said, walking over to the instrument desk that Lionel was operating earlier. "I mean, I didn't understand all of it, but that part about the rights of adopted kids and using time travel to find their real parents was smart. It kinda made me wonder why we haven't had any foster kids asking us to track down their real parents yet."

"Well thanks, um, Jack. Glad to hear you enjoyed it." I was about to ask him a couple of more questions, but the volume of Roger's voice suddenly rose.

"It's an exceedingly bad idea, Lionel," I heard him say. "And I resent the way you've forced my hand like this." He started to walk away from Lionel and back toward where I was standing. I noticed that Jack looked up from what he'd been doing.

"Now, just a moment," Lionel said, "you and I discussed this very thing only the other day."

"We didn't *discuss* anything. You said you wanted to tell him...even bring him here to show off what we're really doing. I said you shouldn't." Roger waved at me resentfully. "And yet, here he is anyway."

"He," Lionel started to say, "that is, Cal, isn't just anyone, Roger."

"He certainly isn't. Up until you unfurled all of our work for him, he was someone who didn't know about any of this. That's the way I would've preferred to keep it."

Lionel held a finger in the air. "Now that's where you're wrong. Cal sussed the whole thing out before I even told him."

Roger stared at me for moment, sizing me up. Then he turned back to Lionel. "*What* did he figure out exactly?"

"How I came to be in that house during the fire. I wouldn't have brought him here otherwise." That was a half-truth. Lionel had brought me into the lab before I recounted my interpretation of events, but I wasn't about to protest.

Roger frowned. "I still don't like it. We can't just bring every Tom, Dick, and Harry in here because they wrote some high-flown article about philosophy and time travel."

"No offense taken," I said sarcastically.

"Steady on, Roger," Lionel said. "Apart from you, Jack, and me, no one else in the world better understands the need for secrecy here. I think Cal appreciates our unique position more than you realize."

Roger rolled his eyes. "So, should the American scientists working on the atomic bomb have just up and told their Russian counterparts about their designs, merely because they happened to be in the same line of work? We can't predict what he's going to do now that he knows."

I'd had enough of being talked about as though I wasn't there. "The Russians and the Americans were *competitors* for the atomic bomb. I'm a lot of things, but I'm not your sworn enemy. Plus, I wouldn't know how to create a time machine even if I did have all the specifications."

Roger sneered. "I don't think time travel is something to make light of."

I took a step toward him. "That makes two of us." He glared at me for a second and started to walk away.

"Just a moment, Roger," Lionel called out to him. "Cal. When you saw me in the burning house, you were rather upset at me for not trying to save the woman who lived there. Remember? I had the breathing apparatus on and everything, but I didn't even *try* to save her."

I hadn't thought of it until just now. "Yeah, I do remember, now that you mention it."

"Okay," Lionel said, rubbing his hands expectantly. "So here we are, all together in the same room. You know for a fact it was me in the house, yet you're suddenly not at all upset. Why on Earth not? Didn't I have some moral duty to save her life?" These questions stopped Roger in his tracks. Even Jack Greenwood made his way over from the control desk and looked on curiously.

I knew what Lionel was asking me, but at first I didn't completely appreciate why. The answer was a pretty simple one, at least to me. Lionel was asking a common question associated with time travel. It was an issue that most people and most perfectly good sci-fi movies got totally wrong.

"Well, if you're hoping I'll say something about unraveling the space-time continuum, you're in for a disappointment," I said lightly. "It's like this: Miriam's family hired you to find her late son's missing Bible. They did this *after* the fire that killed Miriam. So, Miriam did in fact die in the fire. Miriam dying in the fire is what led her family to you in the first place. This means that neither you, nor I, nor any other time traveler that may have been lurking in the past, acted to prevent her death. She *was* killed in the fire, period. It isn't so much that you *couldn't* save her—a better way to put it is that you *didn't* save her. No one did. That things happened the way they did is absolute proof that no one intervened to change anything. So I can't be mad at you for not acting to save her, because it simply wasn't possible."

Lionel smiled approvingly and turned to Roger. "There you are. And we didn't even have to drag him to November of '63 to straighten him out about paradoxes."

35

"November of '63?" I asked.

"Story for another time," Lionel said.

Roger still frowned at me, but his expression softened ever so slightly. "I still don't like him being here," he said, and he finally turned to address me directly. "It's nothing personal, Doctor Sutherland. But I can see that my colleague's mind is made up." He started to walk away and turned back. "You really don't believe the past can be changed?" he asked me.

"Afraid not," I said, wondering why he seemed so concerned about this. "Privately, I've taken to calling this the First Law."

"Oh?" Lionel asked.

"A time traveler cannot alter the past in order to change the future."

"The First Law," Lionel said. "Well, if it's all right with you, I think we'll co-opt that phrase ourselves. It took us a good bit of trial and error to figure out what you've intuited, Cal. Well done."

My mind was awhirl. I'd been toiling in obscurity with philosophical issues that no one took seriously because, according to them, there was no such thing as time travel. Yet here I was, standing among three time travelers with a working time machine just a few feet away! It was tremendously vindicating. It didn't even bother me that I had to keep it secret. Though I'd just met Lionel, the time machine already seemed like *my* secret. I imagined picking Lionel's brain about time travel and discreetly translating that into a future article. The possibilities for additional research which, only an hour ago seemed small and futile, had multiplied immeasurably.

When I came out of my daydream, I noticed Roger had left the room, and Lionel and Jack were bent over the instrument desk talking about something. I figured they had work to do, and I took this as my cue to get going. It was already a beautiful day, and I looked forward to spending the rest of it contemplating what I now knew. After the shock wore off, that is.

"Well, Lionel, thank you very much for showing me all this. To say the least, it's given me quite a lot to think about."

Lionel looked up with a confused expression. "I'm sure it has."

"Rest assured I'll keep this all a secret. But if you're free sometime soon, I'd love to talk with you more about time travel."

"Talk?" he asked with a laugh. "Oh no, I'm afraid we've done all that."

"Oh," I said, disappointed.

Lionel walked over to me and nodded in the direction of the time machine. "Like to have a go?"

I was stunned. Life-altering questions have a way of doing that.

"Are you serious?" Lionel looked at me quizzically as my banal response shook me out of my stupor. "Sorry. That was a stupid thing to say. It's just…"

Lionel placed his hand on my shoulder, and I noticed Jack Greenwood trying to hide a smile. "Easy does it, old man," Lionel said. "This isn't the queen of the spring pageant asking you for a date."

"True. This ranks much higher on the 'too good to be true' meter."

"Nevertheless," Lionel prompted.

I threw up my hands and laughed at the absurdity of it all. "Hell yes!"

"Excellent." Lionel grinned. "I have just the place. In fact, you can help with a bit of business I have there." He took a step back and looked me up and down. "Of course, we can't have you looking like that. You see that room over in the corner? Go to the rack marked '3' and pick out a nice suit. Nothing too formal. Be sure to choose one of the belts as well. Very important about the belt."

I started to walk over to the door Lionel indicated. "Oh," he called out to me. "You'll need an overcoat too. Rather chilly where we're going." Lionel returned to the instrument desk to talk something over with Jack.

I opened the door Lionel had indicated. It was dark inside, and I felt around to my right for a light switch. The room was about 20 feet square with concrete block walls. It was filled with racks of clothes that reminded me of the wardrobe room for a theatrical company, except better organized. Directly in front of me, on a rack marked '0' were articles of clothing that looked like something worn by an English Lord. The jackets, all of which had matching waistcoats, were either black or tweed and cut with very high necklines. There were some walking sticks nearby and an assortment of hats. I also noticed something more subtle. These clothes hadn't been in style for about a hundred years, yet they were brand new. They clearly weren't purchased in some vintage clothing shop. These were the real thing.

"Far out," I said with a smile. I moved farther into the room and found the rack marked '3' about halfway back. The clothes were still authentic, but newer than what I'd seen on the previous clothing rack. The pants were high waisted, and the jackets had lower necklines. The style, along with the number '3,' gave me an idea of where Lionel and I might be going.

Smiling the whole time, I finally selected a slate gray single-breasted jacket with creased trousers, a white shirt, and a blue and white striped tie. As I slipped on the jacket, I looked at myself in the full-length mirror. I felt a little ridiculous in the high waisted pants, even though I'd seen Cary Grant pull off this same look in a dozen different films. I found a matching fedora and slipped it on my head, tilting it forward.

I picked up my own clothes and started back out to the lab. "A belt," I said, snapping my fingers. I saw several belts hanging on the wall. As I grabbed one, I noticed a small box attached to it just to the left of the silver-colored buckle. I slipped it around my waist and flipped off the light on my way out.

"Very smart," Lionel said, giving me the once-over.

I made a turn to show off the outfit. "William Powell, eat your heart out."

"You'll need to empty your pockets of any personal effects, like your wallet and *especially* your mobile phone. Be rather difficult to account for, you know."

"Leave my wallet here?"

Lionel must have noticed my frown. "Not to worry, Cal. I suppose my lot has come to take this sort of thing for granted. Not much time will pass while we're gone. In fact, the clock on the wall will have only advanced about fifteen minutes by the time we return. Now then, Jack. Are we ready?"

"We should be," Jack said, not looking up from the controls. Lionel turned to me, holding his hand toward the time machine.

"Cal, my dear fellow, right this way."

I took a deep breath and pulled open the door to the booth where I'd seen Roger appear a little while ago. It was very warm inside, a combination of my overcoat and the lack of air circulating. On the floor were several seven-sided platforms that were a translucent bluish color. I could just make out some wires and conduit crisscrossing below each platform, and I heard the dull hum of a running motor.

"That's it, Cal. Just stand in the center of any of the Nora Pads you see beneath your feet."

"Nora Pads?" I asked.

"The bloke who designed this part of the apparatus named the components after his daughter."

"Should I do the joke about beaming up?" I asked.

"Quite," Lionel smiled. "This was merely the best design that could be employed for confining and manipulating temporal waves. One of the preliminary designs was actually an egg-shaped container that would have required us to curl up in the fetal position. You'll just need to stand still as the tubes close around you. It's a bit confining at first, but it won't last long. You will feel a bit, shall we say, on edge, but I assure you it's all quite painless. Ready whenever you are, Jack."

The booth's overhead lights dimmed, and the sound of a mechanical latch releasing was audible. I saw the bottom tube rising up and jerked my head back, realizing the top cylinder was coming down simultaneously. The whirring sound, barely audible a moment ago, grew quite loud. Something was clearly happening. Out of the corner of my eye, I noticed Lionel standing there as though he were doing nothing more than waiting for a bus. The tubes were now about eighteen inches apart. My heart pounded, and I felt perspiration under my arms.

What happened next is a little difficult to describe. As the tubes closed completely, all the hairs on my body felt like they were standing on end. It was a tingly sensation, like the shock from static electricity, but not painful. As the whirring hum reached a climax, I felt myself gently pulled in many different directions at once. I don't know how, but I knew I couldn't move. I tried to say something, but there was only a dull echo within my mind.

What is this? What the hell is this! I can't...

Then the physical and psychological cacophony suddenly stopped. Everything was totally black and silent. I pushed myself to form a coherent thought, anything to reassure myself I still existed and was still whole. I felt like I had been painlessly scattered into a million pieces that somehow didn't occupy physical space. A dim feeling of alarm echoed within a thick fog of mental molasses. Then I heard what sounded like...the wind. Everything in front of me became too bright to see. The light dimmed, and the surroundings came into focus. I knew I could move and was somehow whole again.

CHAPTER 6

Thursday January 9, 1930

I BEGAN TO form thoughts, most of which were variations of 'What did you do to me?' My feet weren't on firm ground. It felt like gravel. Even more inexplicably, I was clearly outdoors yet had no memory of leaving Dancy Hall. It was nighttime and very cold. On my left, I saw what looked like the top two floors of a brick building. To my enormous relief, Lionel was standing to my right, looking at me expectantly.

"Not as bad as all that, was it?" he said cheerfully.

"What's going on? Where…"

"Oh, for goodness sake, Cal, take a look round."

I did just that. There were several hollow tubes and three rotating vents coming up from the ground nearby. I knew where we were, but it didn't make sense why we were in this kind of place.

"We're on a roof?"

"Indeed," Lionel said easily. "Most of our travels take us to densely populated areas. We must take great care to turn up somewhere out of sight. Since materializing in a wooded area five miles outside of town is rather impractical, Roger came up with the idea of rooftops. Empty department stores at night may be used in a pinch, but there are night watchmen and alarms to contend with."

I had to chuckle at Lionel's matter-of-fact explanation. Who but a time traveler could have envisioned such a contingency? The upshot was this was all real. We were standing in the past, even if I didn't know when and where yet. I felt as happy as a boy on the last day of school.

"I have about a million questions," I said, laughing.

"I've no doubt you do," Lionel said, looking at his watch. "We'll have time to talk over the how's and why's in a bit. Right now, we ought to be on our way." There was a nearby door that led to the building's stairwell. I watched Lionel try without success to turn the knob. "Damn and blast," he said.

"Don't tell me we came all this way just to get stuck on a roof," I said, bracing myself against a frigid gust of wind.

"Certainly not," Lionel said, examining the doorknob in the twilight. He reached into his inside breast pocket and removed a small black leather case.

41

He unzipped it, took out a couple of small metallic instruments, and began working on the lock.

"So you pick locks too, huh?" I said dryly.

"Tools of the trade, if you'll pardon the pun. A man in my line of work sometimes has to acquire some unusual skills."

"Like breaking and entering."

"To be fair, Cal, we're only breaking into this building so that we can exit again downstairs." I heard an audible click. Lionel easily opened the door. "Ah, there we are."

I shook my head in disbelief and smiled. "After you."

We'd landed—if you could call it that—on top of a four or five-story apartment building. As we made our way quietly down the wooden staircase, I could hear bits of conversation and the occasional notes of instrumental music coming from a radio. At the bottom of the stairs, we exited into a small lobby with hexagonal black and white tiles on the floor and an ashtray to the left of the building's front door.

"Welcome to 1930," Lionel said, holding the door open for me.

I stepped out onto the sidewalk thunderstruck. This was the moment, I would recall later, that time travel became completely real to me. We were in an urban area, which surely still existed in the same geographical place in 2016. Yet everything was different. A black car with running boards and a spare tire behind the fender, driven by a man in a fedora, rumbled past us. It made a guttural sound I wasn't used to hearing cars make. No one on the sidewalk but me took any notice of it or any of the similarly modeled cars that also drove past.

I pressed myself against the side of the building to avoid bumping into the people passing by. Light snow was falling, and everyone seemed in a hurry to get out of the cold. All the men wore overcoats, and many of them carried the evening newspaper under their arms. The women wore dresses that peeked out below their coats. There was a quiet sense of purpose about them that you just didn't see in 2016. I won't pretend to be a sociologist, but the people bustling around me were different. Perhaps it was a kind of maturity that came from living in this period, without the modern conveniences Lionel and I enjoyed.

"Quite an experience, isn't it?" Lionel said.

"It's like waking up in the middle of the Grand Canyon," I said, still looking around in wonderment. An American flag hung over the entrance of a building up ahead. The flag only had 48 stars. I reached out and touched the building next to me, just to make sure it was real. "How is this even possible?"

"What, time travel?" Lionel laughed. "Explaining that would be rather a tall order. Some of the top physicists in the world would be hard pressed to grasp it all."

"How about the abridged version, then?"

Lionel seemed to ponder this for a moment. "One of the most important phenomena used in time travel that we—my lot back at Spalding—have come to understand are called temporal waves."

"Yeah, I heard you mention temporal waves before," I said.

"Just as there are light waves and sound waves, there are temporal waves. As in actual waves of time propagating a given moment. Where different wavelengths of light make different colored light and X-rays and so forth, differing temporal waves also manifest different properties."

"As for instance?"

"This," Lionel said, motioning with his hand at the scene around us. "Our main discovery was twofold. First, in this part of the universe, temporal waves are such that time passes from forward to backward at a certain rate. Second, different periods of time have different wave patterns relative to our own time. As some prior period recedes father into the past, its temporal wavelength differs in verifiable and quantifiable ways. So, we've merely harnessed that phenomenon and manipulated it to travel backwards in time."

"That makes a certain amount of sense, I guess."

"Perhaps it would help to think of it like this. Time is just a dimension, somewhat like the more well-known spatial dimensions. Typically, we move about space with no trouble, while time just carries us along. As it turns out, one can actually travel in another direction through time. A rough analogy is crossing a street on a diagonal. You're moving in two dimensions at the same time: further along on your overall journey, while simultaneously crossing the street. Talking of which."

We'd come to an intersection. Next to me stood a small traffic signal atop a light pole. It was squat and consisted of only a red and green light. The light suddenly changed from green to red as a black and white 'Stop' sign flipped out. After we crossed the street, Lionel unfolded a small paper he'd removed from his pocket.

"Not that I couldn't spend a few weeks marveling at the sights," I said, "but I assume that's not what we're here to do."

"No, I should think not," Lionel said, returning the paper to his coat pocket. "It's just up ahead." We walked another half block before turning into an alley. I was about to ask Lionel whether we'd made a wrong turn when he stopped in front of a dark green door. It was very easy to miss given how little light shone from the street. "Ah, this should be the place," he said, knocking on the door. I was about to ask him where exactly we were when a small panel on the door slid open. A pair of eyes quickly darted from Lionel to me.

"Evening gents," a gruff voice said.

"Hullo," Lionel said cheerfully. "Joe Z sent me." The eyes paused for a moment and the panel slid shut. As I heard a series of locks unlatch, I leaned toward Lionel and whispered loudly, "A speakeasy?"

"Precisely," he said with a grin.

"Who's Joe Z?"

"I'm buggered if I know. Perhaps the proprietor loaned him something and it was never returned. Who can say how these things start?"

As I followed Lionel inside, I nodded at the burly man holding the door. He looked like an ex-boxer or a longshoreman who could take care of himself if things got out of hand. Needless to say, he glared at us. But what did that matter? I was inside an actual speakeasy during Prohibition!

The place wasn't large; you could probably cram about thirty or forty people in here. Tonight, the bar was about two-thirds full with several empty tables nearby. There were two male bartenders wearing white dress shirts and small black bow ties who moved back and forth behind the bar fixing drinks. The walls were brick trimmed in dark wood, and the place was filled with smoke.

"Fancy a drink?" Lionel asked.

"Are you kidding?"

"Excellent. Better make it something simple. These blokes don't have the broad selection of liquor you and I are used to."

I could've drunk a dry vodka martini in this place and died ten minutes later an enormously happy man, but Lionel was right. Who knew whether they even had vodka, which didn't become common in America until the fifties. "Just make it a bourbon on the rocks." As I saw Lionel get the bartender's attention, I instinctively reached around to my back pocket for my wallet. *Damn it.* I left my wallet behind in the lab in 2016. Lionel probably had too. We didn't have any money! I glanced nervously over to the brute watching the front door. Was there a back way out of here?

As I was about to try to get Lionel's attention, I saw him hand the bartender what looked like a five-dollar bill and thank him for the drinks.

"Shall we grab a table?" Lionel asked.

"Sure," I said, glancing back at the bar. The bartender hadn't taken any notice of us and had moved on to some other task.

"Well, I think a toast is in order," Lionel said after we sat down.

"Lionel." I leaned in. "How do you have money to pay for these drinks? Doesn't the currency in the…" I looked around to make sure no one was eavesdropping. "Doesn't 1930's money look different than what we have?"

He smiled as though he'd been anticipating that question. "Not to worry, old man. I'll explain in a moment. But first…" He shook his glass at me. I raised my own. "To your first trip back in time. May you find it agreeable and fulfilling." We clinked our glasses and drank. My bourbon, if that's what it actually was, had more of a charcoal flavor than I was used to.

"Not the quality we're accustomed to, is it?" Lionel said, sipping a clear beverage.

"You could say that. Though the atmosphere more than makes up for it. What are you having?"

"G and T," he said, before adding sardonically, "more or less." Lionel set his drink down and reached into his pocket. He placed a one-dollar bill on the table in front of me. Washington's picture was, of course, much smaller than we were used to, and the treasury seal was red. Lionel provided a very simple explanation. "Counterfeit."

I was shocked. "Are you serious?"

"Of course. Easier than you might think for people in my line of work. All it takes is some special bonded paper and a moderately priced laser printer. Then again, the methods of detection in this time period are embarrassingly unsophisticated."

"Apparently."

Lionel shrugged. "Call it more tools of the trade, if you like. We don't counterfeit money just for the sake of it. Occasionally, our trips to the past call upon us to stay several days at a time. Well, there's a charge for meals and accommodations here just like in our own time. Any effect on the economy from a few counterfeit bills is negligible."

All I could do was shake my head and take another sip of my drink. A man accompanied by a dour-looking woman passed by our table and sat in one of the booths along the wall. I figured they were waiting for someone. The woman had her hair pinned up and wore a lime green hat. She looked vaguely annoyed with the man, while he paid her little mind. He lit a cigarette while she stared quietly at her drink.

This felt all wrong. Time travel—actually being in the past—was like hearing a beautiful song during a happy moment of your life. In this moment, the whole world should be just as happy as I was. Yet this couple wasn't happy. I took another sip of my drink, enjoyed the burn of the liquid, and tried to focus on the rest of the surroundings.

"Rather easy to get lost in all this, isn't it?" Lionel asked.

"Oh yeah."

"If you don't mind my saying so, Cal, you strike me as someone who's thought about a scenario very much like this one."

"You mean where I'd go if I could travel back in time?"

"Quite," Lionel said. He seemed eager for me to go on.

"Of course I've thought about it. But to actually be here..." I trailed off and glanced over to the bar. The bartenders were still working away, and the barstools were now full of men in long coats and fedoras.

"So many times," I continued, "the way you imagine a moment like this is…it's always so much more beautiful in your mind than how it turns out when you actually hold it in your hand."

"And how about this?" Lionel asked. "Better than you imagined, I expect."

I glanced over at the couple in the booth. "No. This isn't better or worse. It's just as good as I imagined it. And in a way, that seems best."

"What were some of the places you dreamed of going?"

"Eh, nowhere special."

Lionel raised an eyebrow. "Oh? Try me."

I drained the rest of my bourbon and thought it over for a moment. "Well," I said, leaning in so as not to be overheard, "have you ever dropped acid?" I could see this took Lionel by surprise, but he recovered quickly.

"LSD?" he asked with a good-natured laugh. "No, I'm afraid not."

"Most people don't have the first goddamn idea what's it like to really groove on an acid trip. They think you need a light show, lots of thumping music, and vitamin C, but that's bullshit. For me, a beautiful trip is all about what goes on in here," I said, pointing to my temple. "Strangely enough, I always imagined time travel would be the same way. I never dreamed about traveling back to some touchstone moment of history. I just wanted to travel to the past. To go there, just to *be* for a little while, and that would be enough.

"I sometimes pictured myself sitting in a hotel lobby, maybe in the 1920's. You know, back when hotels were decadent and posh. I'd sit on one of those cushioned benches with maroon upholstery, next to an ornate ashtray that stood on a pedestal. I'd just watch everyone for a while." I paused for a moment, picturing the scene in my mind. "Or what would really be something is to be present at the time a great work of art is unveiled—some painting, sculpture, or film. I'd love to see everyone's reaction when it's revealed to the world for the very first time, before it's been appropriated by the commentators and shaped by the ether of human history."

Lionel slapped his knee and smiled. "I understand completely. For me it's diners, of all the damned places. Especially diners in America. Don't know why, really. Something about those red and white tablecloths, hooks for one's hat, and a menu with very basic but pleasant food. Plus, they don't bring you a plate of food that could feed the bloody Allied Expeditionary Force."

"That's terrific," I said. Just then another thought struck me. "You know, I didn't realize it until just now, but we're pioneers of a very strange kind."

"Oh?"

"When you think about pioneers in the usual sense—take the Apollo astronauts, for instance—they crossed a frontier. The first to…" I realized my voice had risen a bit, so I paused a moment to quiet down. Who knows what someone would think if they heard what I was about to say. "They were the first men to land on the moon. A place that no one, and I mean *no one*, had ever set foot before.

"But look around where we are. *Everyone's* been here before. This time is part of the genome of human history. We're not pioneers because we've set foot some place no one's ever been. We're pioneers because of our memories. No one else alive right now *remembers* the future. We do. We don't predict it, make educated guesses about it, or imagine it. We *remember* it! Now, how many people can say they've experienced life from that frame of mind?"

Lionel pounded the table with his fist and pointed at me. "I knew you were the right man for this, Cal. Would you like another drink?"

"Absolutely."

Lionel took our glasses up to the bar and returned with two fresh drinks. It was my turn to raise a glass. "Here's to remembering the future." Lionel nodded, and we clinked our glasses. I took an especially long pull from my bourbon and continued looking around the place.

"Good Lord," Lionel suddenly said, sitting up straight. "I'd completely forgotten why we're here."

I snapped back to reality too, which was a shame because the bourbon had started doing its job on me. "Why exactly *are* we here? Not that being here isn't more than enough to keep me happy."

"Well, we have rather a thorny dilemma with regard to the time machine. Of course, keeping it secret is essential, but operating it costs money all the same."

I inadvertently glanced toward the cash register behind the bar. "Uh oh," I said.

"No it isn't 'uh oh' at all."

"Don't tell me we came here to rob the place and then high tail it back to the present."

"Certainly not!" Lionel said, smoothing his jacket. "Anyway, dear boy, you and I can't just up and rob this establishment for reasons which you well know."

Lionel was right. I had let my mind run away with things a bit. "Of course," I said, shaking my head. "It's the First Law again. If this speakeasy hadn't been robbed the quote-unquote 'first time,' then we can't just rob it now." Still, I couldn't help wondering what *would* happen if we tried to rob the place. How far would we get? What would stop us?

"Precisely," Lionel said, adding, "though in some ways a robbery would be a good deal simpler."

I set my drink down and narrowed my eyes. "Simpler than what, Lionel?"

Lionel leaned in closer. "This place, as I'm sure you noticed, doesn't have a giant neon arrow pointing everyone toward this alley."

"It's an illegal speakeasy. They're trying to keep a low profile."

"Yes indeed," Lionel said, nodding toward the bar. "You see that bloke behind the bar? The taller one with the thinning hair and the emerging paunch."

I looked at the bartender Lionel was referring to. He seemed to know what he was doing, occasionally giving a half-smile at something one of the bar patrons said before washing up a highball glass.

Lionel continued. "That man is called Gerald Hardy, and this is his place. Now, despite not having an ostentatious sign out front, this establishment does have a name."

"Okay."

"It's called *The Tumbler*. You're a drinker, Cal. Know what a tumbler is?"

"Uh, not really. Some kind of glass, I think."

"True enough, but not just any kind of glass. When they used to make glassware for taverns—and I mean during the 19th century—the bottoms of the glasses were not flat. This was so a man would be forced to finish his drink fairly quickly, since you couldn't set it down on a table without the glass— wait for it—tumbling over."

I couldn't help looking at the bottom of my bourbon glass, just to make sure it was flat. "I never knew that. That's actually kind of interesting."

"Isn't it, though? Now then, a genuine tumbler with a rounded bottom is a pretty rare thing for obvious reasons. When you set your glass down, you don't want it spilling all over your trousers, do you? In fact, a set of antique tumblers in 2016 is a pretty rare thing indeed."

I was starting to catch on. "Which would make them awfully valuable."

"In a word, yes. Now have another look at the bar. You see that small rack of glasses on the shelf in the middle?" I glanced nonchalantly to my right. There was a dusty mirror behind the bar with a few rows of glasses and unmarked bottles stacked in front. In the center, elevated on a shelf, was a copper rack that held four glasses. They were about half the size of a typical old-fashioned glass, but I could see, even from back here, that the bottoms of the glasses were convex.

Lionel must have been following my glance. "Hardy was in The Great War, you know. What you and I would call World War I. Those glasses were made in Eastern Europe, about 40 years ago. Somehow, he brought them back here, and they're dear enough to him that he named this place after them. I've done some checking around in our time. A set of tumblers of that vintage could fetch between ten and fifteen thousand dollars."

I gave a low whistle. "What about the First Law? We can't just make off with those glasses any more than we can rob the till."

"True, up to a point. We're not actually going to steal them. Rather, we're going to attempt to acquire them."

"What do you mean, acquire them? Even without the First Law, we won't get near them with all those people at the bar."

"There's a forthcoming diversion that will address your concerns, and…" Lionel suddenly looked toward the front door. I turned my head in time to see the portly bouncer hurrying toward the bar wearing an anxious expression which, a little while ago, I couldn't have pictured him having. He elbowed a man aside at the bar in order to get Hardy's attention. Hardy abruptly stopped mixing a drink, sharply ordered the bouncer back to the door, then bent down below the bar. I noticed some of the folks at the bar had confused expressions. Lionel drained the rest of his gin and tonic. "Right," he said, grabbing his coat and standing up. "A bit early, but that should be the cozzers now. Better come with me, Cal."

I had no idea what was happening, but I did as I was told. I figured we were leaving, but Lionel turned away from the front door and headed toward a hallway that led away from the bar. Hardy came tearing out from behind the bar, just a few feet ahead of us. Lionel put his hand out to stop me. To my surprise, Hardy was carrying the rack of tumblers.

"Lionel, what the hell's going on?" Before he could answer, I heard a loud thumping from the front door. Some of the other patrons must have heard it, too, because there were a number of concerned looks directed that way. A few people were even gathering up their coats.

"As I said, that's what sets this all in motion. The place is being raided."

"Raided!" A young couple bumped into us as they rushed by.

"Now, don't worry about it, Cal."

"Don't worry about it? How can you say that?"

Lionel grinned and gave me a poke in the ribs. "Because, old man, you and I don't exist yet."

It isn't often in life that, during a critical moment, someone says precisely the thing to calm you. Back out in the bar, a vibe of panic spread through the bar patrons. Many people had put on their coats and were staring at the speakeasy's front door as if in a trance. Two more people passed us and headed down the hallway. Hardy emerged from a door to our left and shut it behind him. He stopped and looked at us, apparently resigned to the fate of his bar.

"Well, what're you two guys standin' around for? Can't you see what's goin' on? Better high tail it out the back while ya' still can."

"Right," Lionel said. "That's sound advice." Hardy continued out to the bar, not giving us another look.

I started down the hallway in search of the back door, but Lionel stopped at the door Hardy had just come from. He rubbed his hand over the lock and reached into his coat pocket.

"What the hell are you doing?" I asked. "We have to get out of here."

"True," he said calmly, "but not without those glasses." As he removed the case of lock-picking tools from his pocket there was a loud bang out in the bar. I assumed the police just broke down the front door. My suspicions were confirmed when I heard voices yelling for everyone to stay where they were.

My heart raced as all the beautiful images I had of time travel began evaporating. I heard a police officer yell at someone to sit back down, followed by the sound of a chair scraping the floor. Then the same voice sharply called out for a Sergeant Myzska to check the back hallway to make sure no one was trying to sneak out that way.

"Got it!" Lionel said. He opened the door and I rushed in after him, almost knocking him over. It was a fairly small, dank room that passed for an office. We recovered just enough to have a look around. We both saw the tumblers at the same time, sitting on an empty barrel in the back corner of the room. Hardy must have put them there in the hopes that they would just blend in with the background. Lionel hustled around the desk and grabbed the glasses. He smiled and held them up, as if he were showing off a trophy. "Not as bad as all that," he said.

At the same time, I heard footsteps in the hallway. The expression on Lionel's face changed instantly from triumph to horror. We hadn't bothered to re-lock the door, a fact that became quite clear when I heard the knob turning. I instinctively ducked back behind the door jamb and watched Lionel set the glasses on the weather-beaten desk before slipping underneath.

I cringed as the door opened. Whoever it was pushed the door open wide enough so that it pressed against my nose. I slowly turned my head to where I could see a police officer beyond the edge of the door holding a baton. He had dark hair and wore a long coat with sergeant's stripes. Time seemed to stretch out like a puddle, and with each passing moment, I was sure he could hear me breathing.

Finally, he started to close the door and leave, but he stopped suddenly. "Hello," I heard him say. He casually picked up the tumblers from the desk and started to leave. I mouthed a word that rhymes with 'pluck.'

The police officer left the door ajar so I could see him in the crack between the door and door jamb. Another officer came down the hall and stopped when he saw him holding the glasses.

"Hey, check this out, Ed," the sergeant said. "You ever see a pair 'uh glasses like this?"

The other police officer seemed a little confused by the question. "What?

No. I dunno, Sarge. The lieutenant wanted me to see whether you found anyone back here."

"Nah. There's nobody back here," he said, still examining the glasses.

"Well, they want us back up front," the patrol officer said, hesitating for a moment. "How're you gonna get them outta here without anyone seein' you?"

"I'll leave 'em here," the sergeant said, setting the glasses on the floor next to the office door. "I can just, you know, discover 'em later. And you don't know nothin' about this, Kelley. Get me?" Both officers disappeared around the corner and back into the bar. I could hear raised voices out front, along with the occasional sound of breaking glass.

I tiptoed from behind the door. "Lionel," I whispered. He popped his head up from under the desk, immediately spotting the empty place on the desk where the glasses once sat. "It's all right," I said. "I think we can make it out the back way." I eased the door open and peered into the hallway, not seeing anyone. As I walked out the door, I picked up the tumblers the sergeant had set there a moment ago.

"Well done," Lionel whispered with a grin. We turned another corner and found the back door. We practically burst out the door into another alley, being careful not to slam it behind us. In the sharp cold air, I could feel that I'd been sweating.

"Bugger. I thought our number was up on that one," Lionel said, breathing a sigh of relief. I was just about to agree with him when I heard footfalls behind me.

"Hey!" A voice called out. "Where the hell do you two think you're going?" I didn't even have to turn around to know it was another cop. He was stocky and reminded me of the kind of intractable bureaucrat that colleges are teeming with. Damn it, I wanted to hiss. "I asked you fellas where you were going," he said more firmly. He glanced at the tumblers I had momentarily forgotten I was holding. "Whadaya got there?" Lionel and I just looked at each other. Suddenly I remembered what Lionel had said earlier: *you and I don't exist yet.* Everything instantly came into focus.

"I'm Detective Sutherland. This is my partner, Detective Bradshaw," I said before I knew what I was doing. I watched the police officer tense up at this and hesitate for a moment.

"Detectives, huh. What're you doin' out here?"

I tried to project a level of confidence I wasn't feeling. "It was getting a little crowded inside, especially by the front door, so we came out this way." He didn't seem to be buying this. Before he could object, I said, "Good thing we ran into you. On our way out, Sergeant Myzska said he wanted everybody in uniform inside."

"Go back inside?" the officer asked suspiciously. "What the hell for? What about securing the perimeter?"

"They got that all secure from the inside. He needed help with the evidence," I said awkwardly.

"What're you talkin' about, evidence? We're raidin' a speakeasy, for Christ sake. All the evidence is in there behind the bar."

I looked at Lionel a moment, as though he and I knew something the officer didn't. "Don't you know what's going on here?" He narrowed his eyes at me and took a step closer. "The speakeasy's a front. They're counterfeiters!" This stopped the officer cold. "Go ahead, Lionel. Show him some of the bad paper we're on our way to book into evidence." Lionel seemed to jolt awake and reached into his pocket. I hoped he wouldn't say anything. The English accent would be a dead giveaway. He handed the officer a ten-dollar bill.

"Take a look at Hamilton's head," I said, leaning in close.

"What about it?" the officer asked, eyeing the bill curiously.

I elbowed him in the ribs and gave a conspiratorial look. "It's facing the wrong way."

The officer jerked his head back. "I'll be damned."

I took the ten back from him and gave it to Lionel. "You better get inside before the Sarge comes looking for you."

"Yeah," he grumbled, "I know how that damn Pollack is." We watched the officer go in the back door. The instant the door clicked shut, Lionel and I ran to end of the alley, slowing when we got to the sidewalk so as not to arouse suspicion.

"This way," Lionel said, turning to the right. I followed a step or two behind, knowing instinctively not to look back. We reached the end of the block and turned the corner.

"Where are we headed now?" I asked Lionel.

"Some place out of the way," Lionel said. "We can't just disappear into thin air in front of everyone." I had chuckled. "What's so funny?" he asked.

"With everything that's happened during the last few minutes, it completely slipped my mind that..."

"That we're time travelers," Lionel said gently.

"*You're* a time traveler, Lionel. I'm just along for the ride."

Lionel turned to me with an exasperated look. "After what you just did? Good heavens, Cal, you pulled our chestnuts from the fire single-handedly. How in the world did you think to say all that?"

"Don't know," I replied, genuinely perplexed. "It's like when I break up my class with a joke. It's almost always spontaneous. If I try and think of something beforehand, it never works."

"Whatever the cause, it was indecently brilliant."

"So what're you going to do with these things once we get back?" I asked, holding up the tumblers.

"Chap I know is an antiques dealer. He was the one who gave me the idea about glassware in the first place. I'll have to think of some cover story, of course, but he'll be so happy to acquire them, I doubt he'll examine my own tall tale too closely."

I frowned. "I kind of hate to give these up. It'd be nice to have a memento of what just happened."

"I understand, but they're worth far more as a complete set of four. Next time around you ought to buy a copy of the day's newspaper."

He said it so casually that it didn't register at first. *Next time.* I would actually get to do this again, traveling to a different time in the past.

We finally turned into an alley and walked to the end farthest from the sidewalk. "Now then," Lionel said, taking the tumblers from me, "returning is a fairly simple matter. On your belt you'll find a temporal return initiator, or TRI for short." I looked down at the small plastic box on my belt and saw a small gray button.

"Got it," I said.

"Just press that gray button and you're on your way."

I pressed the button and saw a red light change to green. It flashed five times and then remained on. Nothing seemed to happen for a moment, but then I was overcome with a now familiar sensation. As I felt myself getting pulled apart, I fixed my eyes on the far end of the alley, focusing on this little segment of 1930 for as long as I could.

CHAPTER 7

Wednesday September 28, 2016

USUALLY, WHEN I was in a happy, reflective mood, I'd stick around my apartment, listen to some dreamy music, and have a toke. For some reason, tonight I took a walk—more like I was carried along by an invisible wave—to the Green Friar. Jimmy, my weed connection and bartender of choice, poured me a Belgian white ale from Cooperstown, New York.

I thought back on the moments immediately after Lionel and I returned to the present. We parted on friendly terms, and my mind was clear but numb. Even the memories of our trip ran through my consciousness as though they belonged to someone else. Last night, before I went to bed, I looked at myself in the bathroom mirror and said aloud, 'I just traveled back in time' as if that would invest the experience with reality. It was the most profound experience of my life, yet I had no desire to tell anyone else about it. I didn't want the rest of the world knowing there was a working time machine only a few miles from here.

I had nearly finished my beer when an incredible parallel suddenly hit me. Maybe it was because my beer was served in an unusual glass. Not as unusual as a tumbler, but still. Here I was, in a bar in the year 2016. Yesterday, around this time, I'd been in a speakeasy in 1930. Two bars, in two wholly different eras, but they're both bars, full of people with the same emotions, even many of the same desires as 1930. But it was different somehow, and it was more than just because the people dressed differently. *I* was different. Eighty years ago for everyone else was literally yesterday for me. Lionel and I had the unique experience of remembering the future, outwitting a police officer, and bringing some antique glassware back to the present. How in the hell had we actually done all that?

What started as a question asked in wonderment quickly turned analytical. *What we'd done*, I thought again. I could sit here in a bar in 2016 sipping a beer, just as I could in 1930. I now realized, however, there were a great many other things I could do in the past—many more than I'd ever realized. The First Law of Time Travel—that the past could not be altered—bloomed into a host of implications and principles that I'd never before conceived.

This hit me all at once clear as day rather than as a jumble of ideas I'd have to spend weeks untangling. I drained the last of my beer and set the glass down. I had to get some of this down in my notes before I forgot it.

I must have been smiling, because as I slid off the stool to leave I heard a voice ask, "What's so funny?" A woman stood there. She was thin with dark hair and brown eyes. One eyebrow was raised.

I looked at her levelly. "I guess it was an inside joke."

"So I don't get to hear the punchline?"

"Afraid not," I said. "Listen, you're welcome to this stool. I was just on my way out."

"Hope I haven't frightened you off."

"Nah, nothin' like that." I motioned for her to sit down. "Another time, maybe. So long."

It was easy to catch a woman's eye when you weren't trying—one of life's more frustrating truths. Writing papers was often the same. I hadn't come here tonight thinking about ways to revise my article, yet here I was hurrying home to scrap the entire thing and start over.

I couldn't have been more pleased.

Wednesday October 5, 2016

I'd never written an article so quickly and so easily, at least not an article that I thought was worth a damn. This one felt different. I'd just heard back from *Quarterly Journal of Metaphysics* about my other manuscript under consideration. They asked me to make some revisions and resubmit it. I was genuinely relieved they turned me down, and I did not intend to resubmit that version of the manuscript—not with this new one almost complete. I was revising the introduction when I heard a tapping at my office door. I looked up expecting to see Margo.

"Good afternoon," Lionel said breezily.

"Oh, hi." I looked up, surprised to see him. He stepped through the doorway and glanced around at my office.

"Very cozy," he said, stopping in front of one of my movie posters. It was a black and white photo of Barbara Stanwyck hiding behind a door held open by a grim-looking Fred MacMurray. "These two look like they're in rather a difficult situation."

I smiled. "*Double Indemnity.*"

"Oh?"

"They knock off her husband to get the insurance money, only things go awry. The trouble is, now they're stuck together. Neither can leave the other behind or just stop what's already set in motion. 'Straight down the line,' as they say in the film. Beautifully written."

Lionel nodded. "I must check it out some time. Talking of entanglements, are you free this afternoon?"

"How do you mean?" I asked. Lionel winked at me. I caught his drift immediately, and I felt silly that my heart raced as though a girl I'd once gone out on a date with actually bothered to call me back. Then again, if there were a proper way to handle being asked to travel back in time, I'd have to be the one to author that self-help guide.

"Just let me shut this down," I said, turning off the computer.

"Excellent. I'll fill you in on the way."

I grabbed my shoulder bag and turned off the desk light.

Monday May 17, 1993

When the flash of light and familiar sensations of time travel subsided, I was standing in a kitchen. It was moderately sized and rather unremarkable, but for the fact that it was in such disarray. Many of the white cabinets hung open, their contents either spilled out onto the floor or rearranged. A couple of drawers were open as well. What looked to be a junk drawer had been removed from its place with its eclectic contents dumped out nearby.

The owner of the house had been a woman named Laura Dietrichson. Earlier this morning, she'd been murdered upstairs during an apparent burglary gone wrong. Her murder had never been solved. In fact, the police had only ever questioned a few known burglars in the area, but to no avail. None of her property had been fenced as far as anyone could tell, and the case never gained any traction in the press. It was unfortunate, but most crimes were of this type: a tragic death to anyone who happens to notice, but few people do.

Nonetheless, we weren't here to solve the murder of Laura Dietrichson.

Dietrichson's brother had hired Lionel to recover a stuffed bird, of all things. When she and her brother were young, their family had a backyard bird feeder. Apparently, the two of them used to conjure up make-believe stories about the birds, even pretending they had jobs.

For Laura's tenth birthday, her mother had bought her a stuffed raven. Stuffed fowl tended to make people uncomfortable, including an aunt, who thought the gift unusually macabre, especially for a 10 year-old. Still, Laura and her brother treasured it, even if others never really understood the fascination. Later in life, Laura and her brother became estranged. He hadn't heard about her death until several weeks after it had happened.

As they typically do, the police sealed up the house with yellow crime scene tape earlier this morning once Dietrichson's body had been removed. They would return later in the morning to examine the scene further and catalog some of her personal possessions. There was no way for someone to enter or leave the house without breaking the tape and alerting the authorities that the crime scene had been compromised.

Unless, of course, you were a time traveler.

I had to hand it to Lionel for that one. The main downside was that we were stuck inside this house for the duration of the trip. "This isn't quite what I pictured," I said after we looked around the kitchen. It was around 6 am, and the sun was just coming up, casting a dim glow in the house. We both knew it would be unwise to turn on any of the lights.

"Yes, this burglar made an awful mess of things," Lionel replied.

"No, not that. It's 1993 just outside those windows. One of the best years of my life, even if we're nowhere near where I grew up. And here we are tiptoeing around a crime scene looking for a stuffed bird."

Lionel chuckled. "When you put it like that, it does sound rather absurd. This is just the way our business sometimes works. In order to travel to the times we *want* to travel to, we occasionally have to engage in an affair like this. Granted, I didn't invent the time machine with this sort of thing in mind, but it's rather a necessity, you know."

I frowned. "I never thought time travel would seem like a job."

Lionel elbowed me in the ribs. "Admit it, though. You'd kill for a job like this, wouldn't you?"

"Yeah, but a stuffed bird," I said, walking into the side hallway.

"I don't assign the sentimental value to objects people seek."

Lionel handed me a pair of latex gloves. My fingerprints weren't on file, but there was no use leaving behind any unknown prints to give the police something to make them curious.

We exited the kitchen into a short hallway that led to the living room, passing a powder room along the way. The living room was in disarray, just like the kitchen. Couch cushions were thrown on the floor, drawers were left open, and a floor lamp had been knocked down. In addition to this, Dietrichson's television lay on the floor, screen-side down next to a pile of videocassettes that were strewn about. Out of habit, I walked over to the pile of tapes, mildly curious about her taste in movies. It was strange to see all the VHS tapes. I'd grown up with movies on tape, but by 2016 they had become artifacts of another time. *This* time, as it turned out.

It looked as though every tape she owned was dumped out of its sleeve into a pile on the floor. Whoever had broken in even yanked the VCR out of the TV stand, tearing off the cables that attached it to the television. I saw sleeves for *Silence of the Lambs, Ghostbusters, Edward Scissorhands,* and other movies that had been released between about 1980 and now. They were typical of the kinds of movies someone in 1993 would own. I was about to leave when I noticed the corner of another tape sleeve peeking out from beneath the pile. To my surprise, it was *All About Eve,* which didn't seem to fit with anything else here.

I stood up and felt unsettled. We were intruding on another person's life, almost as though we were looking through Laura Dietrichson's private journal or watching a slice of her life she wouldn't have wanted us to see. It made me think of Wendell Correy's line in *Rear Window* when he cautioned Jimmy Stewart that the apartment across the courtyard is "a secret, private world you're looking into out there. People do a lot of things in private they couldn't possibly explain in public." The sum total of the past suddenly felt that way to me. Perhaps there was an ethical principle attached to privacy, time travel, and—

"Cal?" I heard Lionel say.

"Oh, sorry."

"Did you find something?"

I smirked. "Just an idea for a future article."

"Mmm." He moved toward the stairs. "Perhaps we should try up there."

"Lead the way," I said.

There was a full bath at the top of the stairs and bedrooms on either side of it. We went to the bedroom on our left. Lionel took a step into the room. I froze in the doorway and gasped.

"Damn it," I growled.

The shades were pulled, but my eyes had adjusted after being in the dark house for the last several minutes. The bed was unmade, with a quilt lying at the foot of it. The sheets had been white, making the blood covering them stand out in even more stark contrast. I grasped for the first time what people meant when they referred to the 'stench of death.' Not more than a few hours ago—whether we were native to this time or not—Laura Dietrichson had taken her last breath right here. I hadn't even considered that until this very moment.

Lionel placed a hand on my shoulder. "Steady on, Cal. This is sometimes an unfortunate part of what we do. I don't like it either, but it's already happened, and you know as well as I do it's unchangeable. It may help to think of this as looking at a photograph."

"*Standing* in a photograph, more accurately."

"You've got me there," Lionel said. "Try not to disturb any of the physical evidence." He paused, and added, "Even if the cozzers never solve the poor woman's murder."

I nodded and quietly glanced around the room, not really seeing anything. "Uh, there's another room across the hall. Why don't I give it a look?"

"Excellent idea."

I walked slowly across the hall into the opposite bedroom. It had been converted into an office that reminded me of the den at the Maitlands' house in *Beetlejuice*, except it was an utter mess like the rest of the rooms. Drawers had been opened and rifled, and most of their contents were dumped onto the floor. There were utility bills and some correspondence, which I would have given a closer look had we been here to actually solve her murder. I also saw some bank statements with the name 'Winters & Lewis Savings and Loan' at the top. According to the statement, she had a checking account with a balance of around $900, as well as a long-term rental on a safe deposit box. I casually dropped the papers I'd been looking at and moved to the nearby window, feeling like some wannabe detective.

The scene of Laura Dietrichson's demise had been a shock, but it began to wear off. Lionel was right. This had *already* happened quite some time ago as far as we were concerned, and it was a bit like looking into a photograph. Outside of Hogwarts Castle, the people in photos were lifeless and unchanging.

Looking out the window, the sun made that wonderful orange glow on the horizon just to my right. I saw a maroon Ford Probe roll up the street. They stopped making those cars during the mid-90s. Even though this one looked clean and new, those cars were junk. My family had one for a while, during 1993 in fact. Now 1993 was all around me again, yet I couldn't do anything about it. I couldn't go for a walk to see what people wore, what their hair looked like, or what businesses occupied the store fronts on familiar streets. I wondered what was playing on the radio of that Ford Probe that just went by, or in any of the other cars rolling down Beechtree Avenue right now with their windows open. I tried to imagine the music as a flowing melody of gazey guitars and lyrics that made you think of a love scene just before the end of the world.

I heard Lionel quietly exclaim something from across the hall. I was about to go see what it was when I noticed something out of the corner of my eye. "I'll be damned," I said aloud. "Lionel!" I called out. It took Lionel a moment to get here. I must have caught him in the middle of looking for something, because he appeared to snap himself out of a deep thought when he saw me. I pointed to the top of a white bookcase next to the window. "I think that's our bird."

"Indeed," he said. I handed him the bird and watched him turn it over in his hands. "I never was much on bird watching. I suppose this is a raven."

"I don't see any other stuffed birds around."

"Fair point," Lionel said. "Rather a mangy looking thing, but I suppose that's typical of ravens. I believe they're scavengers like crows."

"Edgar Allen Poe's poem will never be quite the same. And look at the bottom of it," I said. Someone had used a bright blue thread to sew it together. "This taxidermist wasn't at the top of his game with that stitching. I don't think it's supposed to *look* sewn together."

"Probably not," Lionel agreed, "but this has to be the bird our man was asking about, even if he didn't mention the awful stitching."

"Just out of curiosity, how are you going to tell him you found it?"

Lionel frowned. "Haven't totally worked that out yet. However, there aren't that many taxidermists in this town. I may tell him I found it in one of their shops. Or perhaps a police evidence tub. Talking of which, we ought to be getting back. I'm sure the police and Lord knows who else will be popping in here in a little while. Nice work finding the bird, by the way."

"No problem," I said, looking at the window.

CHAPTER 8

A S HE EXITED Hardcastle's Liquor Store, holding the door open for an older woman, he didn't notice the stern-faced man with narrow eyes standing by the corner of the building, watching him all the way. Even if he had noticed the man, it's doubtful he would've recognized him. He'd only glimpsed the man two days ago from another room, and his presence here was in an entirely different context.

Fumbling in his pocket for his keys, he didn't see the man hustle to a dark green Honda Civic and quickly exit the parking lot. Had he noticed the car, there's always the chance he would have spotted it a few minutes later, parked at an odd angle two houses away from his own.

He pulled into his driveway and got out of his car, thinking mainly about enjoying a glass of Scotch from the fresh bottle he was carrying. As he walked up the driveway to the house's side entrance, he saw a broken flower pot lying further up the driveway, near the rear corner of the house. He paused for a moment to consider it. It looked like a begonia, of which he had several, but they were all on the porch behind the house. He pondered the possible causes — maybe it had been windier today than he thought — and casually walked toward the broken flower pot.

At the same moment his right index finger touched broken ceramic, a wave of throbbing pain and an ethereal sound like an out of tune bass drum overwhelmed him. Glass shattered simultaneously as he hit the ground.

"Err-awwgg," he groaned, trying to get up on all fours in the midst of the fog. As he got his right knee under him, there was a sudden hammer blow to his ribs. He slumped to the ground, a sharp pain in his side to compliment the emerging knot on the back of his head. The world was wavy and dark, but he felt a hand on the back of his head, holding it in place so he couldn't turn it. Something else also poked him in the shoulder. He knew instinctively that it was the barrel of a gun.

"Did you open the box?" asked an angry voice. Coherent thoughts were at a premium through the pain and the suddenness of what happened.

"What's the…" he started to say, but was cut off by another kick to the side, fortunately just below the previous blow. Whoever kept hitting him pulled him up by the hair so his head was just off the driveway.

"I know you know about the fucking box. Who else did you talk to? Tell me, or you're gonna die right here in your goddamn driveway. Tell me!"

There was more shouting, but he couldn't understand any of it. The waves of pain certainly didn't help, but even what he had understood made little sense. The world contained many boxes, after all. He was about to say something, to try and ask some probing question, but he heard another voice coming from the far end of the driveway.

"What's going on back there…oh, Jesus!"

The hand gripping his hair let go, and he heard footsteps moving away from him toward the side fence. He knew the other man had left. His mind banged around aimlessly, trying to decide whether to let himself pass out or try to sit up. Instinct said to get up, but he felt he ought to take a little rest first. Just a little rest, only until the throbbing in his head subsided and it was a bit easier to breathe. Yes, that's it, he thought.

"Oh God, I'll call 9-1-1," he heard the new voice say, now much closer, probably standing over him.

He smiled at that and settled into the emerging blackness that seemed to welcome him.

Thursday October 20, 2016

I knew my head would hurt when I woke up. I vaguely recalled having a dream where I was planting a garden and a shovel fell on me. *Whack*! Right on the back of the head. Unfortunately, my headache was real and had a less mystical cause than a dreamy shovel handle: bourbon. Two drinks turn into five quicker and more insidiously with bourbon than with any other kind of liquor. Damned if I knew why.

After a shower, a shave, some ibuprofen, and lots of water, I made it to Spalding in plenty of time to teach my undergraduate metaphysics class. My hangover had mostly faded by the time class started, and it wasn't as if I'd never taught with a hangover before. In addition, the students I had this semester seemed to come alive during the last couple of weeks. I didn't think I was doing anything different—it's just that talking with my students lately was more natural and less awkward.

Following class, I returned to my office and cued up Beach House's recent album, *Depression Cherry*. I leaned back and listened deeply to the chorus of *PPP*. Victoria Legrand's dreamy lyrics about the fragility of the things we hold dear, and how easily we sometimes squander them seemed written just for me. My thoughts turned to the time machine during the song's heavenly outro.

Since our trip to recover the stuffed bird, I'd traveled back in time twice more. It was becoming almost as natural as driving a car. Lionel and I had an easy relationship. It was probably our mutual respect for what I once called the "sanctity of the past." It felt like we had known each other much longer than a month. I even spent a little while racking my brain to remember whether I'd ever encountered a strange white-haired Englishman when I was a kid, but to no avail. Anyhow, the First Law made that little more than a fun exercise. If Lionel had never visited me when I was a child "the first time," he couldn't just go back now and tell little Calvin Sutherland about how he'd one day get to fulfill his lifelong dream of becoming a time traveler.

I even felt more comfortable around Lionel's two colleagues. Roger Blanchard, who seemed to take an instant dislike to me when we first met, had softened ever so slightly during a trip the three of us took to 1972 to recover a rare Civil War era rifle. That was fine with me. Time travel suited me well, and I didn't want anything—especially some silly personal conflict—to jeopardize it.

I'd gotten to know Jack Greenwood a little better, too. He was bright, didn't take himself too seriously, and looked upon time travel with a wide-eyed wonder that rivaled my own. Lionel was supervising Jack's dissertation and, like some of the other physics graduate students, Jack assisted Lionel with his research. Jack had inadvertently discovered that Lionel had a working time machine. As Lionel told me, "we had no other choice at that point than to put him on the payroll." Jack had also given me a talisman of sorts. It was a miniature list of major sports champions going back to 1910. One never knew when a thing like that would come in handy, he said.

Of the many significant insights that occurred to me during the past few weeks, the most prominent—and perhaps most paradoxical—was that the past wasn't nearly as predictable as one would assume. One might think that knowledge of the past would give a time traveler every conceivable advantage in getting around and even outwitting people. However, like much of life, that was only the case in the movies. You would need a movie script, a la *Back To The Future,* to arrange for two kids to pass by Lou's Café at the precise moment Marty McFly needed a skateboard to outfox Biff and unwittingly impress Loraine. All this so Marty could later steer her into a situation where George McFly could knock Biff out cold and impress the shit out of Loraine.

The past was still a wonderful, almost magical place, but it shared a very important characteristic with the present: human beings, with all their complexes, whims, and conflicting interests populated it. Knowing who was going to be the next president, what some awful pop culture trend would eventually evolve into, or who would win the next 10 Super Bowls didn't help Lionel and I avoid certain mundane pitfalls.

For instance, on our trip 1930 to recover the tumblers, Lionel and I knew there would be police raiding the speakeasy. Nevertheless, we couldn't have guessed how the proper moment to grab the tumblers would manifest itself. Nor could we have anticipated our encounter with the slow-witted, yet formidable patrol officer in the back alley.

During the aforementioned trip that Lionel, Roger, and I took to 1972, I had chosen to wear a pair of gray bell-bottoms, both because they were in style at the time and because I'd always wanted to wear bell-bottoms. The only belt left in the wardrobe room, however, was brown and didn't match. A minor thing, it would appear. As the three of us walked along a street in Kansas City, a young woman happened to notice my belt, probably *because* it didn't match. She was either on something or lacking in social intelligence— I'd bet the latter. In taking a closer look at my belt, she damn near activated the temporal return initiator and sent me back to 2016 in front of half a dozen passersby. Knowing President Nixon would resign two years later was of no help in dealing with this woman's random fascination with my belt.

Then again, our trips to the past weren't all business and suffering fools. My fourth trip was a very pleasant surprise. It was a trip back to 1954— Wednesday, August 4th to be precise. Our task was purchasing a bottle of wine. It didn't look like much of a trip at first. I had to admit I was growing a little impatient with these snatch and grab forays to the past. After all, you don't take a trip to a far off place just so you can spend your days walking around the hotel property.

My face must have dropped when Lionel first announced this trip, because he quickly reassured me that this was no ordinary bottle of wine. I asked whether the wine bottle contained uranium dust like in *Notorious*, though Lionel didn't get the joke. It was a 1953 vintage from the Joanna Rose Vineyards, extremely rare and, in 2016, extremely expensive. Only about fifteen unopened bottles were known to exist. One had recently sold at auction for almost $40,000.

We traveled to a rooftop in New York City, and it was just as I imagined an early evening on a mid-summer Wednesday would be. The buildings all seemed to be art deco, not yet overcome by glass or the vacuity that would become architecture's calling card during the 60's and 70's. The cars were pastel, and everyone we passed on the sidewalk seemed to be either smoking, wearing a fedora, or hurrying home with a paper bag of groceries. I couldn't get enough of it. Even Lionel seemed content to let me just stroll for a while and take things in.

Three liquor stores and $45 later we had our vintage bottle of wine. Judging by the look on the liquor store proprietor's face, this was a princely sum for a bottle of wine in 1954. I noticed Lionel checking his watch several times going to and from the store and asked him if there was some hurry to get back.

"Not to get back," he answered with a grin, "but there is one more stop we'll need to make."

"Oh?"

"Ever hear of the Rivoli Theater?"

"No," I said. "I've never really been into plays."

"I see," Lionel said, pausing before saying, "Well, here we are in 1954. August the 4th. That date mean anything to you, Cal?"

I tore myself away from watching a couple of kids wearing blue Brooklyn Dodgers hats and jackets with the name of their little league team on the back to consider Lionel's question. I noticed him smiling, and wondered what the big joke was.

"Can't say that I do," I replied.

"I see."

"Do I laugh now or wait for the punchline?"

"Just around the next corner," Lionel said. As we reached the end of the block and turned the corner, I was distracted by the sight of some real life beatniks, sitting on the front stoop of an apartment building. Lionel had stopped just ahead of me. "Do you remember in the speakeasy when you told me you'd like to be present for the unveiling of a great work of art?"

"I think so. I definitely remember feeling that way."

Lionel motioned ahead of us. There was a crowd of people milling about on the sidewalk in front of what looked to be a theater. Sure enough, 'Rivoli' was stenciled in red neon above the marquee. Then I saw the marquee.

"I'll be damned," I laughed.

"Always nice when we can kill two birds with one stone," Lionel said, holding up the paper bag containing the wine bottle. "You know, I've never seen *Rear Window* before."

I laughed. "Neither has anyone else here."

"Shall we?"

I turned to Lionel. "Thank you, Lionel. I can't tell you what it means."

"No need, old man," he said, elbowing me in the ribs. "I see it all over your face whenever we travel back in time."

I still thought about that trip often: how everyone had dressed up for the premiere, the women buzzing over Grace Kelly's wardrobe, and the way everyone gasped as Thorwald looked into the camera and at each one of us as he discovers he's being watched. I watch *Rear Window* once a year—no more frequently than that—but sitting in that theater in 1954 felt like seeing it for the first time. I was as enthralled as the crowd and felt just as much a part of that time as they did.

That was the last occasion time travel and the past seemed so innocent.

CHAPTER 9

Friday October 21, 2016

I HATED CANCELING a meeting with a student at the last minute, especially a bright graduate student who had some legitimate questions about her upcoming term paper. She seemed to understand when she saw me hurriedly gathering up my things. I'd make it up to her next week.

What bothered me more was the sound of Lionel's voice on the phone. There was little trace of his usual casualness, or his dry British way of reckoning with the world. He also gave no explanation. All he said was, "Cal, something's recently occurred, and I need to see you right away."

I hurried across Spalding's campus, even cutting across the grass where I could, a host of possible outcomes fermenting in my mind. Was the time machine suddenly broken beyond repair? Worst of all, had its existence been discovered by someone else?

Slow down, I told myself. No use conjuring up screwy ideas when you're going to find out the truth in a few minutes.

When I arrived at Lab 7, Jack let me in. He looked a little unsettled himself, which didn't bode well.

"Hello, Cal," Lionel said gravely as Jack closed the door behind me.

"Lionel," I said. "What's going on with you guys?"

Lionel sighed. "Roger's in hospital."

"What's wrong with him?"

"He was attacked the day before yesterday."

"Attacked?"

"It happened just after he got home Wednesday evening," Lionel said, harshly adding, "right outside his bloody house!"

"Jesus," I said. "How is he? Is he…mostly okay?"

"He'll live, if that's what you mean. He has a concussion and three badly bruised ribs, I'm sorry to say."

"I don't suppose the police arrested whoever attacked him," I said.

"No," Jack said. "Dr. Blanchard got hit from behind, so he never saw who attacked him. Plus, he's kind of having a hard time remembering everything, you know?"

"One of Roger's neighbors saw the attacker running away," Lionel said.

"Well, that's something at least," I said.

"Not really. Around six feet tall, probably in his early 50s, medium build. Half the middle-aged men in this town in other words."

"Damn it," I said. "I wish there was something I could do to help, Lionel."

"As a matter of fact, there is," Lionel said, smiling for the first time since I got there. Jack nodded as Lionel shot him a knowing look. After a moment, I caught their drift.

"Right," I said.

"Shouldn't be any need for a change of clothes on this one," Lionel said.

As we walked up the steps to the time machine's Nora Pads, I considered asking Lionel if we might need a weapon. I realized that wouldn't be necessary. No shots were fired during the attack, and the assailant got away. Nevertheless, I still swallowed hard and took a deep breath as the tubes closed around me.

Wednesday October 19, 2016

Roger never made it inside his house, and there were no signs of forced entry, so Lionel and I figured the safest "landing spot" was Roger's living room. It contained a chocolate colored couch, two matching chairs, and a couple of pressed wood bookcases that all looked to have been purchased from the same discount furniture store. There wasn't much hanging on the walls except for a couple photos. One of them showed a younger Roger in a British military uniform.

"I'll be damned," I said, staring at the photo. "Though I guess it does make a certain amount of sense."

"Oh yes," Lionel said. "Roger was a member of Her Majesty's Paratroopers. Even participated in Thatcher's silly Falkland Islands campaign in '82. His, shall we say, fighting skills have come in handy on a couple of trips to the past. Still rather hard to believe he was taken by surprise like this."

"Could happen to anyone," I said. "He was outside his own house on a run of the mill Wednesday afternoon. *This* afternoon, as it turns out."

"Yes," Lionel said gravely.

"Sorry. I didn't mean to sound so glib about what happened...er, is about to happen."

After a moment, Lionel said, "I believe in finding out all we can about what occurred, and I suppose we shall. But I can't..."

"You don't want to actually watch the attack," I said. Lionel nodded. "For what it's worth, neither do I. Roger and I didn't hit it off at first, but...well, he sure as hell doesn't deserve this."

"No," Lionel said. "Still, I can understand his initial feelings—about you, I mean."

"Really?" I asked suspiciously.

"Roger and I met at Leeds University, you know. I was there for about a decade or so before he was hired. We knew each other, but not particularly well. Just said 'hello' to one another, that sort of thing. Then one day we got to talking about my research on temporal waves, and that discussion, as you might imagine, quickly turned to time travel. Rather like us, Cal."

"Okay."

"Except Roger was a little more, I suppose 'serious' is the word for it. Suffice it to say, he was of invaluable help in building the time machine. When we were confident that it would work and we could safely travel to the past, he confessed the source of his passion for time travel. And that, I'm afraid, is where you and Roger were at cross purposes."

"I don't understand."

"The First Law, old man. You see, Roger's a widower. I met his wife a few times at department functions. Very nice girl, too. They were married for just under three years when she was killed."

"Killed?"

"Silliest of accidents," Lionel said. "A man backed over her with his car."

"Aw, damn." I shook my head.

"Indeed," Lionel said. "The man was backing out of his driveway. He had a young son in the backseat jabbering away, the way children do." Lionel trailed off, seeming to try and picture the scene in his mind. "He never saw her."

Roger's interest in time travel now made perfect sense. "So, like most people, Roger figured he could travel back in time and save her, right?"

"In a word, yes."

It was what made time travel so appealing. Then again, most people had never actually gone back in time. "Well, you guys must've noticed that there were certain things you couldn't do in the past because of the First Law."

"Why sure, in hindsight, but when we first started traveling in time we just put it down to silly coincidence. On one trip to recover something we were waylaid by an old woman crossing the street."

"I take it Roger actually went back to try and save his wife."

"Twice, as a matter of fact."

"What happened when he did?" I asked eagerly.

"The first time, for all of his planning and care, Roger got the time wrong and arrived a hair too late. It had happened just before he rounded the corner of the street. Fortunately for him he didn't actually see it occur. Nonetheless, this inspired him to try again."

"And the second time?"

Lionel gave a wan smile. "Were you anyone else, Cal, I'd preface this by saying you probably won't believe me. Naturally, Roger got there much earlier this time around. Even walked by the man's house a few times just to get the lay of the land, so to speak. He was milling around a short distance away, sort of keeping an eye on things, probably obsessively checking his watch. Well, this unfortunately aroused the suspicion of one of the neighbors, who promptly called the police."

I rolled my eyes. "Oh, for Christ's sake."

"Not having his wallet with him, or a plausible explanation for his presence there, Roger was actually picked up for questioning. The cozzers left him alone in an interrogation room for a few moments and he disappeared— returned to the present, that is. Very uncharacteristic for him, you know. I'm sure he held out the vain hope that there was some way to save his poor wife. Perhaps if he'd only planned things a little better or gotten there even earlier or something. Then along came your colloquium paper, and that forever slammed the door on Roger's hopes. I must say, we'd never pondered time travel as a logic problem before."

"I'm sure Roger would've preferred to keep it that way," I said. Just then, I heard a thud toward the rear of the house. Lionel and I looked at each other. Then there was another thud. Through the curtain, I saw a figure walk past the window toward the kitchen.

"Kitchen window," I whispered. We made our way to the back of the kitchen, behind a small folding table. I edged over to the far right of the window to try and peer out from an angle where someone outside couldn't see me. I saw a broken flower pot in Roger's driveway, which ran next to the kitchen.

"I'm going to the front of the house to watch for Roger," Lionel whispered, tiptoeing out of the kitchen.

It suddenly hit me how bizarre this was. Lionel must have felt some urge to shout out, warning Roger of the attack. Yet, there was no report of anyone calling out to Roger, and we knew that the attack took place. For all of Lionel's and my talk about the First Law, we'd overlooked a fundamental question: *what* is it that prevents the past from being altered? Is there some physical, thermodynamic force preventing Lionel from exercising his vocal chords to warn Roger? Does Lionel merely believe he shouldn't call out because of what we know? Is it all just a matter of fortune and happenstance?

I didn't have a chance to continue that train of thought. A man suddenly appeared at the edge of the window next to me. He stood too close to the window frame, so I couldn't get a good look at him without moving the curtain. I kicked myself for not opening the window a crack so that I could hear whether anything was said during the attack. Just then, Lionel silently bounded into the kitchen. He mouthed the words, "Roger's here," and crouched down below the window. He took a deep breath and seemed to steel himself for what was about to happen.

The man outside moved toward the center of the window. I could tell he was facing away from me, so I peered between the edge of the curtain and the window frame to get a look at him. He was just under six feet tall with graying hair, thick arms, and an emerging paunch. His nose was a bit large and his eyes were small and narrow, which gave him the look of someone permanently scowling.

In a flash, I saw Roger bending over to examine the broken flower pot in the driveway at the same moment the man lunged for him, violently swinging his arm downward. He held what looked like a small black metal pipe that crashed down on to the back of Roger's head. Roger seemed to tense for an instant, then dropped flat on the ground. I winced audibly and turned away. Lionel just crouched on the kitchen floor with his head down and his eyes closed.

I stood up to where I could see outside, hoping that this guy was just going to take some money from Roger's wallet without hitting him again. Unfortunately, I saw him kick Roger once in the side of the chest. Roger looked on the verge of losing consciousness, and for his sake I hoped he would. It was downright awful seeing him like this. The man removed a gun from his belt and pointed it at the back of Roger's head. Even though the window was closed, I heard Roger moan.

"You opened it!" the man growled. As he did, Lionel picked his head up and gave me a quizzical look, probably wondering the same thing as me: opened what? More importantly, this changed the tenor of the assault. Whoever this person was, he wasn't just out to rob Roger.

Then the man yelled, "Did you see the tape?"

Lionel got to his feet, apparently ready to see for himself what was going on, when we heard a faint voice call out from the other end of the driveway. This must have been the neighbor who had called 9-1-1.

I watched Roger's attacker freeze and look momentarily toward the end of the driveway. Then he lowered the gun and started to hurry away from the scene. Lionel and I ran into the next room to try and get one last glimpse of him. We watched him climb up onto the fence separating the two yards. As he did so, he briefly glanced down at the ground, his head facing us.

"Oh my good God," Lionel said. He didn't even bother to whisper.

"I know," I said. "At least we know Roger will be all right. And we got a good look at who attacked him."

"I already know him, Cal."

"What? Who is he?"

Lionel closed his eyes and pinched the bridge of his nose. "He's the one who hired us to recover the bird."

CHAPTER 10

Thursday October 27, 2016

I HADN'T SLEPT well since the attack on Roger. One night I drank too much to make the uneasiness go away. The next night I didn't touch a drop, worried I would overlook something like figuring out the reason Roger was attacked or that someone was looking in my window. Today, during my afternoon seminar, I actually lost my train of thought right in the middle of a lecture and made up some wild-ass claim on the spot. Time travel wasn't supposed to make me feel this way.

This past Saturday I imagined using the time machine as a "solution" to these problems. Why not live in the past for a while? I could take some of the counterfeit money and go to 1947, maybe San Francisco. I'd lie low and work as an usher in a movie theater. I could even squat in a posh apartment I knew would be abandoned for a couple months.

But then what? Even if I could stay in the past forever, I'd never leave Lionel to deal with this all alone.

My mind snapped back to my office and the paper I was grading. My pen ran out of ink just as I wrote a grade on the last paper from my undergraduate metaphysics class. I tossed the pen in the trash on the way out of my office and went to get a fresh one from the supply closet. Margo must have seen me pass, because she was waiting for me as I returned to my office.

"I've told you how I hate sneaks," she said.

"Sorry Margo, I wasn't aware you'd appropriated all of the blue ink pens. Seems like an abuse of your position."

"Oh, you can keep the pen, Cal. I have a special stash of premium pens I keep under lock and key. I was talking about a certain manuscript that was recently accepted for publication."

I felt my face redden. "Oh, that."

"Yes, that," she said. "Were you going to wait for some dramatic moment during your next tenure review meeting to finally tell me about it?"

"That's actually a good idea, but the truth is I just forgot about it." Margo probably figured I was being falsely modest, but I wasn't. My real life encounters with time travel had overtaken any issues I'd discussed in the paper.

"The *Quarterly Journal of American Philosophy*," Margo said. "Well done, Cal. You know, you're the first faculty member to get an article accepted there in about five years."

"No, I didn't know that."

"I'm glad to see you took our talk last month to heart," she said. If Margo knew what motivated that article—and how quickly I'd written it—she'd never believe me. Anyhow, she meant well, and I wasn't going to try and talk her out of it. "Believe it or not, I actually read some of your manuscript."

"You're right Margo, I don't believe it."

"Speaking of which, I'm not sure I believe in this so-called First Law of Time Travel that you get so much mileage of out of in your article."

"Article?" a voice said from behind. I turned to see Bruce Hardwick, my colleague who took such a dim view of my research at Margo's party last month. What the hell was he even doing here? Probably searching for a desperate graduate student to teach his classes for him while he jetted off to some circle-jerk conference. "Are you working on an article, Margo?" he asked, not paying me any mind.

"Actually, I was just congratulating Cal on a forthcoming publication," she said.

"Oh?" Hardwick asked with a skeptical tone. "And which journal gets the honor?"

"*Quarterly Journal of American Philosophy*," Margo said after a pregnant pause. Hardwick's eyes betrayed his surprise. He glanced at me unsmiling. I gave Hardwick a look like Jack Benny just after he zinged someone.

"Q-JAP is publishing something of Cal's?" Hardwick said, using the overly cute acronym for the journal.

I poked my head in front him, tired of being talked about as though I wasn't there. "Yes, as a matter of fact, they are publishing my article."

"Hmph," he said, quickly adding, "Well, I'm just finishing up something for them myself. Has to do with the ethical similarities in cloning and genetic alteration for…"

"That's fine, Bruce," Margo said, cutting him off. "You'll have to let me know how the manuscript progresses."

"I'm curious," Hardwick said, turning to me with a frown, "just what was it you were writing on."

"The implications of a logical law that pertains to time travel."

Hardwick snorted. "I wouldn't have thought Q-JAP would be interested in a subject like that."

"Like what?"

"It's very, shall we say, left field. I haven't met a philosopher apart from

76

you that even gives it a second thought. I mean, if it were at least a little more interdisciplinary that would be one thing. But as it stands now, it's just a lot of idle thought experiments."

"On the contrary, Sonny Jim," a familiar voice said from behind me. We all turned to see Lionel walking up to us with a smile. "Cal's research has been invaluable to some cutting edge work in physics and quantum engineering." He turned to me with a smile and shook my hand, purely for dramatic effect. "So, I take it you heard back about the manuscript we were discussing."

"As a matter of fact I have," I said, giving a thumbs up.

"Excellent," Lionel said.

"I don't believe we've met," Margo interjected, probably wondering whether I'd staged all this as a prank.

"Oh, quite right," Lionel said apologetically. "Lionel Bradshaw. I'm with the Physics Department."

"The Physics Department?" Hardwick asked, clearly surprised.

"Indeed. Cal and I have been collaborating on a project for the last little while." I could see Margo glancing at Hardwick and trying to not to smile.

"Nice to have met you." Hardwick excused himself, clearly defeated.

"Quite," Lionel replied. After Hardwick sulked off, Margo turned to Lionel and shook her head.

"You know, if you're thinking of stealing Cal away from us to help with your scientific research, I wouldn't bother. As far as I know he can't even balance a checkbook, and he bought his first cell phone two years ago, only because I kept after him about it."

"Which I often forget to turn on," I added.

Lionel chuckled at this. "I'll be sure to keep that in mind." We chatted amiably for another minute, and then Margo excused herself. Lionel and I went into my office.

"You have impeccable timing, Lionel. No pun intended," I said after we got inside.

"Always my pleasure to un-starch a stuffed shirt," he said, pushing my office door closed. "I wish that was my main reason for dropping by, though."

"Okay," I said warily.

"Roger's out of hospital, you know."

"How's he doing?"

"Oh, all right, considering. Face is still healing, and he moves a bit stiffly, but nothing too serious. He and I were discussing an alternative way to pick up this man's trail."

I shifted in my chair. "Lionel, don't take this the wrong way, but have you considered that maybe we ought to just leave this alone."

Lionel narrowed his eyes. "Leave this alone? We can't. I mean…not after what happened to Roger."

"I'm not trying to minimize that, believe me. It's just that, I'm having a hard time seeing where it would lead."

"Maybe there's more to all this than meets the eye," Lionel said.

"There's always more going on than meets the eye. We don't know why that bird was so important to this guy, and we don't know why it would motivate him to attack Roger. My point is the answers may not be worth the trouble it will take to find them."

"Aren't you the least bit curious?"

"I'm curious about lots of things, Lionel, but I can't investigate them all. Besides, we don't even know this guy's name."

"Yes, that would be of invaluable help," Lionel said. "However, there is another known connection to this man."

"Don't keep me in suspense."

"Funny Cal, I thought you would have been the one to see it first."

I narrowed my eyes at Lionel. For a moment, he reminded me of my father, though they looked nothing alike. Often, when I encountered a puzzle as a kid, especially if it concerned why a person did something a certain way, he always folded his arms, sat back in his chair, and left me to figure it out on my own. The trouble was, I'd already been wrestling with this problem for several days, and I had no idea why Roger was attacked. So what connection was Lionel so sure of that I was missing?

"I'm still not seeing it. This guy might as well be a ghost."

"I don't believe in ghosts, Cal. Besides, take your focus off the man for a moment and consider the thing he wanted."

"You mean the bird?"

"Precisely," Lionel said. "At present, we don't know who or where our man is, so we can't just ask *him* about the bird. But it did belong to someone else for a number of years, didn't it?"

"You mean the sister? But she's dead."

Lionel rolled his eyes. "Oh good heavens, Cal. Sometimes it's as though you've never traveled through time before."

I shook my head and frowned. "Shit. I should've already figured that out. But how exactly would we do this?"

"Well, I'm afraid that's up to you, old man."

"What're you talking about?"

"Roger and I talked it over, and we think you're the man for the job."

"Job?"

"Encountering Laura Dietrichson sometime before she was killed, during the summer of 1992. There's a good chance the bird was still in her possession by that time, and she might be able to shed some light on its significance."

It made a certain amount of sense. All except the part about me flying solo in the starring role. "Why me?"

"Let's just say I'm an excellent judge of such things."

"Really?" I asked dubiously.

Lionel gave me a wan smile. "You seem best suited to the task. Whoever goes back is probably going to be there for a little while. Roger's still recovering, I'm unfortunately a bit too grandfatherly for the role, and Jack lacks the requisite experience."

"I'm not exactly a grizzled veteran of time travel myself."

"True, but I've seen you in the past, Cal. What you lack in experience, you more than make up for in intuition. Plus, you're the right age."

"Right age?"

"About the same age as Laura Dietrichson."

"Oh," I groaned, "so that's what this is about."

"It is and it isn't," Lionel said.

"Look, past or not, picking up women out of the clear blue and getting them to tell me all their deepest secrets isn't my strong suit. 'Good evening, ma'am. I'm from a special branch of the Audubon Society. Got any mysterious stuffed birds whose origins you'd like to discuss?' I wouldn't know where to begin."

Lionel paused, and looked at me sympathetically. "Cal, you'll just have to trust me on this. You *can* do it. I know. We can talk over some further practical considerations at the lab. You'll likely be in the past for a while, maybe a month or more, so you ought to pack a suitcase."

I sat quietly for a moment, trying to think this through. How would I even meet Laura Dietrichson? If I did, how would I casually inquire about a stuffed bird that someone else would come looking for all these years after her death? Dozens of scenarios flashed through my mind, but they all had one thing in common.

I looked at Lionel and smiled. "The early 90s, huh? I do remember that time fondly."

CHAPTER *11*

Friday June 5, 1992

YOU'RE THE ONLY *man for the job, Cal.*

When Lionel said this five days ago, I swelled with pride. Even Roger shook my hand before I walked up the steps to the Nora Pads, which seemed strange and out of place for him. I set my suitcase on one pad while I stood on an adjacent pad. I'd get the chance to inhabit the early 90s all by myself, and for a significant duration. It was strange packing clothes and toiletries as though I were merely going on a vacation. My own clothes were suitable for this trip, as my usual choice of attire was pretty nondescript. I didn't tell Lionel, but I packed a supply of weed, too. I'd never gotten stoned in the past before, and I wasn't about to let the opportunity go by. If I got to experience the 90s all over again—and 1992 may have been the decade's zenith—I was damn well going to *experience* it.

Then I arrived in 1992 only to wonder, *now what?*

Our plan was simple enough. I could stay here for as long as I needed to, try to get to know Laura Dietrichson, and find out what I could about her brother—especially why he would want the stuffed raven in 2016. Jack had collaborated with his roommate, a computer science major, to provide me with a fake credit card. Outwitting the anti-theft technology of the early 90's was a snap using early 21st century technology.

Even the fact that I would be in the past for an extended period wasn't an issue. Jack explained the Delaney Axiom to me, which governed the amount of time that passed in the present when one went back in time. As long as I kept the same temporal return initiator that I departed with, only about fifteen minutes would elapse in 2016 while I was gone. Since I departed on a Friday afternoon, I would return fifteen minutes later on the same afternoon, with the whole weekend to decompress—assuming I even needed to decompress.

That was all well and good, but there was still the matter of somehow befriending Laura Dietrichson. I couldn't just walk up to her and start asking her questions about her estranged brother, a stuffed raven, and who she thought would have a reason to murder her next spring. Approaching her seemed very much like approaching a woman for the first time in a romantic context.

I had only one chance to make a good impression. If she blew me off, then I'd have to return to 2016 with my tail between my legs and an array of excuses.

I spent my first couple of days in 1992 on sort of a vacation, smoking weed and hanging out in the area just south of my later Beechtree area residence. Unlike 1930, I had a living memory of this time. Back in the present, my memories of the early 90's seemed timeless. Now that I was in 1992, the people I encountered appeared out of style. Beyond the obligatory flannel shirts and long hair, I didn't remember the early 90's having a unique style to them. Yet they did—everything from the cars, to the radio jingles, to the signs on storefronts all seemed off key. As a teenager, I had simply been immersed in the time. If I tried to fit in back then, it was by using something given to me by the zeitgeist. I hadn't been able to compare anything then to some related item from the future.

Nonetheless, it was wondrous being here at first. I spent the better part of my first few afternoons at a music store on Beechtree Avenue—in 2016, it was a Tapas restaurant—sampling discs and talking music with the young clerk behind the counter. His face lit up when I mentioned my interest in bands like Ride, The Stone Roses, and Slowdive, even if their greatest album was still a year away. He introduced me to a band called Curve and asked me where I thought music was headed "once this grunge thing peters out."

I said there would probably be a bunch of fifth-rate Eddie Vedder imitators, and that music from across the pond probably wouldn't take hold in America like it ought to. I also suggested he keep an eye on the electronic music scene. Saying all that was cheating, but I didn't care. It felt good. I told him I'd be in town for a while and we should hang out and get high some time. The trouble was, getting high in 1992 got old after a couple days. I couldn't just groove in the past forever, as idyllic as it sounded.

On my third day in 1992, I saw Laura Dietrichson.

I passed by her house on foot several times during the day to get a sense of her routine. I caught a glimpse of her car backing out of the driveway one morning, probably on her way to work. She drove a gray Pontiac Grand Am, with all the plastic paneling that was supposed to make the car look futuristic but inevitably fell off and made it look ultra-cheap. If she had friends or a bustling social life she did that somewhere else, because I never saw anyone at her house.

I got my first good look at her that evening when she returned home. I was across the street, and I felt my heart race as her car rolled past me into her driveway. She got out of her car as she'd likely done thousands of times, without so much as a glance at the surroundings. She had chestnut hair pulled back in a ponytail and wore a light blue dress with black sandals.

It was one thing to read about murders in true crime books. Sometimes they contained photographs of the victims while they were alive. You might even see a documentary with the victim on video, like the footage of Ron Goldman at that wedding all the news outlets would be repeatedly showing two years from now. The victim had a life; photos or a video were merely evidence of that life. But that's all it was. The person was still dead as you watched them.

Yet here I was looking at a *future* murder victim, as real, as alive, and as wholly unaware of the date she would die as I was of my own. I could have called out to her just to watch her react, the way anyone would. Her murder in ten months somehow made her seem even more alive. I slept badly that night, thinking I'd have some trippy dream like Jimmy Stewart in *Vertigo*. However, Laura Dietrichson wasn't a live woman pretending to be a dead woman. The live woman I was following was the very same woman who would soon be dead.

Watching her coming and going the next several days muted the eeriness of that initial encounter, though I still felt very uneasy. Equally troubling, though in a different way, was that I'd been here over a week and wasn't any closer to learning anything of value. I had to figure out a way to approach her.

As I was about to turn the corner on my usual evening walk past her house, I saw her coming up the street towards me, carrying a stack of papers in a folder. I stood off to the side pretending to look in the window of a yarn shop as she came to the corner. She turned away from me and walked down Beechtree Avenue. I followed her about two blocks to a coffee house called Café Anne. It wasn't a large place, so I worried that if I went inside she would notice me and my cover would be blown. On the other hand, maybe it was time I forced my own hand a bit.

In I went.

Laura was standing by the back counter, waiting to receive her order. She wore a gray V-neck t-shirt and the kind of pants people would refer to as "mom jeans" in about fifteen years. The barista handed her a dark green ceramic mug with steam coming off it, which Laura carried to a table in the second row from the window, near the middle of the café. I ordered a café au lait when I got to the register, trying all the while to watch Laura out of the corner of my eye. I still had no idea how to approach her, or even whether it was a good idea to have followed her in here.

After my order was ready—it cost me a whopping $1.41 with tax, about half what it would cost in 2016—I walked to the rear of the café to add some sweetener to my drink. To my chagrin, a college aged couple sat down at the table behind Laura. There was nowhere I could sit to watch her without being seen.

I decided to walk past her table to see what she was working on. I turned myself sideways to fit between the two rows of tables. At the same moment I glanced down at her table, she stood up without looking and bumped me, causing me to spill most of my drink. A good bit of it landed on my left arm, burning me.

"Ow, damn it," I said, shaking my arm.

"Oh, my gosh, I'm so sorry," she said, her neck turning red. "I wasn't looking. It was totally my fault." I just stood there with my lips tight in a frown, shaking my left arm. She must have thought I was going to yell at her, because she backed off a step and said, "I'm really sorry, okay? It was an accident."

"It's all right," I grunted. "It just burns a little. You don't have a napkin, do you?" She seemed to relax and hustled to the rear of the café to grab some napkins. By this time, the barista had come over with a rag to wipe the floor.

"Here you go," Laura said, handing me the napkins. Her voice was higher pitched than I had imagined. I wiped off my arm and the side of my pant leg. Somehow, the coffee had completely missed my shirt. "Can I at least buy you a fresh drink?"

All at once, who she was and the reason I was here came back to me. I had completely botched this, blowing whatever pathetic cover I had. Now I just wanted to get out of here. "Uh, no. That's all right."

"Please. It was my fault it spilled. It would make me feel better."

I thought this over for a moment. The toothpaste was already out of the tube, so to speak. "Café au lait," I told her reluctantly. She nodded to the barista who went off to make it. I stood there with a blank expression on my face, trying not to look at Laura.

"If you like, you can sit here while you're waiting," she said, pointing to the chair across from her. The other tables had filled in during the brief time I had been here.

"Okay," I said, sitting down. She sat across from me but didn't pick up her pen. Neither of us said anything. I looked toward the counter, hoping my drink would soon be ready. I noticed her staring at me quizzically, expecting me to say something. I hated making small talk at the best of times, and the awkwardness at our table was palpable. Then I noticed the papers on the table in front of her.

"Oh, you're a teacher," I blurted out more eagerly than I intended. Her arched eyebrow told me she mistook it for some kind of cheap icebreaker.

"I hope you're not going to say something about how a woman like me shouldn't be alone on a Friday night, grading papers."

I shrugged. "It's not like I expect every woman to spend her Fridays doing Jell-O shots in a bar on half-price yoga pants night."

She seemed to laugh in spite of herself. "Well thanks, I guess. Although I'm not sure what yoga pants are."

Shit. I guess they're not called that yet. "Forget it. So what do you teach?"

She looked down. "I doubt you'd be interested."

"Oh, oh I see," I said, feigning offense. "Just the typical Neanderthal male, eh? No taste for anything apart from tractor pulls and jock straps."

She let out a laugh that drew stares from the couple next to us. She put her hand over her mouth to cover it. "Where in the world do you come up with this stuff?"

The barista set down a fresh café au lait in front of me. "Must be the coffee," I said, giving a crooked smile like William Powell in the *Thin Man*. "So, what *do* you teach? I'm guessing it's not home economics."

"Very perceptive. It's European Literature."

"No shit," I said, relaxing even more. I didn't read much of it anymore, but I remembered some books from when I was an undergrad.

"No shit," she repeated. "Now your eyes are probably going to glaze over while you think of a way to change the subject, right?"

"Actually I was going to point out that café au lait is sometimes drunk by people in a European country whose name I can't recall." She laughed again. "You're not having them read anything by Albert Camus, are you?"

"Mmm," she said eagerly, putting down her coffee. "You know Camus?"

"I'm hanging around a coffee house, aren't I?"

"Touché." She smiled. "But no. These are high school juniors. That may be a little much for them. We're actually finishing up *Brave New World*."

My eyes brightened. "I love that book. That was one of the first books in high school that I 'got,' you know?"

"I wish some of my students would get it. A lot of them are just wondering when we're gonna invent Soma," she said, shifting some of the papers. She pulled her hair back behind her ear and took a sip of her coffee.

"I guess every high school literature class has its share of Delta Minuses." It was a reference to the rigid class structure of the characters in the book. Delta Minuses were at the bottom of the hierarchy. She was still looking down, but I saw her smile and then try to hide it.

"I guess so," she said.

"Still, better your students than friends or family, right?"

"Oh? Are you related to any Delta minuses?"

"Distantly," I said. "I have an older sister; she's definitely an Alpha. You?"

She smiled. "Only my younger sister, but she's okay. A solid Beta-Plus."

"Oh."

"So, what do you do?" she asked. "Don't tell me you're a teacher, too."

I felt myself stiffen. I'd been here over a week and hadn't thought of a cover story for who I was. "I do teach. Philosophy, believe it or not."

"Oh really?"

"So, I know a little about eyes glazing over and the 'I never did very well in that class,' routine whenever you tell someone what you do for a living."

"I bet you do," she said. "My name's Laura." She stuck out her hand. I hesitated a moment before shaking it. Touching her hand broke my train of thought.

"I'm Cal," I said automatically. Should I be telling her my real name? Then again, what did it matter? In ten months…I shook the thought out of my mind. I told her I was on a visiting summer fellowship to Spalding, figuring it was probably a good idea to mix in a few half-truths with whatever tall tales I'd end up telling her. At least I was familiar with Spalding in case any direct questions about the campus arose.

"Well Cal, it's very nice to meet you," she said after my partially-fake biography.

"Likewise." I smiled.

She seemed to hesitate for a moment and then nodded at my coffee. "Don't take this the wrong way, but would you like to get something stronger?"

"You mean like an espresso?" I asked, adding a dry laugh.

"Cute." She smirked.

Suddenly I felt my face go blank. I was so caught up in the rhythm of the conversation that something she said completely passed me by. I sat there for a moment wondering if I'd heard her correctly.

She must have noticed my expression change. "Never mind," she said, shifting her papers. "It's all right."

"What? No, it's fine, sure. Sorry, did you say you had a younger sister?" She nodded. "Not an older brother?"

"Uh, no," she drawled. "Why?"

"Just made me think of something else," I said. "Forget it."

She mentioned a bar a couple blocks away. I knew the location she was referring to—it was a comic book and card store in 2016—but I was only nodding without really listening. Something else was on my mind as she packed up her papers.

Laura Dietrichson doesn't have a brother.

It could have been a lie, but why lie about something like that? It was yet another puzzle to untangle: If Laura didn't have a brother, who was the man who hired Lionel to recover the bird in 2016?

Saturday June 13, 1992

The clock read '7:52,' and the sun already peeked through the Venetian blinds. I lay there for a few moments, trying to imagine the light showing up the dust in the air as if I was in some ornate living room in a 1940's film noir. It would look different from the present setting, but something about the feel, the heaviness of it, would be the same.

I was fully awake, as I usually was on Saturday mornings when I would've preferred to sleep in. Laura's steady breathing reminded me that it was my first night in a different bed. She lay on her side, facing away from me. Her arm hung off the right side of the bed, and some of her hair fell on my pillow. We'd seen each other a few times during the previous week, but this was the first time we'd spent the night together. We had gone to a bar as planned last Friday night—even closed the place down. At the end of the night, I walked her to her front door but didn't make a move to kiss her, though my instincts told me she was hoping I would have.

I called her on Sunday for dinner. As I dialed her number from my hotel room, I wondered why I was doing it. My reason for being in this time had become blurry. I was supposed to find out about the man who hired Lionel and later attacked Roger. Laura was a way to do that. Yet, when I knocked on her door last Sunday, those thoughts were overshadowed by other feelings I didn't want to examine more closely. Every time my hand brushed against the temporal return initiator on my belt, I suddenly recalled who I was. It must have been similar to the way an adulterer felt when he was with his mistress and happened upon some place that had a connection with his wife.

I quietly slipped out of the bed and put on my T-shirt. As I stood up, I stared down at my empty side of the bed. I remembered the terrible sight the last time I looked down at this side of Laura's bed. Ten months from now, I'm going to stand in this room again and...

STOP IT! I screamed in my head.

I went into the bathroom, used the toilet, and washed my face. I needed a haircut. Fortunately, my barber in 2016 had been in the same location nearby since the mid-eighties, so that wouldn't be a problem. I came out of the bathroom and was about to go downstairs to make myself breakfast—I fancied some eggs—and read the newspaper. Next to me was the door to the second bedroom, which Laura used as an office. The door was partially closed.

I tiptoed across the hall and went in. Unlike the last time I saw it, her office was pretty well organized. The school year ended last week, so the desktop was free of papers, and all her books stood neatly on the bookshelves. I hadn't paid them any attention last time, but she had a number of classic works of literature. I even saw a copy of Plato's *Republic*. A diploma from an out of state university hung on the wall to my right.

The stuffed raven sat directly in front of me.

It was on the middle shelf of the bookcase to the right of the window.

Last time it was one shelf above this. I walked around the desk, cautiously picked up the bird, and turned it over in my hands. Like Indiana Jones and the golden idol at the beginning of *Raiders of the Lost Ark*, I couldn't just walk out of here with it. I wouldn't be hounded by giant boulders and pygmies with poisoned arrows, just the First Law.

Since Lionel and I would find the bird here next year, I couldn't make off with it now. Instead, I looked at it and frowned. What was the significance of this damned thing? Did it even have any significance?

"Cal?" a voice said from behind. I whirled around with a guilty look on my face. Laura looked at me quizzically, wearing a long T-shirt with an owl on it.

"Morning," I tried to say as naturally as I could.

Her eyes moved to the bird. "What are you doing with that?"

"I was on my way downstairs. This is a nice office. Quite a few good books."

She took a step into the room. "What're you doing with that bird?"

"Nothing. I was just looking at some of your books and saw the bird on the shelf." Without thinking, I set the bird one shelf above where it had been.

"All right," she said sleepily, "don't worry about it."

"What is it, a family heirloom or something?"

She hesitated a moment. "A reminder."

CHAPTER 12

H E GULPED DOWN the last of his beer and drew a fresh cigarette from the pack next to the empty glass. It was one of the few bars in town where you could smoke, somehow grandfathered past the anti-tobacco zealots as a "cigar bar." He didn't see anyone in here smoking a cigar and didn't expect to. He did notice an arch look from the middle-aged, PTA-looking woman at a table nearby. He blew the smoke over his shoulder in her direction. The bar wasn't that crowded, which was good. A middle-aged couple sat a few seats to his right, and a college-aged kid in a Pittsburgh Steelers hat sat around the corner to his left. The bartender appeared, asking if he wanted a refill. He answered with a curt nod.

"Hi ya', Nick," a piping voice next to him said.

"Hey."

"Well, I made it. Right on time."

"Yup," Nick said flatly. The kid's cheerfulness was grating. It was probably a put on anyway. He knew the kid was desperate.

"So, you still need me to do that thing for you, right?" The kid said this just as the bartender got there. The kid ordered a Jack and diet—also grating.

As the bartender left, Nick glared at the kid. "Don't say that shit where anyone else can hear you." He liked seeing the hurt look on the kid's face.

"Sorry," the kid said, rubbing his arm near the crook of his elbow.

"Are you sure you're up for this?"

"For this? Pshaw, hell yeah," the kid said, just as someone ordering a drink bumped into Nick.

"And you can't talk like that with this guy. He's gotta believe your story. If you walk in there like some junkie douche bag, he's not gonna go for it."

"I know, I know."

"No! You don't know. That's why I've gotta tell you all this shit. So just listen up, okay?"

The kid put his palms out in front of him. "Okay. Sorry."

Nick frowned. He hated the thought of counting on this kid to do anything other than hit his parents up for money. After a moment, he took a folded sheet of paper from his pocket and laid it on the counter. "Here."

The kid picked up the paper and looked at it for a moment. "This is what I'm supposed to ask about?"

"That a problem?"

"No. It's just...well, isn't there some, like, government organization you can get this stuff from?"

"Maybe. Why, don't you need the money?"

"Sure."

"Well, okay then."

The kid looked at the paper and read it aloud. "Service records, discharge form, medical records, and commendations. You think this guy will be able to get this stuff?"

"Yup."

"How? I thought you said he was a like a science teacher or something."

"He's a physics professor. And I have no idea how he does what he does."

The kid looked back at the paper. "Is this guy, uh, Sergeant Arnold Paulson, a friend of yours or something?"

"Nope. Never met him."

"Then, how come..."

He was getting annoyed with the kid and his questions. "Someone I used to know. Paulson was her husband. Okay?"

"All right. No worries."

"You know where you're going?"

"Yeah," the kid said with a laugh. "I took some classes at Spalding for a while. But I never heard of this Bradshaw guy."

"Don't worry. You just tell him what I told you to say, got it?"

"Yeah, I guess so."

Thursday June 18, 1992

"You don't have to hang around here tonight if you don't want to," Laura said to me.

"I know," I said, "but it's either lounging here on your living room couch—"

"—Love seat," she interrupted, "and you look like an overgrown child with your legs hanging so far over the armrest."

"At any rate, I can either hang my apparently gangly legs over your love seat or over the side of the bed in my drab hotel room."

"It can't be that bad. At least the university is putting you up there until next month."

"You'll have to come see it some time," I said, flipping the page of the book I was reading. "You can help me count the semen stains on the comforter."

She gave me a repulsive look. "Oh gross, Cal."

"Which is why I'm hanging around here." I wiggled my legs. "No pun intended."

She gave me a sly smile. "You should've said something like, 'Even if I had a beautiful mansion, I'd still choose to spend the evening in your cozy living room by your side.'"

"If I had a beautiful mansion, we'd be spending the evening there." She laughed at this. "Thanks again for letting me borrow the book."

"No problem," she said. "Glad you're enjoying it."

I was reading *The Sun Also Rises*, which I found on Laura's bookcase upstairs. Though I genuinely wanted something to read—and enjoyed this story in particular—the book was just a pretense for going into her office again to look at the stuffed raven. Why not just take it, I wondered; let the First Law sort out how Lionel and I would be able to find it here next May. I still wondered whether it had any significance. It was a stuffed bird, for crying out loud. Did you have to show it to gain admission to some secret place, like that creepy orgy mansion in *Eyes Wide Shut*?

I'd been in 1992 for almost a month now, which was longer than it sounded. At least it seemed that way. I noticed myself taking the past for granted in some respects. In many subtle ways, it became my present. When I went out for a walk, I barely noticed the young guys with long hair, flannel shirts, and jean shorts with combat boots. Every radio seemed to play a steady mix of Pearl Jam, Soundgarden, and Metallica to the point where I absent-mindedly anticipated it.

I'd also begun taking for granted how easy it was to talk to Laura. Worse still, I felt happy whenever she laughed at something I said, which was often. Too often.

Even without my cover story about being at Spalding on a visiting summer fellowship, this little frolic had an expiration date before next May. Whenever I found out what I came here to learn, I was supposed to push a button on my belt and disappear. That was how time travel worked. Except I'd be leaving someone behind, someone who would miss me. I hated entanglements. Death is Laura's fate. Even if I wouldn't cause it, that cast a shadow over this. Was it ethical to have foreknowledge of the moment someone will die and not tell her, even though it wouldn't change anything? Was her death even my secret to keep? Would I want to know, if our positions were reversed?

"I guess sometimes it is hard to know why people are attracted to one another," I heard her say.

I looked up startled. "What?"

"Jake and Brett," she said. "In *The Sun Also Rises*. You were staring off into space. I thought you might be wondering what Jake could possibly see in Brett in the book. I know I sometimes have."

"Maybe neither of them are ever satisfied obtaining what they claim to want. Getting it takes all the zest and adventure out of it. Isn't that one way they're all so lost?"

Laura sat up. "So you think she falls for Jake because he's impotent, and therefore she can never truly have him?"

"Why not? Mike's a drunk, and Robert Cohn is Robert Cohn. So, there you are."

"That's a very…practical explanation of Hemingway. Not really what I would've expected from a philosopher." She smiled slyly. "That was a compliment, by the way."

"I doubt even Hemingway would recognize his own work if he read what counted as literary criticism of it."

"No argument there," Laura said.

"So what's on your summer reading list?"

"*East of Eden*," she said.

"Really?"

"I try to re-read it once every couple of years. There's just something about northern California during that time that always stays with me." She seemed lost in thought for a moment. "It's funny sometimes, the random things that stay with you."

I smiled. "I know what you mean. I always loved *Grapes of Wrath*, but for the life of me I can't recall any of Tom Joad's famous speech. Yet I vividly remember Tom and Al replacing that bearing in their jalopy by the side of the road. I can even remember when I read it. It was during the summer—" I was about to say 'summer of 2003,' "of my first year in grad school."

"Is this what they call philosophy of mind?"

"Hardly. It's just how nostalgia works. Memories and sentimentality are local. Unless it's some monumental event like nine-elev… er, the Kennedy assassination, you mostly remember *you*, and something of yours—certainly not the state of geo-political events. If you asked a man to recall the late 1940's, his first response wouldn't be anxiety over the hydrogen bomb or even Jackie Robinson's first game for the Brooklyn Dodgers. He'd probably talk about the old neighborhood and the day so-and-so fell off his bike; how it felt going to work at the plant for the first time; how the old Hudson Terraplane used to run like a top, or some late spring day when everything went exactly right."

Laura looked at me quizzically. "You're very unusual, Cal. Now I see why you like all those old movies."

I sat up. "Speaking of which, we ought to watch *All About Eve* tonight."

"I've never seen it. Is it on TV tonight?" she asked.

"What're you talking about? You have a cop…" I turned to look at the cabinet next to the TV where she kept her VHS tapes. *All About Eve* wasn't there. I know I remembered seeing it when Lionel and I came here for the first time in May of '93. I could've sworn it had been here. I stared blankly at her collection of tapes.

"Staying in and watching a movie. So predictable." She smiled.

"Am I?" I said, turning reluctantly back to Laura.

"Sometimes it's good to be predictable."

"Sometimes," I said flatly.

She got up from her chair and slowly walked over to me. Then I saw what she left behind on the chair.

"What're you doing?" I asked.

"Sauntering over to you."

I pointed to the chair. "No, that."

"Oh, I'm darning a sock. Women still do that in the nineties, don't they?"

The socks were navy blue, but she was using bright blue thread to stitch them. I'd seen that shade of blue once before. "The color doesn't match." As I said it, she bent down to kiss me.

"Doesn't matter, Cal. The hole is on the bottom of the sock; no one will see it." She kissed me again.

"What about the movie?"

"Oh, if we're not busy later, we can see what's on." She kissed me deeply. I allowed my resolve about the blue thread to fade away for a little while.

Friday June 19, 1992

Laura had to leave for a faculty development seminar just before nine. We said our goodbyes, she got in her car, and I pretended to get in mine. After she drove away, I casually walked around to the back door and let myself into the kitchen using a spare key she kept hidden out back. I took a small paring knife from her knife block and went down the hall into the living room.

Every time I'd snuck a peek at the stuffed raven during the last week, I knew there was something different about it from when Lionel and I would find it next May. When I saw Laura with the blue thread, the penny dropped. Between now and next May, someone would cut open the bird and hastily resew it.

That someone turned out to be me.

I'd briefly considered substituting a fake bird for Lionel and I to find next May, but that wouldn't work. The man who hired Lionel wanted *that* bird. Therefore, taking it wasn't an option. I sat at Laura's desk and turned the bird over in one hand while I held up the knife in the other, ready to make a cut. For a moment, I just stared at the bird, pondering the strange circumstances. If I was wrong about being the one to cut the bird open, the First Law would intervene to stop me. I couldn't help wondering about that. I pictured everything from the knife handle breaking to an earthquake.

"Only one way to find out," I said aloud, and effortlessly plunged the knife into the underside of the bird. Even as the knife went in, I half expected some magical force to grab the knife from my hand and hurl it across the room. Once I made a slit along the underside, I slipped my fingers inside. It didn't take much probing until I felt something hard. Whatever it was, it wasn't part of the bird's body. I eased it out of the bird, being careful not to spill too much sawdust on to the desk. When I finished, I set the bird down and stared blankly at what I found.

It was a gold-colored key.

Saturday June 27, 1992

I didn't know whether it was foolish or prudent to keep the key on me at all times. I considered leaving it back at my hotel room for fear I might lose it, but then I worried a maid might accidentally take it out with the trash. I stuck it in my hip pocket and hoped for the best. It wasn't like Laura was doing my laundry, though she had offered.

Once my initial shock at finding the key wore off, I hurried to a locksmith to have a copy made. Sewing up the bird was an absolute nightmare. I remembered saying to Lionel how bad the stitching job was when we first saw the bird, but I didn't remember it being quite as jagged and disjointed. Needless to say, sewing was more difficult than it looked. I replaced the bird at Laura's, went back to my hotel room, rolled up a joint, and pondered this new puzzle. What did the key open?

As if that wasn't enough to contemplate, I passed a Circuit City store yesterday and decided to go in and check out the state of the art of electronics in 1992. All the televisions were shaped like boxes, and I even did some comparison shopping for the laser disc players they had on sale. An overzealous clerk did his best to convince me that laser discs would replace VHS tapes within five years, if not sooner. He didn't take kindly to me pointing out that the discs were too big and the resolution wasn't *that* much better. As he walked away, I noticed that they sold movies on VHS. I remembered mentioning to Laura the other night that we ought to watch *All About Eve*. Without thinking about what I was doing, I easily located it in the drama section and went to pay for it. The instant the cashier handed me the bag with the movie in it, I gasped, realizing what I'd done.

Laura had a copy of *All About Eve* in May of '93. I saw it during Lionel's and my first trip, but it wasn't there the other night. Even now, it seemed preposterous that during Lionel's and my trip here in May of '93, I had encountered

evidence of my own presence in Laura's life during the previous summer—
this summer. As I walked along the sidewalk with *All About Eve* in a shopping
bag, I kept thinking something would prevent me from giving Laura this
movie. I'd forget it, accidentally lose it, she'd reject the gift for various
reasons, or maybe I'd chicken out and buy her some flowers instead.

None of that occurred. She thanked me, gave me a kiss, and promised
we'd watch the movie together soon. If I had realized this while I was in the
store looking for the movie, would I have still bought it? Running into these
kinds of issues seemed to be a symptom of spending so much time in the past.
It was as though time was slowly closing in on me, and I didn't like that. How
much longer would I be here? Would I even be able to leave?

"There you go again," Laura said as we walked along Beechtree Avenue.
We'd spent the morning hiking at a nearby nature preserve and had just
finished lunch at an Italian restaurant that would later become a Starbucks.
We had a nice walk in the woods, even stopping to make out for a while in a
secluded spot by a small creek. Laura got what I assumed were some nice
photos of the wildlife habitats. After one picture, I slipped and asked her to
show me the photo she'd just taken as though she were using a digital camera. Fortunately, I was able to laugh this off.

"Huh?" I said as we walked along the street after lunch.

"I spent the last couple of minutes talking to you, and you haven't heard
a word I said."

"I was listening," I lied.

"Okay. So what do you think I should have ordered at lunch instead?"

"Something with pasta and sauce," I said. She swatted me on the shoulder and rolled her eyes. "I said I was listening. I didn't say I could offer wise
words or answer any follow up questions."

"Penny for your thoughts, then? Although I'm entitled to know for free."

"It was nothing really. I often get these random ideas for research and
papers whenever I'm doing something totally unrelated to philosophy." I
watched her face drop ever so slightly. "I'm not trying to insult your intelligence, Laura. I just didn't think you'd be interested."

"It's not that."

"What then?"

"You mentioned your research and… it's nothing."

"It pretty clearly *is* something, especially to you."

It took her a moment to answer. "Whenever you mention philosophy, it
just reminds me that you're only here for another month or so."

"Oh," I said awkwardly. I didn't want to think about this, let alone talk
it over with her.

"Do you," she started to say, and then hesitated. "Do you still have to go?"

"I'm afraid so." I never wanted this. Why had I agreed to come here? Why had Lionel asked me?

"What about Spalding? Wouldn't they maybe hire you on full time if you're doing a good job?"

I chuckled. "They just might, funnily enough."

"Yeah?"

"Well not this coming academic year. Still, I've gotten to know a couple people there. We seem to get along pretty well. I guess you never know."

"What's the university like where you teach now?"

I couldn't help smiling. "Believe it or not, it isn't all that different from Spalding. Even some of the faces around campus remind me of the folks here."

"You'll have to give me your number before you leave." She must have seen me flinch, because she pulled away and hastily added, "It's okay, you don't have to."

"I didn't say that."

"Your face did."

"It's not that," I said. I had no phone number to give her in this time, unless she wanted to talk to the teenage me. I didn't remember ever getting such a phone call.

"You're just not the long-term commitment type," she said sarcastically.

"I don't deserve that."

"You're right. I'm sorry."

"You caught me off guard. I just wasn't thinking that far ahead. I know this is going to sound strange, but it never really occurred to me that you might miss me when I leave."

"What?"

"Seriously. It just didn't."

She chuckled at this. "I'll miss how you make me laugh, especially when you're not trying."

"Careful. That's a lot to live up to. Besides, I can't be the first guy to make you laugh." I quickly added, "And I don't mean to imply that you've been with an overabundance of guys."

She smiled. "Thank you. And no, you're not the first. Just the first in far too long."

"Oh?"

She gave me a quick look, and then her eyes darted away. "Let's just say the last man I was with…"

"Ended badly?" I offered.

She shuddered. "That's an understatement."

"If I didn't know better, I'd say there was more to it than that."

"There was." She sighed and looked all around at the neighborhood. "That's how I ended up here."

"What do you mean?"

"After what happened, what he did…I couldn't stay."

"What did he do?" I asked, intensely curious.

"He used me, Cal. I mean literally." She said this just as we passed Café Anne. "I wasn't even with him that long, but it seemed a lot longer, you know? Maybe it's because of how long I've lived with the memory."

"How long have you been living with it?"

"I don't want to talk about it, okay?"

"But it had something do with you moving here?"

"Yes."

I was trying to keep her talking. "It was pretty bad, huh?"

"Absolutely terrible." I saw her wipe away a tear. "He's the one who gave me that stuffed bird."

"What?"

"It's stupid too. The only famous author he probably ever heard of was Edgar Allen Poe. One day, right as things were cooling off between us, he gave me the raven as a gift. So transparent, when I think back on it." She laughed ruefully. "He just needed me around for a few more days. It worked. I didn't see him, *really see him*, until it was too late and…everything had happened."

I was trying like hell to organize and process all she was telling me about this guy. Some incident. That she felt used. And *he* gave her the damn bird.

"That's why I keep that stupid bird around. It's a reminder to not get involved with the wrong man again. And of everything else."

I was weighing whether or not to just ask her about the key, to tell her the whole thing. Who I really was, why I was there, even what would happen to her in ten months. She had a right to know, didn't she? I could make her believe me. Maybe she wasn't really dead. I never actually saw her body when Lionel and I were here. Maybe I'd been busier here than I thought, looking for ways to bend the First Law.

"Let's get a picture," she suddenly said, rooting through her bag.

"A picture?"

"Mm-hmm. Right here. It'll remind me of how much you like movies." She stopped in front of a video rental store called Movie Gallery.

"Holy shit. An actual video rental store," I said.

"Don't they have those on your planet?" she asked playfully.

"Sure. That's how we're able to disguise ourselves by adopting your silly catch phrases like, 'Show me the money!' and that kind of crap."

"Show me money?" she asked.

"I know, right?" I said, covering myself, only to put my foot in my mouth again. "Can we even take a selfie with that camera?"

She arched an eyebrow. "You mean a self-portrait?" Just then a guy with a ponytail and pleated pants—the 1992 version of a hipster—passed by. Laura got him to take our picture. She brushed her hair back with her hand, smoothed out the brown top she was wearing, took my arm, and leaned in against me. I smiled, trying hard to disguise all that I was thinking about her.

Monday June 29, 1992

Why couldn't I stay in 1992 for a while longer? I'd been sent here to do something, and so I hadn't properly appreciated this time. Why not stay here for a while longer, in this time and with…yeah, I guess with Laura, too. What was the harm in staying here for another couple months, even if I didn't find out anything further about the key or the bird?

Maybe it was the song I'd become absorbed in. I tuned Laura's radio to Spalding University's station, WSPL. The DJ said he'd gotten hold of some demo tapes from a band called Ozean. It was a very dreamy song called *Scenic*. The lead vocalist reminded me a little of Liz Fraser from the Cocteau Twins, as if she were singing from some far-off place through the morning fog. Really beautiful stuff. It put me in an introspective mood. *This* is the kind of thing I should be doing in the past. Discovering hidden gems like this song. When I got back to 2016, I could research whether Ozean ever cut a record and leave Lionel and Roger to worry about this damn key.

The song ended, and I snapped out of it, as though I were staring out my office window and suddenly remembered work I had to do. The key was my problem, too. The copy I made was in my right hip pocket. I felt it as I slipped on my jeans. I genuinely wanted to find out its significance. Laura would be going out later in the morning, so I would have at least an hour to poke around her house. I buckled my belt and glanced at my Temporal Return Initiator out of habit, just to make sure it was still there. I was only vaguely aware of the door slipping open behind me.

"What the fuck, Cal! What the fuck!"

I whirled around to see Laura glaring at me. Her eyes were wide, and she looked as though she were a wholly different woman than I'd known for the last month. She held the stuffed raven in her right hand. For a moment, I thought she was going to throw it at me.

"I can't believe you *did* this!" she said.

I'd been caught. Completely and irrevocably. I felt genuinely ashamed, as if I'd disappointed my parents. Unconsciously my hand drifted down to the TRI on my belt, and I momentarily considered pressing it and ending this in a literal flash.

"Calm down, okay," I said foolishly.

"Calm down? Are you fucking kidding me!"

"I'm sorry, all right. I just...my curiosity got the better of me."

"Oh, Jesus. Maybe I can dig out my teenage diary for you to look at, too!"

"I'm sorry," I said again. "You were just being so cagey about it."

"That's because I didn't want...because it's none of your business!" she yelled. I could see tears in her eyes.

"I was worried," I said. It sounded banal, even to me.

She rolled her eyes. "Oh God."

"I'm serious, Laura. The way you talked about all this...a mystery guy, an awful incident from the past, and a stuffed bird being given as a gift. How could I not wonder at least a little bit?"

She walked toward me. "Don't! Don't you try to make out like this is my fault—that I caused all this."

But she *had* caused this. Her death brought me here. "I already said I was sorry and that it was *my* fault. Look, shake the bird. The key's still inside. I didn't take it."

This seemed to give her pause. If there was ever a time for the direct approach, this was it. "Laura, what's that key for?" She seemed to consider this for a moment, though I could tell from her eyes that she was still very angry. Finally, she just looked at me and shook her head 'no.'

"Is it something that's here? In this house?" I asked. She stared at me, apparently thinking over how to answer. I took a step toward her. "It's all right, you can tell me."

She closed her eyes and turned away. "No. I don't want you to know."

"It has to do with what happened in that other town, doesn't it? It has to do with...that guy you told me about."

"Okay, Cal, that's it."

"Laura—"

"No," she said. "No more. It was my fault. I knew he was...I should've known it would happen."

"Known *what*? When?"

"It's mine, Cal. I have to live with it and not make the same mistake with anyone else."

"I'm not 'anyone else.' You know that."

She looked at me strangely, holding the bird out in front of her. "Aren't you? It just occurred to me: I don't really know anything about you. What town are *you* from? Who's the dean at the school you apparently teach at during the rest of the academic year?" I could've lied to her, made up something, but I didn't. I just stood there feeling helpless. She took this as confirmation of her suspicion that I was deceiving her. I walked toward her to hold her, but she tightened up.

"Don't," she said quietly.

"Do you want to—"

"I have to leave soon, Cal. You better finish getting dressed."

"So that's that, then?"

There were tears in her eyes. "You should have left it alone. It's *my* past."

"The past sometimes has a way of not *staying* past, Laura."

"Whatever that means," she said, walking away.

I heard her walk down the stairs. I finished buttoning my shirt and felt the key in my pocket. I thought for a moment of leaving it behind or throwing it out. Keeping it suddenly seemed dishonest. But I held onto it anyway.

When I got to the bottom of the stairs, I heard Laura moving around in the kitchen. I thought of going in there, but there was nothing I could say. I had been deceiving her, all this time, even with the best intentions. I slipped out the front door without saying good-bye.

Thursday July 2, 1992

It was early evening and beginning to rain as I walked along the sidewalk, carrying my suitcase. I pictured Michael Rennie as Klaatu in *The Day the Earth Stood Still*, walking down a pleasant Washington, DC area street, on his way to the boarding house where he meets up with Helen Benson and her son, Bobby. I suppose it may have looked similar, but I sure didn't feel like Klaatu. He had knowledge of advanced technology and extraterrestrial civilizations. The novelty of my own brand of unique knowledge had worn thin several days ago. Maybe when I got back to 2016, the memory of my time here would grow upon reflection. Right now, it felt like it was late at night, the music had stopped, and people were yawning and leaving the party.

I could return to the present any moment I chose. Yet something felt unfinished. I rang Laura's doorbell as the rain fell loudly on the porch roof. She opened the door wearing jean shorts and a navy blue tank top. She seemed about to greet me and then glanced down at my suitcase.

"Hi," I said.

"Hello, Cal." She looked me up and down. "I didn't know you were coming by or I would have—"

"No worries. I always said I wasn't one for pop-ins."

"And yet here you are."

It might have been a provocation, but I wasn't taking the bait. "Can I come in for a minute?" She didn't say anything, just moving back and holding the door open for me.

"A suitcase. I guess you're leaving." I nodded. "I thought you said your fellowship ran through the end of the summer."

"I did. It does. But I've, uh, exhausted the research I came here to do. Spalding was pretty understanding."

"Good for them," she said with a noticeable edge.

I sighed. "Is that how we're going to do this?"

"Do what?" she asked. I looked at her harshly. She was probably feeling many of the same conflicting emotions I was, but I couldn't stand seeing her act like a high school sophomore who'd just been told she wasn't allowed to stay out as late as the other kids.

"I do care for you, Laura," I said, getting a skeptical look in return. "It's the truth. Why the hell do you think I bothered coming here today? I could've just blown town without saying a damn thing after the other morning."

"What, because I drove you away?"

"Because whatever we had this summer seems to have ended."

She stopped for a moment, and I saw tears in her eyes. What she said surprised me. "*Does* it have to end, Cal?"

I closed my eyes and nodded. I heard her sobbing. "I'm sorry, Laura. Sorry for what I did the other day and for all of it."

"For what it's worth, I had already forgiven you."

"I'm glad to hear it."

"You always seemed so, I don't know, real. You *always* made me laugh."

I felt the room, the house, and Laura closing in on me all at once. "You're an easy person to be nice to."

"Neil Roback," she said after a moment.

"You mean the guy who gave you the bird?"

She nodded. "That's probably not his real name. Or if it is, he changed it after what happened."

"Does the key go to something that he gave you?"

She nodded again. "I don't even know why I kept it."

"*What* is it?"

"The reminder of a terrible mistake. Maybe a way to prove it wasn't all my fault." She seemed lost in thought for a second, and then asked. "Will you keep in touch with me, Cal?"

It was no good pushing her, and in any case, I didn't give a damn about the key at the moment. Whatever I'd come here to do, and how well I'd done it, didn't matter much. "I'm not always good at keeping in touch. I always figure everyone else has gotten on with their lives while I've been trying to live mine. I will be thinking of you, though."

She suddenly hugged me. "Oh, Cal." I took her in my arms. Each moment that passed made it harder for me to leave. Finally, I pushed her away and kissed her as long as I could. I wiped her face and felt my throat tighten up.

She took a step back and looked me up and down. "Good bye, Cal."

I looked at her for what felt like a long time—Laura alive, breathing, standing there looking at me and feeling something. *That* was the image of her I wanted to carry with me. I was determined to carry this 'now' back with me to my own present.

"So long," I said. I picked up my suitcase and trotted down the front steps, feeling like I was moving against the great tide of my own will.

I looked back through the falling rain, just in time to see her shut the door softly.

CHAPTER 13

Friday October 28, 2016

UCH INK HAS been spilled by poets about the myriad ways we're swept along by time. As I materialized on the Nora Pads, all I could think about was how un-poetic time felt. Lionel was his usual self, smiling warmly, shaking my hand, and welcoming me back. He was completely charming and courteous, and for the first time it seemed totally misplaced. Did they even know me anymore? Did I?

Jack and Roger were there too, dressed exactly as I remembered. Only fifteen minutes had passed in 2016, just as the Delaney Axiom said would be the case. Jack was even sitting in the same place, with the same bottle of water he'd brought to the lab, though it was now half-empty. The sun shone through the window in the same place I remembered it. It made me think of my rain-dampened shirt. It was as if I'd never left.

Yet I had over a month's worth of memories pressing upon me.

I felt hollow as I stepped down from the Nora Pads, back into my incongruous but equally real life. I would've much preferred to be alone for a while, to retreat into myself and reemerge more slowly into the present. However, Lionel and Roger were eager to discuss what I'd found out and had made dinner reservations at Apollonia's, one of my favorite restaurants. Postponing our inevitable discussion of 1992 until dinner was, I suppose, their way of letting me settle back into the present. The restaurant was near my apartment, so I dropped off my things after leaving the lab, changed clothes, and walked to Apollonia's to meet them. Even my apartment felt alien to me, though it looked no different than when I left it earlier that morning, over a month ago.

Lionel, Roger, and Jack had gotten to Apollonia's ahead of me and were sitting at a round table. I ordered a vodka martini as soon as I sat down. When my cocktail arrived, Lionel made a toast to my safe return. I winced when our glasses clinked. I wasn't in a festive mood and downed half the martini in one gulp. I had recounted part of the story back at the lab, including the name of Neil Roback that Laura had given me just before I departed.

"We weren't able to find out much, I'm afraid. And what we did find out was less than helpful," Lionel said.

"She said Roback probably wasn't his real name," I said.

"Something may still turn up, Dr. Bradshaw," Jack said before turning to me. "He's dead. Someone by that name was killed in a car accident in Florida in early 1988."

"That makes it officially a fake name," I said. "Laura probably knew him some time after '88."

"Let me guess, no next of kin." Roger said flatly.

Jack shook his head. "Nope. Both his parents are dead, and he didn't have any brothers or sisters."

"You're positive about this, Jack?" I asked.

"According to the death notice I found, he was killed in a car crash and was an only child."

"And this man, whoever he is, gave her the bird?" Lionel asked.

"That's what she said."

"When?"

"I didn't think to ask her that," I said.

"Never mind," Lionel said, "although it might have been of great help in determining the significance of that damned bird."

"Oh," I said, suddenly remembering, "this may help answer that." I took the key out of my shirt pocket.

"A key," Roger said.

"Hidden inside the bird."

Lionel put his hand to his forehead. "Good Lord. That must have been what our man was after. How on Earth did you think to look there?"

"Remember the awful stitching job we noticed when we recovered the bird?" Lionel nodded. "Guess who did it?"

"No!" Lionel said.

"Oh yeah."

Lionel slapped his leg. "Well, I'll be damned. Must've been quite a thing to carry out *after* you'd seen the results of your handiwork. I even mentioned to our client that we noticed the jagged stitching on the bottom of the bird. Little did I realize that the tailor was with me when we nicked it from 1993."

"Wait a minute. You mentioned the stitching to the guy who hired you?"

"Yes."

I leaned in closer. "What did you say, Lionel? Can you remember exactly what you told him?"

Lionel thought for a moment. "I don't remember the precise wording. Something about how my colleague noticed the haphazard stitching job on the bottom of the bird, or something like that. Maybe a dig about taxidermy, that sort of thing. You were there, Roger."

"I don't really remember," Roger said disinterestedly.

"*You* were there?" I asked Roger.

"Yes," he said uncertainly. "Why?"

"Christ," I sighed. "When Lionel told him 'my colleague' or whatever it was, this guy must have thought you cut open the bird, Roger, and that Lionel was trying to cover for you." I looked at Roger sheepishly. "I guess in a round-about way you being attacked was my fault."

To my relief, Roger smirked. "Forget it."

"What's the key for, Cal?" Lionel asked eagerly.

I frowned. "I don't know."

"Well, did you at least ask her?"

"Yeah, but she wouldn't tell me anything useful. Whatever it is, it's something that bothers her a lot." I pictured her face the final time I saw her. "She was angry at me for even asking about it to begin with, but…terrified at the same time. I don't know." As I looked up, I thought I noticed Lionel and Roger exchange furtive glances.

"I suppose we can get to the bottom of that eventually. Besides, there's still plenty about this that doesn't make any sense."

"You mean like who our client really is," Jack said.

"Yes," Lionel replied, "and why he asked us to recover that bird. I'd even settle for knowing how the devil he got my name. Although answering any of these questions is like trying to grab hold of smoke. Still, Jack, maybe you can find out a little more about Roback himself."

"There's always the girl," Roger said.

"Girl?" Lionel asked.

"Laura Dietrichson," Roger said, turning to me. "You could go back again, say, a week or so after you left and talk to her some more."

"I'd really rather not," I said.

"But Cal, this could break everything open," Lionel said.

"We didn't part on those kind of terms," I said, fixing both of them with a grave look. "No."

Roger was about to protest, but Lionel shook his head and said gently, "It's all right, Cal. We'll sort something else out. We do have that key. Perhaps Jack can dig out a little more information on this Roback bloke. And if Ms. Dietrichson mentioned some terrible turn of events, that might show up in the newspaper archives. Now then, to change the subject a bit, we've been hired to find something else. Should be a snap."

"Oh yeah?" Jack asked.

"Military records this time," Lionel said. "Young man came in on behalf of his grandmother. Apparently, her late husband was a World War II vet, and somewhere along the way all his things went missing. Old uniforms, medals, even the identification medallions of one of his fallen comrades."

"You mean dog tags," Jack said.

"Right. According to the grandson, she last saw them when the couple moved to their present home in 1975. He died in 1983. That was when she first noticed their disappearance. Should be a fairly straight-forward affair."

"And," Roger interjected, "we were sure to get the man's name and address."

"Even made a copy of his driver's license," Lionel added cheerfully.

I sat there quietly, half-listening and sipping my cocktail. I could feel Lionel looking at me. "How about it, Cal?" he said. "Up for a jaunt to the seventies?"

"I don't know. I'll let you know."

I was relieved Lionel didn't push for an explanation why I was suddenly hesitant to travel back in time. Maybe he already understood. He just quietly said, "It's all right, old man. Take the weekend to think it over and let me know."

The conversation went on around me. I didn't say much, and none of them really pressed me for any further details. I excused myself and went home at the first decent opportunity. I sat on the couch in my living room, smoking part of a joint leftover from the previous night in 2016, just over a month ago. I didn't bother turning on the lamp as it grew dark. I left someone behind along with what felt like an entire other life. Tomorrow I'd wake up and have to be me again; that is, the 'me' connected with this strand of my life.

Monday October 31, 2016

The weekend passed, but there was a strangeness about it. I kept waiting for some long-neglected task that required my immediate attention to manifest itself. After all, I hadn't spent a night in my apartment or done any philosophical work in over a month. But it only *felt* like I let things atrophy. In reality—which is to say, the collective reckoning of the people in my primary timeline—I'd only been gone for part of an afternoon. Things hadn't been neglected at all, nothing that mattered anyway.

Were Laura alive now, she would remember spending part of a summer with a guy named Cal Sutherland. To her, it would be a flickering memory over twenty years old. To me, our time together had ended just yesterday. If we bumped into each other in 2016, she would be startled by my appearance. I would look like I hadn't aged a day. Like closed causal loops, it was another of the peculiarities of time travel.

Had I fallen in love with her? I'd never know for sure. I don't know that I wanted to know, really. From the moment we met in Café Anne, I had wanted it both ways with her. I wanted her as a girlfriend, someone to spend time with and to hear laugh when I said something amusing. For that, she had to be a real person, with needs, feelings, and boundaries. Yet I also wanted her as a mystery to solve, a puzzle to unravel. I needed her in order to suss out the purpose of the stuffed raven, Lionel's mystery client, and even the reason behind Laura's own death. In that sphere, she *couldn't* exist as a real person. That summed up my feelings about her, even if it didn't resolve anything.

What seemed worse was that I knew the truth about her, about what had been her future. Yet I hadn't told her about it. I wasn't one for kitchen-sink drama, but I had used her, too. Maybe not in the way that men and women typically use each other, but it was still something of which I wasn't proud. I had affection for Laura, the bright young woman. All the while, I'd grown tired of Laura-the-key-to-unlocking-what-was-becoming-an-annoying-mystery. Since I couldn't have the one Laura without the other, I endeavored to put her away completely. Whatever else, she was long gone. Whatever her death meant to the present, it no longer interested me.

Or so I told myself.

Tuesday November 1, 2016

Today felt like the first day I was truly back in 2016. The light snow on the way to campus helped. It was a little early for snow, but it was a nice reminder that the season was late fall and not summer. My morning metaphysics class went well enough, though I had to spend more time looking over my notes than usual since I hadn't seen them in over a month. A few students had questions after class about their upcoming papers, which I was able to answer, somewhat to my relief.

I spent my office hours mostly focused on preparing for my afternoon graduate seminar. Every now and then, my thoughts turned to Lionel and the time machine. He'd asked me again yesterday if I wanted to go along to 1975 to recover those military records, but I declined. He sounded surprised by my refusal, but took it in stride. The trip didn't hold much appeal right now. We'd be there to work, and that, it began to dawn on me, cast a shadow over time travel's appeal.

My mood improved during my afternoon seminar. This seemed to rub off on my students as well. As sometimes happened, the course of our discussion happily went in a direction I hadn't anticipated. A couple of them even gave me a gentle ribbing when I trotted out yet another quote from *Double Indemnity*. I thanked them for keeping track of my references to this movie, while they wondered aloud whether I was aware actual films had been produced after the 1980s.

I was enjoying things so much I almost hadn't noticed Jack Greenwood standing in the doorway near the end of class. He'd picked my brain about the philosophy of time a couple weeks back, and I told him he was welcome to sit in on my seminar whenever he wanted. Seeing him there felt like a continuation of the positive vibe I was now feeling. The present was becoming mine again—becoming real again. As class ended, I motioned him inside while I answered a couple brief student questions.

"Glad you could make it, Jack," I said after my students left. "It's too bad you weren't here about 20 minutes ago. You missed an interesting discussion about fate."

It suddenly struck me how ill at ease he looked. "Oh, um yeah," he said.

I glanced up to make sure we were alone in the seminar room. "What's the matter?"

"Doctor Bradshaw's been arrested."

§ § §

Jack wasn't able to provide many details on our drive to the jail. He'd been on his way into Dancy Hall just as Lionel was led out by a detective and a uniformed patrol officer. Lionel seemed chipper and even slightly amused by it all, but I suspected that was just a bluff. Jack hadn't been able to get a hold of Roger, so he called me instead. By the time Jack and I got to police headquarters, Lionel was in the process of being released on his own recognizance after posting $300 bail. If there had been any bluster on Lionel's part earlier, it had since been replaced by a look of somber concern.

"Tell me this is just some silly mistake, Lionel," I said as we exited the building. We walked a few steps away from the entrance before he answered.

"I'm afraid it isn't," he said, "at least not totally. The charge itself is rather minor. Receiving stolen property."

I almost laughed from relief. "That doesn't seem so bad."

"What did you steal, Dr. Bradshaw? I mean, what do they think you stole?" Jack asked.

"That's the worrisome part," Lionel said with a grave look. "It was those military items. You remember the trip back to 1975?"

"Did anything unusual happen during the trip?" I asked.

"Not at all. I was there and back in no time, pardon the pun. Right after the couple moved, they put some boxes out for trash. It seemed that by mistake they placed the box with the husband's things among them—exactly what I suspected happened. Not the first time we've been hired in a case like that either. At any rate, apart from a local busybody passing by and admonishing me for poking through someone else's rubbish, nothing out of the ordinary occurred."

I thought this through a moment. Lionel arrested for possessing military records that were last seen in the curbside trash almost forty years ago? "This doesn't make any sense," I said.

Lionel laughed morbidly. "The cozzers weren't forthcoming with details, though they seemed rather pleased that they got to detain a university professor in a suit. All they said was they received a report early last week that the items had been stolen."

"Early last week," I repeated aloud. Something was wrong.

Lionel nodded. "Yes, the timing is rather suspicious. They were reported stolen just *before* I was approached about recovering them."

"And if you actually found them in 1975, they couldn't have been taken from someone in the present day."

"Precisely," Lionel said. "If that wasn't worrisome enough, I have the impression the police believe there is more where that came from."

"What do you mean, 'more'?" I asked.

"Additional, quote-unquote, stolen property, Cal," he added gravely. "They wanted my permission to search the lab."

"Oh God. You didn't let them, did you?"

"Certainly not! They were none too pleased. Made noises about getting a search warrant and coming back some other time to give it a good going-over."

"They were probably just bluffing about a warrant," Jack said.

"Possibly," Lionel said, "but that's not the kind of bluff I want to be called on." Lionel's concern brought a chill to all three of us.

"If they did start poking around the lab, do you think they could discover what's really there?" I asked. Lionel paused to consider this.

"It's highly unlikely. Then again, police do seize evidence and write up reports. Who's to say how many different people might look over what they found." Lionel stared ahead. There was a chill in the air, but there were still many people coming and going on the downtown streets. "This is the closest that the time machine has ever come to being exposed." We walked on in silence, stopping at my car.

"So what do we do now?" Jack asked.

Before Lionel answered, I spoke up. "We have to get to the bottom of this."

"Agreed," Lionel said.

"Starting with whoever hired you to recover those military records."

Lionel seemed to brighten at this. "This time we have the young man's name and address on file."

"Do you think he was the one who called the police?" Jack asked.

"Who else could it be?" Lionel said. "I can't imagine why he'd report us to the police."

"Let's ask him," I said, trying to sound more confident than I actually was.

§ § §

Tracking down Steven Millard, the kid who hired Lionel to recover the military paraphernalia, proved to be one of the easier feats we'd tackled lately. The address he'd given Lionel was in an area of town euphemistically referred to as "working class." In actuality, it was a neighborhood long past its prime that consisted of large old houses with peeling paint, unkempt yards, and front porches that sloped in unnatural ways.

As we pulled up in front of a faded yellow house with white trim and a moss-covered roof, Millard just happened to be walking down the sidewalk. He was a thin, twitchy kid who looked to be grappling with a dependency on drugs that was in a class above my recreational weed. Roger had recovered sufficiently to come along with Lionel and I. I got the feeling that being taken by surprise was a blow to Roger's pride. He was eager to demonstrate that he could still take care of himself.

"Right," Lionel said, opening the car door.

I frowned as we crossed the street to the house. "Do you really think this kid's gonna tell us anything useful?"

"We'll make him talk," Roger said, walking in front of us.

"Steady on, Roger," Lionel said, "we didn't come here to rough anyone up. Remember, he *knows* us."

"Don't forget, Lionel, you're an ex-con yourself," I said, trying to lighten the mood. Then, doing my best impression of Scorpio from *Dirty Harry*, I added, "It was Bradshaw, the Englishman. He did this to me!"

"Yes," Lionel said dryly. "Perhaps Roger is merely going to hold his legs and dangle him from the upstairs window."

"If you two are finished, none of that should be necessary," Roger said. "Look how gaunt the boy is. He's probably a drug addict and quite paranoid too. We're not the only ones who have materials in our possession we'd rather the police didn't find. We can use *that* against him, if need be."

The dank front hallway smelled like a garden shed on a wet day and was just as cluttered. Millard's apartment was on the second floor. We heard footsteps inside but they stopped as Roger knocked on the door.

"Who is it?" a voice asked tentatively from inside. Roger responded by knocking louder. After a time, the door opened a crack and Millard peeked out. Roger pushed the door open with his left forearm and walked in.

"Hey, what the fuck, man?" Millard said as Roger barreled past him, looking around.

110

"Good evening, Steven," Lionel said cheerfully as he and I walked in. I closed the door behind us. "You remember Roger and me, don't you? This is another of my colleagues." Millard's eyes darted uncertainly back and forth among the three of us.

"What're you guys doing here?" he asked. "I paid you what I owed."

"Bet your aunt was pleased to have those items returned to her," Roger said.

"Uh, yeah. She was, real happy," Millard said, rubbing the back of his neck.

"Was she?" Roger asked. "Because you told us it was your grandmother that wanted those things." Millard's eyes widened.

"Well yeah. I mean…it was my grandma, you know. But we always called her auntie."

"Bullshit," Roger said. "Why did you call the police after we gave you what we were hired to find?"

"What're you talkin' about? I didn't call the cops." Millard said indignantly. Maybe it was years of sifting through flimsy excuses from students, but I instinctively believed him. At least about this.

"Funny," Lionel said, "because I spent the better part of this afternoon at the police station, accused of stealing those items."

Millard seemed to consider Lionel for a moment. "I'm tellin' ya', I didn't call the police. I don't even like cops."

"Well, somebody did," Roger said.

Millard gave a nervous laugh. "Well, I don't know who it would be."

"How did you find out about us and what we do?" Lionel asked. Millard didn't say anything; he just looked at the floor.

Roger took a step toward Millard. "I'd wager there's a lot of gear lying around this apartment you'd rather the police didn't find, eh? Shall I call them and find out?"

"Hey, c'mon man. The cops can't just go busting in here because you told them to."

"They could if I reported my wallet was snatched by a young man fitting your description who just happened to run into this building."

"Shit," Millard said, "that'd never work."

Roger started for the door. "You don't think so? Let's find out, shall we."

"No wait, wait," Millard said as Roger grabbed the doorknob.

"Someone put you up to this, didn't they?" Lionel asked. Millard just nodded. "Who?"

"I don't know his name," Millard said.

"Sure you do," Roger said harshly.

Millard sighed. "Are you gonna tell him I told you?"

"I shouldn't think so," Lionel said gently. "It sounds as though this all happened without your knowledge. We just want to know why the police were called."

"Nick Murdoch," Millard said despondently.

"Where does he live?" Roger asked.

"I don't know. Really I don't. He just told me he wanted to find this army stuff or whatever that used to belong to his landlady. He said you'd be able to find it, but we were never at his house or anything."

"What else did he tell you?"

"Nothing, I swear. He told me to go see you, well him," he said, pointing to Lionel, "and to tell him that they used to belong to my dead grandfather and that my grandma really wanted to get them back."

Roger and Lionel looked at each other, apparently uncertain what to say next. This name, even if it weren't made up, wasn't much to go on without an address. How could we pick up the trail, I wondered.

Suddenly I had the answer.

"*Where* did you meet him?" I asked abruptly.

"Huh?" Millard asked.

"You said you didn't meet him at his house or apartment, so where did you meet him?"

"AJ's bar over on Call Street."

"When?" I asked.

"I don't know. Like a week ago."

"No, when," I said. "Give me the date, the exact date."

Millard seemed to think this over. "Monday. Last Monday night."

"You're sure about that? Last Monday, the 24th?"

"Yeah, man," he said, a little exasperated. "I remember going home to watch the Monday night game afterwards, all right?"

"One final question, and it's very important you tell me the truth. Look at me." I took a step towards him so that we were less than a foot apart. "Have you ever seen me anywhere prior to tonight?"

Millard looked taken aback by this, but he recovered enough to say, "Nah. I never saw you before. Just them."

"Okay then. You have a nice night, kid," I said, pulling open the door. I was already part way down the stairs when I heard Lionel call out to me.

"Cal, wait."

I continued down the stairs and out to the sidewalk, pausing to wait for Lionel and Roger.

"Damn it, Cal," Roger said when he got there. "We have what is likely a fake name and no address, and you just decide on your own that's enough?"

"Hold it, Roger," Lionel said. "Jack can search the usual databases for the name 'Nick Murdoch' and perhaps turn up something. But Cal, you really shouldn't have done that. We could've gotten a lot more out of that young man if we'd stayed."

I smiled. "We've got everything we need to pick up the trail, Lionel."

Monday October 24, 2016

"So what was it like in 1992, I mean to actually live there for so long?" Jack Greenwood asked me from across the booth."

"It had its ups and downs," I said, trying not to revisit too much of my trip.

"Damn." Jack smiled. "That must've been sweet. You didn't go to any concerts or anything while you were there?"

I relaxed at this. "Afraid not. I spent some time hanging around a record store that used to be on Beechtree, but that was it. I hadn't thought about it before, but it'd be great to go to a concert in the past. See a band, *just* before they break. Like Led Zeppelin in the late sixties."

"Oh, totally!" Jack said. "If I go back to the early nineties, I'm definitely seeing Soundgarden. Maybe even Nirvana. Kurt Cobain died, what, like two years after you were there?"

"Pearl Jam was way better," I said, sipping my bourbon and trying to hide a smile.

"What?" Jack said. "No way."

"Look at Pearl Jam's and Nirvana's first two albums side by side. *Ten* and *Nevermind* is a dead heat at the least, but *Vs* crushes *In Utero*. Nirvana was already a spent force by the time Cobain died. His death was tragic, but legacy-wise it was the best thing that could have happened to the band. Plus, there was a lot happening in music during that time that wasn't grunge or whatever people took to calling it."

"Like what?"

"Shoegaze, dream pop. Bands like Mazzy Star, Slowdive, Ride, or The Cocteau Twins. I mean, it's not for everybody, but you ought to check them out. All their stuff is on YouTube."

"I've never heard of them."

"I'm not surprised. Don't get me wrong, '92 was a great time. I wish I could've spent a month there just…on my own, with nothing else to do. But back in the day, if a band wasn't played on terrestrial radio, then you'd never know they existed. Plus, those bands I mentioned were all British, except for Mazzy Star. Heavy distortion, feedback, kind of dreamy lyrics that sound melancholy but leave you feeling hopeful in the end. They never fully caught on in America. Music critics had this comically negative reaction to them. God knows why, but it was pathetic. At any rate, '92 to '93 really was the pinnacle of that scene, and...son of a bitch!" I put my hand to my forehead to hide my face.

"What is it?" Jack said, starting to turn around.

"Don't turn around, Jack," I said.

"What?"

"It's the guy that attacked Roger. He just walked in." The balding man with narrow eyes who I last saw fleeing Roger's backyard slowly walked over to the bar and sat down. He took out a pack of cigarettes and lit up, making me wish I had one myself. You could still smoke in this bar for some reason. Probably some silly combination of local regulations and political favors.

"What do we do?" Jack asked nervously.

"Nothing," I said. "We know him. He doesn't know us. That gives us the advantage. Let's just sit tight and see what happens." I took a long look at the man sitting at the bar who Steve Millard called 'Nick Murdoch.' He reminded me of several bald character actors sprinkled in movies during the nineties.

"If he's here to meet Millard, then he must've set up Doctor Bradshaw with the cops," Jack said, working out what I was thinking.

"Probably."

"But why?"

I didn't have it all worked out, but I could guess part of it. "It's gotta be some kind of threat. He's worried we'll find out more about the bird and the key. He probably thinks we've had the key from the very beginning, especially after seeing my awful stitching job. And he's right, even if he has no idea how or when we got it."

"So why have Doctor Bradshaw arrested?"

I narrowed my eyes and took a long look at Murdoch, who stubbed out his cigarette just as the bartender placed a fresh glass in front of him. "Probably to keep Lionel from going to the police. If Lionel is a wanted man, he's less credible in the eyes of the police."

"That makes sense," Jack said, "but you and Dr. Bradshaw don't really have much you could tell the police."

"Murdoch doesn't know that. He's probably lying awake at night trying to figure out how we got that damn bird." I nodded in the direction of the bar. "Here comes Steve Millard." Jack turned around to look at him. Millard looked all around the bar, but it seemed to be more of a nervous twitch than actually searching for anyone. He sat down next to Murdoch and said something to him. I saw the smile fade from Millard's face as Murdoch gave him an arch look.

"So, what do we do now?" Jack asked.

"Same as we planned. We follow Murdoch to wherever he's going next. Hopefully home."

Jack glanced over his shoulder at the bar. "I wish we could just go up and surprise them right now."

"Kind of like slipping Thorwald the note that says, 'What have you done with her?'" I said with a smirk, thinking of *Rear Window*. "Doesn't work that way, Jack. If either of them remembered one of us busting in on their conversation at this particular date and time, Millard never would have turned up at the lab with that story about finding the lost military records. And since he did turn up at the lab—"

"I know, but it still sucks. I mean, they're right there!"

"Yeah," I said, staring at them sitting at the bar. Before I knew what was happening I stood up from the booth.

"What're you doing?" Jack said anxiously.

I smiled. "Getting another drink." I walked toward the bar, my eyes fixed on Murdoch and Millard. My heart beat faster as I got within two feet of them. Millard sat closest to our booth, and there was an empty stool next to Murdoch. I could feel my eyes widen as I moved toward the gap between Murdoch and the empty stool. I leaned in.

"Oh sorry," I said as I deliberately brushed up against Nick Murdoch. He frowned slightly, but he made no effort to look over and acknowledge me. It was exactly what one would expect to occur when accidentally bumping a bar patron. Millard barely looked my way either. I suppressed a smile as I ordered another round of drinks and tried to listen in on what they were saying. They talked in very low voices, so it was difficult make anything out. Murdoch especially tried to keep his voice hushed. I did manage to overhear him tell Millard he'd have to be careful how he talked to someone. If he "sounded like a douche bag," whoever it was would never go for it. I knew this someone else was Lionel.

When the drinks came, I took them back to the booth and sat back down. I could feel my hand shaking slightly as I sipped my fresh bourbon.

"I can't believe you just did that," Jack said, impressed.

"You mean that I went through with it or that I was able to do it?"

"Both, I guess."

"As long as we don't try and change anything, there are lots of things we can do here in the past." I took another sip of my drink before adding, "And the list of things we can do seems to grow all the time."

Jack leaned in closer. "Before we left, I looked up the score of the NFL game tonight. The Broncos beat the Texans twenty-seven to nine. You know the Broncos were only nine-point favorites? We could totally clean up!"

I smiled at this. It was hard not to like Jack. "Do you happen to know any bookies around here?"

"No." He frowned.

"S'all right. Not really what we're here for anyway."

"One of these days I'm gonna do it, too. Travel back and lay down some money; walk up to the bookie like I really know something he doesn't."

"How come you haven't already? I'm sure the money would come in handy with the time machine. The portion you'd hand over, anyway."

"Eh, Dr. Bradshaw doesn't want us doing that. He says it would be ill-gotten. We only find things people hire us to find and valuable items that are lost." I wondered how Lionel squared this policy with that vintage bottle of wine he managed sell for a cool forty grand, but I didn't press the point. Inventing a time machine gave Lionel the right to be inconsistent here and there.

"Whoa," I said, looking to the bar. "Millard got up and left. Murdoch looks like he's finishing his drink. Don't…turn around," I gently cautioned Jack, who downed the second half of his beer in one gulp and took a deep breath when he was done.

I watched Murdoch stand up slowly and place all but one of the bills on the bar into his pocket. I was relieved to see that he didn't look around. He seemed to have a perpetual frown on his face, as if he had little time for anyone or anything.

"Take it easy, Jack. Let him get outside first." I drained the rest of my bourbon, happy to feel it burning the back of my throat. "We'll follow him *French Connection*-style, just like I described. I'll walk twenty yards behind him, and you walk on the opposite side of the street, parallel to him in case he crosses somewhere. And remember, he's not looking for us. If things really get hairy, we can just run into an alley and disappear into next week."

"Got it," Jack said.

As we got up, I saw Murdoch turn left and pass the window of the bar. Jack went out first and dashed across the street. I waited a moment and then started following Murdoch. It was dark out, so I wasn't worried about him getting a good look at me. He didn't seem to be in much of a hurry and walked at a comfortable pace. I glanced over at Jack who was a step or two behind Murdoch on the opposite side of the street.

At the next corner, Murdoch stopped and looked around. I quickly ducked into a doorway as he crossed the street, heading straight for Jack. Jack saw this and froze. "Keep goin' Jack," I said under my breath. Finally, Jack crossed the street in the same direction he'd originally been moving. I don't think Murdoch noticed him. I crossed the street behind Murdoch and was now about thirty yards back. We were on a side street that only contained houses and very few passersby.

After two blocks, Murdoch ducked into a building. I quickened my pace and caught up to where he'd gone just as a second floor light came on. It was a four-unit brick apartment building, about three miles north of where I lived. I heard footsteps coming up behind me and turned to see Jack hustling over.

"Shit, that was close," he said breathlessly. "I thought he was gonna see me when he crossed the street."

"Don't worry about it; you did fine." It disturbed me bit how often I'd been following people in various time periods over the course of the last several weeks. However, I couldn't help smiling as I noted the address on the building and thought about Murdoch inside.

"Got you, you bastard."

CHAPTER 14

Thursday November 3, 2016

BAD IDEAS ONLY look truly terrible in hindsight. A man can talk himself into anything so long as he desires the intended result strongly enough. I'd spent over a month in 1992, trying to learn all I could about the true nature of a stuffed bird. Yet the sum total of what I discovered was a key whose purpose was still totally unknown. Nonetheless, I convinced myself that this Nick Murdoch was connected with Laura's death. Moreover, I felt I owed it to Laura to find out whatever I could. It was equal parts noble, delusional, and foolhardy.

I stood in the dark, about three houses up from Nick Murdoch's brick apartment building. I had surprise on my side, I reasoned, plus the fact that I knew a great deal more about him than he did about me. I took a deep breath and walked toward the apartment building. The front door to the building should have been locked at night, but as was all too typical, the landlord couldn't be bothered.

I walked up a flight of stairs that looked like they hadn't been swept in at least a year and stopped in front of a dark wooden door with a gold-colored '3' tacked just below the peephole. I could tell there was a light on inside Murdoch's apartment. There was another apartment door behind me, but no one appeared to be home.

I knocked loudly on Murdoch's door, hoping this would rattle him a little. My heart raced as I heard footsteps coming closer. In that moment, I almost chickened out and ran. Laura's face flashed through my mind. Murdoch opened the door a crack, and I saw his narrow eyes peeking out at me. Finally, he opened the door all the way. He was dressed in a baggy long-sleeved green shirt and cheap black slacks. As we stared at each other for a moment, his head jerked back suddenly.

"You? What the hell do you want?" he said angrily. Something about this, other than his tone, bothered me.

"Hello, Nick," I said, trying to sound like I held the upper hand.

"What do you want?" he said louder, taking a step toward me.

"I want to know about the bird." He was clearly taken aback by this, but only for a moment.

"What bird?"

"A stuffed raven that recently came into your possession. There was a—" I started to say, but I was cut off as his right arm swung out to hit me. I managed to block it, but as I did he swung a fist hard into my abdomen. I immediately fell to my knees, trying to protect my head and draw a breath at the same time. My lungs felt the size of corn kernels. I put my left hand on the floor to get up. He kicked my arm out from under me, and I dropped to the floor still gasping for air. I faced the wall and felt Murdoch kneel down on my back, pinning me to the floor. My chest was a wave of pain, and I thought I was going to pass out.

"How the hell did you find me?" he growled. Even if I could talk, he'd never believe me. I just lay there, struggling to catch a breath. He gave me a hard kick in the thigh. "*How do you know where I live?*" I felt the pressure on my abdomen relax slightly. "Oh," he said, "it was that Millard prick, wasn't it?"

"Who?" I huffed. He kicked me again, this time in the ribs, hard enough that I was back to square one with trying to breathe.

"Why're you so curious about that fuckin' bird? You, Bradshaw, and that other limey that cut it open. How did he find it anyway? How did he do it!"

"Do what?"

Murdoch seemed to consider this. He spoke in a more even tone. "That thing should've been long gone. Years ago. *I* should've—but it doesn't matter." He pulled me by the hair, picking my head up off the ground. His face was pure menace, the narrow eyes yellow with anger. "It's all gone. I *got* what I wanted, you hear me? You tell that to Bradshaw, tell it to his limey fuckin' face." He let go of my head, but kept his weight on my back. "Now, let's see who *you* are."

I was trying to process what I heard. It made a strange sense. He'd gotten what he wanted, whatever it was, and didn't seem worried anymore. Which means he must've destroyed something…something connected with the key!

"Nice to meet you, Calvin Sutherland…of Spalding University!" I felt my body go cold. He had my wallet. I could hear him flipping through it. "So you *didn't* hire Bradshaw. You work with him." I stayed quiet and still. "Not for long," he added.

Why would he think I hired Lionel? I turned my head and saw him looking at the other cards and papers in my wallet.

"All right, get up," he said. I hesitated for a moment, trying to think of what to do next, whenever I got out of here. *If* I got out of here. He took a step back as I got up on one knee. I saw him glance at my wallet. Before I had a chance to think it through, I swung my fist in an uppercut, right between his legs. He let out a shrill 'Oooo' sound and simultaneously dropped my wallet and staggered back, falling through the doorway into his apartment.

I grabbed my wallet, shoved it into my pocket, and started for the stairs.

There was a painful knot in my right thigh, and my chest still ached, but I didn't care. He tried to stick out his leg and trip me, but he missed. I practically jumped down the stairs and ran out of the building and out to the sidewalk. A couple walking by gave me an alarmed look as I flew past them. I didn't stop running until I got to my car, cursing myself all the way.

Friday November 4, 2016

I didn't turn on any lights when I got home last night. I just stood at the front window for about an hour, drinking whisky and looking up and down the street. I even placed a folding chair up against my front door, but it didn't help me sleep. I finally felt exhausted enough to fall into a fitful sleep about two hours before I needed to get up. Nick Murdoch showed up in all my dreams. Of course, that wasn't the only thing that cost me a night's sleep.

What the hell was I going to tell Lionel?

I'd taken a reckless gamble, confronting Murdoch when I held none of the cards. Worse still, it jeopardized the secrecy of the time machine. I'd done it on my own, without talking it over with anyone whom it might affect. I didn't know what I'd say, how I'd apologize, or what effect this may have. I was, however, pretty sure I'd taken my last trip back in time.

On the other hand, if I did nothing and kept quiet, it was entirely possible Lionel and the others would never find out what happened last night. However, that was a bad idea on many levels. If Murdoch did suddenly turn up at the lab, what was I supposed to do, just pretend I forgot about our confrontation? As Joe Cabot said in *Reservoir Dogs*, "You know how to handle that situation: shit in your pants and dive in and swim."

I spent several minutes looking out my apartment window, watching the sidewalk before I went downstairs to my car. My eyes were glued to the rear view mirror for most of the drive to Spalding, making sure I wasn't being followed. I made it into the building and to my office without anyone seeing me. Margo's door was ajar, but she didn't look up as I silently walked by. I wasn't in the mood for chitchat anyway.

I probably should've gone straight to see Lionel, but I wanted to stop here first to collect myself. It would be a long walk to Dancy Hall. I sifted through some emails for a while, and straightened and re-straightened the things on my desk. I even searched for a few movie posters online in case I wanted to replace the ones currently hanging in my office. This was just a half-assed attempt to put off the inevitable. Disgusted with myself, I shut down my computer, gathered up my things, and turned off my desk lamp. I walked into the hall, half-closing the door behind me, when I froze.

There was a uniformed police officer and another man standing outside Margo's office. I saw her walk out and point in the direction of my office. I managed to duck back inside before any of them saw me, but they must have noticed my door closing. Murdoch had sent the police after Lionel; now he probably told them I was an accomplice, and they were after me.

Maybe I could play dumb and talk my way out of it. That would never work. Police may sometimes appear a little dim, but an allegedly bright university professor like me stood zero chance of outwitting them in this situation. Some students passed by on the sidewalk outside my window. I wished could have switched places with them.

The window! Just as I unlocked it and started sliding it up, there was a knock at my door.

"Cal," Margo called in a singsong voice. I then heard her add, "I haven't seen him around. He usually doesn't come to campus on Fridays." She knew damn well I was here. I'd have to thank her for that later. As I prepared to climb out the window there was another knock at the door and a male voice I didn't recognize said, "Professor Sutherland?" I stopped for a moment, one leg over the window ledge, and considered how ridiculous this would look to any of my students who happened to be passing by.

Unfortunately, I knocked a book onto the floor with my other leg. Another knock immediately followed. I didn't care about being quiet now; I just climbed out the window and closed it. Some students outside the building gave me curious looks, but I just nodded and smiled as if it was some big joke they were in on too.

Going to my car would have taken me past the entrance to Noll Hall. I decided to circle around to the rear of the building and make a break for Dancy Hall. Even if I was about to be taken into custody, I had to tell Lionel what was happening. I tried to walk as fast as I could without running, which wasn't easy. When I got some distance away from Noll Hall, I turned to look back and saw the two police officers. For just an instant our eyes locked, and both men started after me.

I tucked my bag under my arm like a football and started running. I managed to keep far enough ahead of them to burst into Dancy Hall with a fifty-yard lead. I ran down the hallway to Lab 7. Lionel, Roger, and Jack were all there. Lionel gave me an understandably startled look.

"Cal! Didn't expect to see you today…" he started to say, but must have noticed how frazzled I looked.

"The police are after me," I said, catching my breath. "This was the first place I thought to come."

"The police? Oh God."

"They'll probably find their way to the lab any second."

"What do the police want with *you*?" Roger asked.

"I screwed up, Lionel, I'm sorry. I went to Nick Murdoch's apartment last night to confront him and —"

"Oh no, Cal," Lionel said, putting a hand to his forehead.

"What the hell did you do that for?" Rodger asked harshly.

"I don't have time to explain. Is there a back door or something?"

Lionel shook his head. "Only the fire door."

"Damn! Is there somewhere I can hide?" I was looking around frantically.

"What about there," Jack said, looking in the direction of the time machine. Lionel gave both Jack and I a skeptical look.

"Why not?" Roger grumbled in an exasperated tone.

"It wasn't totally powered down anyway," Jack said, pushing buttons and rapidly clicking through on-screen menus.

"You better hurry, Cal," Lionel said pushing me toward the Nora Pads. "Where are you sending him?" he asked Jack.

"I don't know," Jack said. "I hadn't thought that far ahead."

"Send me back to late September, some place close by, so I don't have to change clothes," I said, stepping on to the Nora Pads. "Shit! I don't have a belt!"

"Don't worry, Cal," Lionel said. "Is there a familiar place you can go for a while in the past? I can come get you later with a TRI." There was knock at the lab door that caused us all to stop whatever we were doing.

"I'll try and stall them," Roger said, walking toward the door.

"Put me on a roof near AJ's bar," I said to Jack. "I'll just wait for you in the bar." He nodded. "I'm sorry about all this, Lionel. I never wanted —"

"I know," he said somberly.

"We're ready. Here goes," Jack said as the pad lit up and the whirring sound grew louder. As the tubes closed around me, the last thing I saw was Lionel looking at me with an expression that seemed to be a mixture of disappointment and sadness.

Thursday September 29, 2016

I didn't think it would take Lionel very long to come get me, so I just stood around outside AJ's Bar. After waiting for about fifteen minutes with a perfectly good watering hole right behind me, I went inside. Despite what I'd done in the present, this was *still* the past, so why not enjoy myself a little? The consequences of my stupidity at confronting Murdoch wouldn't occur for another month. At this point, Murdoch hadn't even hired Lionel.

It was about 6:30. Most of the happy hour crowd had cleared out, and I easily found a stool at the bar to the right of the entrance. I was about four seats down from where Nick Murdoch and Steve Millard would be sitting a few weeks from now. I glanced back to the booth Jack and I would eventually occupy and smiled. Déjà vu—literally.

I ordered a bourbon on the rocks and downed it in a matter of minutes, wanting to get in a drink or two before Lionel showed up. I was halfway through my second drink when I realized I'd been here about a half hour. Where was Lionel? Was he planning to leave me here for a while to let me stew about what happened? Had they all been arrested and the time machine shut down...or worse? I hadn't exactly left them in a favorable position.

On the other hand, the police were looking for *me*, and I wasn't anywhere to be found. They would think I found another way out of the building, and Lionel and Roger would be only too happy to encourage this. I swallowed the rest of the second bourbon and told myself not to worry about it. I was in the past for Christ's sake. None of that had even happened yet, so why worry about it?

"Gettin' an early start on the weekend?" the bartender said. He looked about my age and had an impressive array of tattoos up and down both arms.

"You know it man," I said. "Tomorrow's Saturday, so why wait?"

"Uh, it's only Thursday, boss."

Oops. It had been Friday when I left the present. "Oh yeah. But I'm off tomorrow, so it might as well be Saturday, you know?"

"I hear that. Another one?"

"Please." He returned with my third bourbon, which I resolved to drink more slowly. I chatted with the bartender, whose name was Dusty. The alcohol must've been getting to me, because small talk came unusually easy to me. I tried to recall whether he'd been tending bar on the night Jack and I were here, a few weeks from now.

People had been coming and going for about an hour, but still no Lionel. I occasionally glanced over to the front door to check for him, but otherwise stayed focused on my bourbon. Without intending to, I'd nearly drained glass number three. My head was spinning, and I could tell that if I didn't make a deliberate effort, I'd slur my words. I knew full well that drinking bourbon often got away from me, but I never thought I'd be here long enough for that to happen. As if by magic, Dusty made a fourth glass appear in front of me just as I finished the previous one.

The buzz of conversations swirling around me was comforting. I had left some serious problems behind in the present, but they seemed to vanish. Maybe it was the alcohol. On the other hand, maybe being in the past had become sweet and bucolic-like it had been when Lionel and I first traveled back in time. Memories of the speakeasy brought a smile to my face.

A snippet of a nearby conversation filtered hazily into my consciousness.

"Yeah, I don't know where they went. I think my fuckin' roommate took 'em," I heard Dusty telling someone. I saw him talking to a heavyset man wearing a San Francisco Giants jersey who said something I couldn't hear. "Eh, what're you gonna do? They're long gone."

"What's long gone?" I asked. "Did you lose something?"

"Just some rockets."

"Rockets? You mean...what do you mean?"

"*Model* rockets," Dusty said. I nodded in understanding. "I built 'em when I was a kid," he continued. "It was a set of the rockets from the sixties. I had the Saturn V and whatever that one was they used when NASA got started."

"The Redstone," I said, making a mental note to re-watch *The Right Stuff* when I got the chance.

"Yeah right," he said. "Anyway, I had these models, and I planned on giving them to my kid one day. He's seven now."

"Only you lost them somewhere."

"I didn't lose 'em. Like I was tellin' him, I think my roommate took 'em a while back. No big deal."

I leaned in closer. "If you don't mind me asking, when do you think your roommate may have taken them?"

"Damn," he said thinking it over. "I think I moved out in '97. Yeah, 'cause I remember all that shit with Princess Diana was going on. My roommate was an ass too. I had to chase him down for the rent half the time."

"Well Dusty, if you want those rockets back, this may be your lucky day," I said, confidently taking a sip of bourbon.

Dusty gave a skeptical laugh. "Oh yeah? Do you hang out with my old roommate or something?"

"I'm serious. I have a friend who has a side business recovering things like this. I mean, he charges for it, but only if finds what you're looking for."

"How's he going to track down a bunch of model rockets? They're probably in the bottom of a landfill somewhere."

"Don't ask me how he does it, but he's very, very good at what he does. He's found some stuff over the years that you wouldn't believe." I couldn't help feeling a little full of myself, being in on the secret of Lionel's success.

"So who is this guy?"

"His name's Lionel Bradshaw. He teaches out at Spalding. Here, let me give you his number." I wrote down the number on a bar napkin. Dusty stared at the napkin for a moment.

"Eh, maybe it's worth a try."

"Definitely. If those rockets are there to be found, he'll find them for you."

"Cool. Thanks."

"Don't mention it," I said, taking a drink. Dusty put the napkin in his pocket. I turned to look at the door, but still no Lionel.

"Did you say you knew a guy who could find stuff that people lost?" a voice behind me asked.

"Sure," I said, turning around to answer.

Nick Murdoch stood there, waiting for me to reply.

The glass of bourbon almost slipped out of my hand. Whatever I was going to say next caught in my throat.

"Yo," he said more loudly, "did I just hear you saying you knew a guy who could find things for people?"

"Yeah," I managed to say. I felt like I was going to hyperventilate or have a heart attack. So much about the last few weeks of my life instantly made sense, including Murdoch's initial reaction to me when I turned up at his apartment.

"You all right?" Murdoch asked, probably thinking I was drunk. I wasn't. Seeing Murdoch standing here sobered me up in a flash. Just leave, I told myself. Just get outta here. However, if I was right about what happens next, either I couldn't just leave, or it wouldn't matter if I did. This is it! *This* is the moment it all starts. There has to be a way to stop it. All I need is to…

"I got it right here, man," Dusty said, coming over. He turned to me. "You don't mind if I give the name to this guy, do you?" I closed my eyes and shook my head 'no.' What did it matter anyway? I watched Murdoch take a pen from his pocket and copy down Lionel's name and number from the napkin in Dusty's hand. He nodded at Dusty and seemed to consider me for a moment. Then he shuffled away without bothering to thank me. I stared at the place where Murdoch had been standing. My mouth hung open.

"Hey, you all right?" I heard Dusty ask from what seemed like far away.

"I gotta go." I laid some money down on the bar, probably too much, and went to the door. Murdoch was sitting in a booth somewhere behind me, but I didn't turn around to look. The world spun as I got to the door, and it had nothing to do with the bourbon. It felt like the scene in *Lock, Stock, and Two Smoking Barrels* where Ed just lost all his friends' money in the card game and The Stooges' *I Wanna Be Your Dog* is playing.

It was eerily quiet outside. I felt like the world should have changed abruptly in light of what I'd just done. Even if it had *already* happened before I got here; even if it couldn't be undone, that made little difference. I was numb. I put my hand to my forehead and closed my eyes, falling back on the brick wall behind me.

"Cal," I heard a familiar voice say, "are you all right? I hope I haven't kept you waiting long."

"It's my fault, Lionel," I said, aghast. "Everything that's been happening this whole time is all my fault."

CHAPTER 15

I STILL DON'T see how that's possible, even if you did run into him there," Jack was saying. "What about the First Law and all that stuff you told me about closed causal loops?"

"This isn't a *closed* loop. It's not an instance where a past event causes something to happen at a later time, and that later event in turn brings about that past event. I didn't know I was going to run into Murdoch in early October until it happened. Yes, he got Lionel's name from me at that time, and that's what led him to hire Lionel in the first place. But it wasn't *that event* which caused me to travel back in time and run into him. My traveling back and running into him was just…a cockeyed way that things naturally occurred. I didn't travel back in time to alter anything; this is just the way it all unfolded."

"That's all well and good, Cal, but we need to figure out what to do about this," Lionel said. "Whatever Murdoch is up to it's been in progress for some weeks now, even if we've only just become aware of how he came to hire me. Yesterday with the police was a very close call."

That was understating it a bit. Following my encounter at the bar, Lionel and I hadn't immediately returned to the present. We walked around the block a few times while I sipped some coffee and he filled me in on what happened just after I departed. The police burst into the lab looking for me just as the cylinders on the Nora Pad started opening again. Lionel and Roger bluffed the police into thinking that the time machine was some highly technical apparatus for, as Lionel had put it, isolating and studying quantum filament waves. This was a fictitious phenomenon he borrowed from an episode of *Star Trek: The Next Generation*. The police swallowed it, but they didn't leave happy.

Lionel reasoned that, because the police missed me on campus, the next place they would try was my apartment. He had waited until the following morning to come back in time to retrieve me. Because I didn't have a TRI belt with me when I traveled back, more than fifteen minutes had passed between my departure and return to the present.

"Here," Roger said, handing me a business card. "You'll likely want to hire a lawyer at some point." It was a downtown firm called Person & Baab that specialized in criminal law.

"Thanks," I said, pocketing the card. "Hopefully I won't need it." The room was silent for what seemed like several minutes. I caught Lionel looking at Roger and nodding toward the door. Roger frowned at me and asked Jack to come with him to look for some equipment they apparently needed. My time traveling days were probably over. Lionel sat down opposite me.

"Cal, I have to ask. Why on Earth did you confront Murdoch the other night?" It was a blunt question, but I deserved it.

"I don't know. I shouldn't have done it without us talking it over."

"You shouldn't have done it *at all*. I'm merely wondering why the impulse arose in the first place."

I smirked. "Ask a psychiatrist."

"Cal." He frowned.

"Because I want an end to this," I said indignantly.

"To what?"

"This!" I waved my arms frantically. "Look at that. Over on the back wall there's a time machine. *A time machine*. When was the last time any of us just paused for a moment to reflect on that, huh? It's a gateway to strange and wonderful beauty. Yet all we're doing is popping in and out of the last couple of weeks, ducking around corners like a bunch of teenage sneaks. Well, wasting time in the past is no better than wasting time in the present."

"That's true, up to a point. But wherever we go in time, the present day, *this* present day, is always our frame of reference. No matter what we do in the past, our tasks aim at the present, whether we're recovering some object or, as you'd likely put it, just grooving on the scene for a while. I can understand how you feel, but it wasn't frustration about time travel that led you to Murdoch's apartment the other night."

"Sure it was."

"What you said a moment ago about time travel is far too thoughtful to motivate such a rash decision." Lionel paused for a moment, seeming to consider what he was going to say next. "You spent quite a while in 1992, didn't you?"

I looked up sharply. "What're you, Columbo now? What the hell's that got to do anything?" I thought I noticed a faint smile on his face.

"Rather a lot, I should think."

"Well, I'm sure you'll tell me my jaunt to 1992 was all worth it."

"It clearly wasn't." He paused before adding, "After all, Laura Dietrichson is still dead."

"I never mentioned her, did I?"

"You didn't have to. But that *is* what motivated you to confront Murdoch."

I sprang up from the chair and turned my back to him. This was too personal. My mind and my feelings were my own to contemplate, and I did more than my fair share of that without anyone's help.

"You shouldn't have sent me back to 1992," I finally said.

"You *had* to go, Cal."

"Only because I was naïve enough to picture the early 90's the way I remembered it." I turned angrily to face him. "And you knew I'd see it that way, didn't you? You knew exactly what I'd think, and you offered it all up in a way designed to make me swallow it!" Lionel looked away and didn't say anything. I knew I was right. Here I'd been blaming myself for everything, and all the while Lionel was behind everything that happened, manipulating me the whole time. Then I remembered something he'd said to me.

"You know your best work was that bit about me being 'the only man for the job.' That was fucking brilliant. It actually convinced me I was up it, even *destined* to do it. Well, you're in it now, aren't you? Right up to your pressed collar. You haven't seen the last of Nick Murdoch, but I'm sure you'll think of something. As for me, I'm done." I started to walk to the door. "Oh, good luck with the key, by the way. Have you tried the locks on your desk drawer? Stranger things have happened."

"Cal," Lionel called out. I turned on him.

"*You* should've gone back Lionel," I shouted as Laura's face filled my consciousness. "*You* could've gotten to know her, smiled at how bright and clever she was, and woken up next to her in the room where she took her last breath. I'd like to see how you would've learned to live with it. I had no business being there, no reason to ever encounter her alive!"

A sympathetic smile came over Lionel's face. It reminded me of the look he gave me during the fire at Miriam's house, which seemed like a million years ago. "As a matter of fact, Cal, no one but you *could've* done it." He put up his hand to stop my onslaught of vitriol and walked to his office on the other side of the lab. I watched him pause at his desk before opening the drawer. He emerged carrying a small manila envelope. He undid the flap on the envelope and handed it to me.

"Open it," Lionel said quietly.

I figured it was just more bullshit, some way to keep me here a little longer while he tried to save face. I opened the envelope, and its contents took my breath away. I felt the envelope slip from my hand and fall to the floor.

"Should I have told you about this in advance?" Lionel asked rhetorically. "I don't know. I only know that I didn't."

"Where did you get this?" I finally managed to ask.

"I found it on our first trip back to Laura Dietrichson's house—May of '93.

You were in the room across the hall where you found the bird. Of course, I didn't expect to come across this. Then again, I wasn't looking for it. It was just sitting on her dresser propped up against a jewelry case."

"A little brown one with a rose engraved on it, right?"

"I suppose it could have been. Once I saw this, I wasn't paying all that much attention."

I sat down and stared dumbstruck at the photograph of Laura and I that Lionel just handed me. "I remember when this was taken. It was right before I came back to the present in front of a video store on Beechtree. We'd gone on a short hike that morning and were walking back to her place after lunch. Some guy took the picture for us. I...I didn't even know she had it developed, let alone kept it all that time."

"It looks like it meant a great deal to her," Lionel said. I nodded, still immersed in the photograph. It was haunting and yet somehow liberating all at once. "I'm truly sorry, Cal. For everything that happened, even if it did seem inevitable somehow. I should've told—"

I put up my hand to stop him, but couldn't take my eyes off the photo-graph. "I understand. If you *had* told me about it, it would've constantly been on my mind. I'd never stop thinking about when that photo would be taken, and whether I'd be in the right place and time to have it taken. I probably would've gone in search of the video store right after I got to 1992. Trying to figure out...something."

I stood up, slipped the photo in my shirt pocket, and turned to leave. "I was angry before, Lionel. I shouldn't have said any of that stuff."

"Never mind," Lionel said, dismissing it. "Water under the bridge."

I started to leave. "You haven't seen the last of me, Lionel."

CHAPTER 16

Monday November 7, 2016

S O LIKE I said, Margo, it was just a misunderstanding." As I'd expected, Margo came to my office moments after I'd arrived. It wasn't every day that the police happened by the Philosophy Department intent on questioning a faculty member. All things considered, Margo took the whole affair rather well.

"You do have the distinction of being the first fugitive we've employed."

"I wouldn't go that far. Even if 'fugitive' has kind of a nice ring to it."

"Do you often use your office window as a shortcut out of the building?"

"Oh, so you did know about that."

"Of course I did."

"Well, thanks again for not blowing me in."

"The hell with the police. Let them do their own sleuthing." She leaned in closer. "But I am curious, Cal. What is it you're trying to sell on the black market? A first edition of Aristotle's Collected Works?"

"Actually that's not a bad idea," I said truthfully. Lionel and I had never discussed it, but I assumed it was possible to travel that far back in time. It would be difficult, however, to just 'blend in' in the middle of Ancient Athens, especially not speaking the language. Nevertheless, recovering the lost works of Aristotle would probably net Lionel and me a king's ransom.

"Cal?"

"Sorry, got distracted for a moment."

"Well, don't. The last thing I want is to be an accessory in all this."

"The police wanted to ask me about some military paraphernalia that had been reported stolen."

"How did the police connect you with something like that?"

"Damned if I know. Anyway, I went down to the station earlier, and it's all sorted out." That was a lie. What I had done was pay a visit to the Person & Baab Law Firm. Stacy Baab, one of the partners, agreed to handle my case, such that it was. She told me not to say anything to the police but to refer them to her. The advice hardly seemed worth the money, but the possibility of having a lawyer run interference was invaluable. Getting the police off my back would give Lionel and me time to think about what to do next. There was no way we'd heard that last of Nick Murdoch.

"I have to ask this, Cal, but is everything all right? I mean, with you."

"Apart from having to deal with this nonsense, sure." I noticed a faint look of skepticism in her eyes. "Why do you ask?"

"I was just thinking it's been an interesting couple of months for you. You have that forthcoming publication, which is very welcome news. Especially because it gets me out of calling you into my office to give you a good wigging about your tenure review."

"Happy to help."

"But I don't see you around here as much these days, aside from when you have class. I rarely see you working in your office. Plus, you had that situation with the house fire back in September."

"Oh, that," I said, thinking about how the two events were related even if Margo couldn't.

"Is it really just 'oh that?'"

"Yeah, Margo, it is. Honestly, I thought of the fire the other day for the first time in weeks. As for not being around here as much, you remember that guy I introduced you to the other day? The physicist? He and I have been collaborating on some research."

"Really."

"He finds philosophy of time a lot more interesting than most of the people around here."

"No counting for taste," she said dryly as she stood up to leave. "Even so, Cal, keep me informed if anything comes up. I'd hate to think of the police beating a confession out of you and my not doing anything to stop it."

"Thanks, but I don't really think my case rises to the level of jack-boots and rubber hoses."

"I'm sure that still happens from time to time," she said.

"Confessions under duress don't stand up in court anyway. The only truly foolproof kind of confession—I saw this on an episode of *Dragnet* once—was when…" I stopped talking abruptly.

An answer to a question I'd been wrestling with for days occurred to me all at once. Without any further consideration, I knew it would work. At the same time, I hated myself for thinking it.

"Yes?" Margo prompted. "What is this so-called foolproof confession?"

"Oh, Joe and Bill, uh, tricked this guy into spilling the beans about something. I was just trying to remember exactly how they did it. Eh, it'll probably come to me on the drive home. It was pretty clever though."

"Well, keep your nose clean."

As soon as she left, I grabbed my phone. "Lionel," I said when he came on the line. "I know how we can find out about the key."

§ § §

Being here made him very uneasy. It reminded him too much of his own brushes with death and misfortune. He closed his eyes, arched his back, and summoned all the resolve he could muster. It wasn't easy, given what was happening inside the house. He clenched and unclenched his right hand, hoping that they had planned this correctly, especially the timing.

He flinched at a bang from inside the house and felt his heart rate quicken. Gunshots hadn't made him flinch since he was a kid. He peeked around the back corner of the house. He couldn't go in until the man inside left. That was a roll of the dice, too. They'd anticipated him coming out the front door, but that was just a guess. Once the man left, getting inside wouldn't be a problem; he knew where the owner kept the spare key. There was a border of round stones next to a planter. He picked up the third stone from the end and found a small black box underneath. He slid the top open and found the key inside, replacing the rock where it had been.

Another minute went by. Too long. By the time I get in there, this will have all been for nothing, he thought. Then again, maybe it's possible to speed things up a bit.

"Right," he said aloud, banging on the back door. The faint sounds of movement inside the house came to an abrupt halt. He pounded on the door again for good measure and then resumed his place at the rear corner of the house. After a minute, he heard the front door open. He crouched down and peered cautiously around the corner. A man came into view and stopped for a moment to look up the driveway toward the rear of the house. He looked back up at the house, apparently considering whether to go back inside. Then he gestured angrily and ran off. He was empty-handed.

The man at the rear of the house opened the kitchen door, wiping the doorknob with his jacket as he went in. The kitchen was a mess, just as he'd anticipated. Every cupboard and drawer looked to have been opened and its contents rifled. He made his way down the hall, pausing at the bottom of the stairs. It was still possible to leave, he thought. We could find another way. But no. This plan, he had to admit, was brilliant. Cruel, but brilliant.

He sighed and walked up the stairs. As he got near the top, he could hear panting sounds and a moan. He turned slowly into the doorway on the left, trying not to betray alarm at what he saw. It wasn't the first time he'd encountered the victim of a gunshot. A woman lay on her side. She wore a long blue shirt that served as a nightgown. Most of the nightgown, along with the sheets on the bed, were covered in blood. The woman gave him a terrified look when he appeared in the doorway and inched toward the bed, away from this strange man who didn't belong here.

"It's all right," he said quietly but firmly, "I'm not going to hurt you. I promise." He bent down next to her. She'd been shot once in the chest. There was also dried blood on her face and some bruises beginning to develop.

"Hel…" she started to say before coughing and swallowing hard. She gave him a plaintive, desperate look. "Help me, please."

Saving her was beyond hope. He knew that. The goal here was to buy time and get her talking. The pertinent thing now was to keep her calm. "I'll do what I can," he said, taking a surgical dressing from the small bag he carried. He pressed it against the wound in her chest.

"Did you call 9-1-1?" she managed to say.

"Yes," he lied.

"Please don't let me die," she pleaded, trying to sit up. "Please…"

"Shhh…it's all right. Just try and lie still."

"How did you get in?"

He hesitated. "The backdoor."

"I…" she started to say before coughing up some more blood. He wiped her chin.

"I used the key you'd hidden under the stone around back." He looked at her for a long moment, knowing it was time for the whole truth. "Cal told me it was there."

"Cal?" she asked, wide-eyed, "Is he here?" She coughed a few more times, seeming on the verge of tears at the strange threads of her life that were suddenly coming together. "Who the hell are you?"

He took the dressing from her chest, placed it into a plastic bag, and replaced it with a fresh one. "I'm going to tell you, Laura, but there isn't much time and you have to listen to me very carefully, no matter what. Do I have your word?" She nodded weakly.

"My name is Roger. I'm a time traveler. Cal was too." A look of disgust came over her face. He could tell what she was about to say. "Wait a minute, I can prove it." He reached into his pocket and slipped something out.

"Have a look at this." He held up a thin rectangular object. "Believe it or not, this is a phone. In 2016, we call them Smartphones, even though people use them for the silliest things." As he turned on the phone, he noticed her looking on with wonder as he swiped through the pages with his finger. "It does lots of things other than just make phone calls. For instance, this." With a few finger swipes, he brought up a digital photo. "There's Cal. Notice the cars in the background. Have you ever seen cars that look like that?" She seemed calm, but wary. The color had drained from her face. This was taking too long.

"Look, here's another one." He brought up another shot of Cal with a sad, troubled expression on his face. "Now look closer at what he's holding." Roger zoomed in and reoriented the picture to reveal what Cal had in his hand. She gasped. "That's a picture of the two of you, isn't it? The same one that's on your dresser right now. It would take too long to explain how we got that photo, but the important thing, Laura, is that you believe what I'm telling you. Do you believe me?"

"Yes," she said faintly.

"Good. In the future, people hire us to find things for them, things they believe are long since lost. They don't know how we do it, of course. A man hired us to find the stuffed raven that you keep in the room across the hall. We didn't know it contained a key until Cal was here last summer and recovered it. However, we have no idea what the key is for. Can you tell me? This may be our only chance to find out."

Her head fell back on the floor and she stared at the ceiling for several moments. "Am I going to die?"

"I'm very sorry," he said softly. "Time travel is rather different from the movies. I'm afraid we're powerless to change the past."

Tears rolled down her cheeks. "There's a safe deposit box at Winters & Lewis Savings and Loan. It's box number 1106."

"Can you tell me why this man believes the key was hidden in the bird?"

She covered her eyes with her hand and wept. "Because I just told him. He was hitting me and he…It was just…"

Roger tried to soothe her. "It's all right. I understand. It wasn't your fault."

"He was," she started to say, then began coughing again. Roger wiped some of the blood from her chin. "I think, uh, he was gonna go get it, but then there was this pounding downstairs."

Roger fell back in disbelief. "You mean the banging on the door stopped him from getting the bird?" he said almost to himself. Laura gave him a confused look. "Never mind. You say the key is for a safe deposit box?"

A combination of wheezing and gurgling came from her throat. "Does Cal have to see it too, what's in the safe-deposit box?"

"Probably."

She grabbed Roger's arm and squeezed it. "I never meant for it to happen. I wanted to go back inside. I didn't want to just leave them. I tried, but he grabbed me…" she started coughing again.

Roger patted her arm and spoke gently. "I'm positive Cal will understand."

"I hope so," she said through tears. He could see she was very near the end. His first instinct was to keep her calm and wait for her to expire, but that didn't seem sufficient.

"You should know that Cal cares for you very deeply, Laura. He hasn't been the same man since he returned to our present. My coming here was the only way, the only time, we could find out about the key. I volunteered to make this trip back in time because I know what it's like to lose someone. I also knew Cal couldn't bear to see you like this."

She seemed to calm suddenly. "Please tell him…tell him I was very happy last summer, and I miss him a lot. He was so lovely." A faint smile came over her face. "Tell him I'm sorry we'll end up like Jake and Brett." She began to cough uncontrollably and stopped suddenly. Her body relaxed, and he watched her eyes go blank. She lay on the on the floor, limp and motionless.

He shook his head somberly, removed the surgical dressing from her chest, and placed it into the plastic bag. He looked around to make sure he hadn't left anything else behind or made any footprints in the blood on the floor. The whole affair suddenly seemed very cold-hearted. Roger wasn't religious, but he couldn't help thinking she deserved something, some kind of eulogy or kind words from someone who knew her well. However, he wasn't the one to do that, and anyway it was time to leave. He moved to the phone on the nightstand and dialed 9-1-1 with his knuckle. He placed the phone on the floor next to her and quietly left through the back door.

Wednesday November 9, 2016

I'd been pacing around the lab ever since Roger disappeared on the Nora Pads about 15 minutes ago. What did I have to be anxious about? Laura's death was engraved in the past and couldn't be undone. Perhaps it was the thought that one of us was now there—*had been* there all along, as it turned out—when it happened. It was as if she was dying all over again.

It was odd to have Jack Webb to thank for inspiring this trip. I had once seen an episode of *Dragnet* where an armed robber is dying, and Joe Friday bends over to see if the crook has any last words. Friday mentions in a voice-over that anything a person confesses just prior to death is taken as the hard truth and is even admissible in court as evidence. Of course, you didn't often know when and where a person would be taking his last breath until it was too late. Unless you had a time machine.

I made it clear from the outset that I wasn't going back to watch Laura die. I figured Lionel would try at least once to talk me into it, but he never got the chance. To my surprise, Roger volunteered to go. I was still trying to figure out why when I heard a familiar clicking sound. The cylinders over one of the Nora Pads began to drop. I joined Lionel and Jack at the control desk as the cylinders closed together and a loud whirring sound filled the lab. Roger stepped off the pad as the cylinders returned to their fully open position. I cringed as I noticed a small streak of blood on his shirt, just above the waist.

"How'd it go, Roger?" Lionel asked.

Roger gave me an embarrassed look before answering. "As well as could be expected."

"Were you able to…" Lionel started to say. Roger nodded. He reached into his shoulder bag as we all looked on eagerly. When he showed us what he retrieved, none of us knew what to say at first.

"It was in a safe-deposit box at a local bank," Roger said.

"A tape?" Jack said incredulously as Roger held up a black VHS cassette. All three of them turned to me.

"Don't look at me. I know just as much about this as you guys do."

"We'll have to make a copy of it after we're done. I'll need to return it so Murdoch has something to find in the present," Roger said.

"Good thinking," Lionel said. "Now we just need a VCR."

"I think there's one in the empty office at the end of the hall," Jack said. He hurried out of the lab.

"I'm going to wash up," Roger said.

"Here's hoping that tape will yield some answers," Lionel said to me after Roger left.

"I'm sure it will raise just as many questions," I grumbled.

Jack wheeled in an AV cart with a television and combination VCR and DVD player. He plugged it into a floor outlet next to the desk. "Looks like the tape's already rewound," Jack said, inserting it into the VCR just as Roger returned. It took a few moments before there was any picture

"What the hell?" I said as a picture came on to the screen. The video showed a large rectangular table in the center of a tile floor. Two people stood on opposite sides of it with their heads down. Near the top of the screen, a counter ran the length of the screen. One person stood at the counter talking to someone on the other side, and I could see a few other people walking back and forth behind the counter.

"A surveillance video?" Lionel said.

"I guess so," I said. "Looks like a bank."

"Can you make out which bank it is?" Roger asked, apparently wondering the same thing.

"Afraid I can't," Lionel said, squinting. "We can watch it again if need be."

"There's a clock on that wall," Roger pointed out. "Looks like it's just before '10:30.'"

We watched for a while longer, but it was more of the same. At one point there were three people waiting in line to see the tellers. A couple of minutes later, the lobby was empty again. Of all the possible things that key could have led to, this never entered my mind. Even when I first saw Roger holding the tape, I figured it was some kind of home movie, probably shot by Laura. I imagined her giving some videotaped account that neatly explained everything.

I could see everyone's attention beginning to wane as the tape droned on. Jack glanced over at the instrument desk, Roger shifted around impatiently, and Lionel kept straightening his tie.

"Why would she be hiding a bank surveillance tape?" Jack asked, speaking for all of us. No one answered. "Do you want me to fast-forward through this and see if anything happens later on?"

"No, I shouldn't think so," Lionel said. "There's the chance we might miss something." I could tell even he wasn't convinced. My patience was fading too. *This,* I said to myself. This tape is what Nick Murdoch was so eager to get his hands on? This is what Laura was so ashamed of in 1992?

"Shoulder pads were really a thing twenty years ago," Jack said. I snorted at this while Lionel and Roger smiled faintly. Jack had a point though. The bank customers' fashions were the most interesting thing about the video so far.

"Any idea how much longer this tape is?" Roger asked.

"Nah. This VCR just has one of those counters that doesn't give the time," Jack replied.

I shook my head disgustedly and glanced over at the time machine. Lately it seemed to be taking us in circles, rather than *to* some place worthy of discovery. I turned back to the video. The lobby was mostly deserted now. Then four children who looked to be elementary school age entered the picture from the left, walking single file. This seemed to catch Lionel's attention as well, especially when a few more kids followed them.

A plump woman entered the frame. She had her back to the camera, but she held out both of her arms as if she was trying to keep the children in front of her in an orderly way. Some more children entered the picture, and they moved into a group between the bank counter and the table in the foreground where customers picked up deposit slips. Some of the children were now out of the frame.

"A school field trip?" Lionel asked, turning to me.

"I guess so...oh my god! Pause it," I yelled while at the same time reaching for the VCR myself. I took a moment to make sure what I was seeing. "Look at the other woman who just entered. It's Laura!" The others turned to the TV, now looking on very intently. Her hair was shorter than it would be when I encountered her however many years later, and she was dressed more formally than I was used to seeing her. The back of my neck tingled.

"Is it really her?" Lionel asked.

"It is," Roger answered somberly before I could. "I recognize her, too."

"Cal. Are you..." Lionel started to say.

"I'm fine, don't worry. Keep the tape going."

Someone dressed in a suit came around from behind the counter to meet the group of children. He talked briefly with Laura and the other woman and then turned to address the children directly. It was probably the bank manager. He seemed to enjoy talking with them. He was very animated, waving his arms here and there and occasionally pointing to something nearby when one of the kids spoke. Finally, he clasped his hands and pointed off to his right in the direction of the counter. The children followed him with the woman I didn't know in front and Laura in the back. As they walked, Laura chatted with another man who accompanied the group of children. His back was to the camera. He was probably one of the dads volunteering as a chaperone.

It was a little cramped behind the counter, but they managed. One of the tellers came over to address the class. I kept watching Laura. She called this tape her "reminder." But of what? What past sins were contained on this tape? She wasn't doing anything remarkable. Occasionally she bent down to talk to one of the children, but that was it.

After a few minutes, the group moved further away from the counter toward the rear of the bank. Laura followed them. The dad who was chaperoning the group said something to her just before he went off to the right, probably to use the bathroom. The children disappeared from view and business in the bank went on as usual.

A minute later the tape suddenly stopped.

"That's it?" I said indignantly. "Isn't there anything else?"

"I don't think so." Jack pressed the fast forward button, but there was only static. He stopped the VCR. No one said anything for a little while. I saw Lionel and Roger stealing glances at me, but no one offered up any explanations for what we'd seen.

"I know what you're all thinking," I finally said, "but that tape means *something*. Someone wanted to get his hands on it all this time after it was recorded. I can tell you Laura was deeply troubled by it the last time I saw her. She's in the tape, for Christ's sake! It *has* to be important. She even—"

"Steady on Cal, we believe you," Lionel said. "Even if it's little more than blind faith at the moment. Jack, how soon can you copy that tape to disc?"

"Should be able to have it for you by tomorrow," Jack said.

"Excellent," Lionel said.

141

CHAPTER 17

HE KNOCKED GENTLY on the door, reminding himself to be light and friendly, but not so much that it would arouse suspicion. The door opened a crack, and an eye peeked out fearfully. He expected this.

"What's up, kid?" he said evenly. The eye darted back and forth.

"Uh, it's not really a good time right now. The place is kind of a mess."

"Got another job for you."

The face behind the door seemed to think this over. "What kind? Like last time?"

"Open up and I'll tell ya'." There was a pause, and then the kid removed the chain on the door and opened it. As the man walked in, the kid made a beeline for an end table. Though his view was partially obscured, he could see a baggie and a spoon being hastily put under a copy of the local alternative newspaper.

"Catch you in the middle of something?"

"What? No. Well, you know..." the kid said. The man gave a half-smile and sat on a tattered love seat on the opposite side of the room. The apartment was neater than he would've expected from a kid like this. It wasn't terribly big—there was probably a bedroom down the hallway to his left—but it was in pretty good order despite the mismatched furniture that had seen better days. He was sure the kid was scamming money from mom and dad. Typical. He probably told them college was going fine, too, even though God knows the last time he'd been there.

"Are you gonna sit down, or are you still deciding if you're gonna shoot up that shit?"

"Oh, that's just—"

"What're you so nervous about?" he asked, though he already knew the answer.

"When I saw you at the door I figured it was because those guys came here."

"What guys?"

"That British dude from Spalding."

"He was here?" he asked, feigning surprise.

"Yeah, him and two other guys were here last week. Surprised the shit out of me."

"What did they want with you?"

The kid hesitated, rubbed his right arm, and looked down at the floor. "They kept asking me about you."

"Me?" he asked, allowing himself to show a bit of anger. "Why the hell would they be asking about me?"

"I don't know, Nick. I didn't say shit."

"What did you tell them?"

"Nothing. I—"

He put out his hand to slow him down. "Just tell me what you said."

"Well, they came up here, right. They started asking me about those papers you wanted me to get. And I told 'em just what you told me to say."

"Then what?"

"I don't know, they just left."

He stood up from the sofa. "Oh, bullshit. What happened? Did you give me up?"

"No. I swear. I told 'em I thought your first name was Roy."

"Did you tell them where I live?"

"I don't even know where you live," the kid said. Maybe it was true. He'd never been to his apartment with this kid. However, that didn't explain how this Sutherland prick turned up there. "They thought I called the cops on them."

"Hmm."

"It's the truth, Nick."

"So what happened? They didn't leave here without you telling them something."

"It wasn't anything." Nick looked at him sharply. "Seriously. The one guy just asked where and when you and me met the first time. So I told him. I mean, who cares? It was like over a week before they came here anyway. Then they just left. The guy who asked me walked out and the two British guys followed him."

"And that's it?"

"Yeah," the kid whined.

"Okay," Nick grumbled after a moment. "Forget it." The kid seemed to relax a little and sat down in a yellow chair. He kept glancing furtively at the end table, rubbing his hands nervously on his legs.

"Did you still need me to do that thing?"

"Huh? Oh, yeah. You just gotta pick something up for me. There's a hundred and fifty bucks in it."

"One-fifty? It was two-hundred last time."

"Smaller job, smaller pay, kid. Besides, it looks like you still need the money." The kid looked down, somewhat embarrassed. "Get a pencil, I'll write down where you gotta go." The kid turned away toward the end table and started moving around some of the papers. Nick stood up slowly, slipped a small revolver out of his waistband, and was on the kid within two steps. As the kid turned back around to say something, Nick swung the butt of the gun down hard just above his temple. The kid let out a yelp as his hands flew up to protect his head. Nick grabbed the kid's wrist and angrily swung the gun down at him several more times. Each hit was accompanied by cries of pain that faded with each blow. One blow seemed to fracture the kid's jaw, but by this time, he was unconscious with blood dribbling from his mouth.

Some blood splashed onto the gun. Nick wiped it on the kid's shirt. He grabbed the lamp off the end table, yanking the plug from the wall. He wrapped the cord around the kid's neck, pulling it back savagely. After a few moments there was a gurgling sound followed by some involuntary movement. Then the kid was still.

Nick dropped the cord as the kid's lifeless body fell awkwardly over the chair. His face and head were already swollen and bruised. Nick brought his own breathing under control and calmed himself. He wiped his hands on the kid's legs before taking a handkerchief from his back pocket. He doubted there were any usable prints, but he wiped down the lamp just in case.

Then he reached into his hip pocket with the handkerchief and took out a small white business card. He crumpled the card a little and touched the corner of it to some of the blood coming from the kid's mouth before placing it discreetly under the end table like it had been dropped there.

He looked around one last time to make sure he hadn't left anything else behind. Then he walked casually out of the apartment into the empty hallway.

Friday November 11, 2016

I didn't have any classes today so I stayed home. Snow was in the forecast this weekend, but today was just a crisp, late autumn day. The sun was even shining, which would become rarer as the weeks went on. I should have been out enjoying it. The DVD sitting next to my TV was keeping me indoors. Yesterday Jack had given each of us a disc that he burned from the original VHS tape.

The copy was surprisingly clear, considering the source material. Not that it did any good. I'd watched that damn video a half dozen times since Wednesday, and I was no closer to figuring out its significance. I began doubting whether it had any. I even watched the beginning twice, before Laura and the class got there, hoping to find some hidden clue. There was nothing, not even a hint about what bank it was. Even the uneasiness of seeing Laura before we first met faded with each viewing. I was so sour on the whole thing I probably wasn't giving the footage my honest attention anymore.

Still, I woke up this morning refreshed. I resolved to give the disc another honest try and then go out for a long walk and hope one of the others discovered something this weekend. I figured I'd watch the tape once more sober and then watch it once through stoned. What the hell, it worked with Miriam and *Strangers on a Train*.

As expected, nothing stood out the first time I viewed it. I even began packing up my pipe halfway through watching it, right about the time the bank manager finished talking to the kids and started leading them behind the counter. Every time I saw Laura on the tape, I couldn't help wondering what was going through her mind in these moments. She was just an anonymous schoolteacher, taking her class on a field trip. Did she have any idea that these few minutes at a bank would be so significant in the future, long after she was killed? It was always this way when pondering any momentous event from the past. You couldn't help looking at it through the lens of the present, imposing a history upon it that had yet to occur.

Laura's future was both inevitable and well known to me. It was easy to start contriving ways it would have seemed inevitable to her too, like imagining she had a premonition of things to come merely because I happened to know her fate. I found myself wishing there had been audio to accompany this video. It would've been sweet to hear one of these little kids call her 'Miss Dietrichson.'

I finished packing my bowl and glanced up at the TV. Just as I was about to spark it up, the phone rang. I briefly considered taking a hit before answering the phone just to be adventurous, but decided not to. It was a good thing too.

"Hullo, Cal?" I heard Lionel's voice say over the phone.

"Morning, Lionel. What's new?"

"Rather a lot, as a matter of fact."

"Oh?"

Lionel seemed to pause for dramatic effect. "Are you up for a trip back to 1990?" As he said '1990,' random scenes flooded my mind. Muted sunlight, wavy hair, ordinary people dressed in gothic clothing watching films that took place in large art deco spaces, and strains of Ride's *Vapour Trail* playing over the whole scene. It was an overlooked period where the 80's had mercifully died but the 90's hadn't become the 90's yet.

"Yes," I said into the phone, "I believe I am."

"Splendid. I can fill you in on the particulars when you get here."

I'd already showered and shaved, so all I had to do was clean up my gear and grab my coat. On the way downstairs, I tried to keep my mind from picturing all the awful and unlikely scenarios that awaited us in 1990.

When I got to my car, I looked at the road ahead and took a deep breath. I had the feeling that the next time I saw my apartment and this neighborhood, my life would be different. All because of what I would learn.

As I would discover later, an unmarked police car had turned onto my street just as I pulled away from the curb and prepared to turn the corner.

Wednesday March 7, 1990

We'd been searching online and in university library databases all week for some lead on the location of the bank we'd seen in the video, but we'd come up empty. When your search consists of 'something going wrong at a bank, late eighties or early nineties,' you really have nothing to go on. Then Jack came to the rescue when he noticed something the rest of us missed. As the children entered the bank, a customer on his way out held the door open for them. Only the right half of one door is visible at first, but as the door was held open, Jack noticed a slanted line on the glass. It was one side of a large capital 'A.'

We checked up on the banks in the town of Rothsburgh, where Laura mentioned to me she'd lived previously. Only one of them had a capital 'A' in its logo: Bruhl & Anderson Savings and Loan, or B & A Savings. It was now defunct, having been swallowed up by a larger conglomerate some time during the late 90's. There were two branches close to the school where Laura taught, so all four of us made this trip back. Roger and Jack staked out one branch, while Lionel and I took the other one about two miles away from the first branch.

We parked in front of a payphone and left the car window open. Roger had taken down the number of this pay phone before driving off to the other branch. Once he'd gotten there, he called us with the number of a nearby pay phone. Since a cell phone from 2016 wouldn't work in the past, this would serve as our rather convoluted relay system to let each other know which branch Laura arrived at.

Lionel and I sat in a Buick LeSabre. The branch of Bruhl & Anderson Savings and Loan occupied a parcel in the front corner of a large shopping center. A one-stop grocery store anchored the left side of a vapid strip plaza shaped like an L. When I was a kid during this period, plazas like this were all the rage. All people cared about then was having lots of parking and an array of forgettable stores that seemed to go out of business every other month.

We had rented cars using a fake credit card like the one Jack's roommate cooked up for me when I went to 1992. The cryptic video, oddly enough, gave us some clue to our actions. A wall clock read just before 10:30 when the tape started. None of the four of us appeared on the surveillance footage, so we knew we never actually entered the bank during the period shown on the tape.

The dashboard clock in our car showed '10:18.' Business at this bank branch was light. A crew of brick masons lumbered into the parking lot in a weather-beaten red truck. Four men, each wearing a flannel shirt, filed inside. They were probably there to cash their weekly paychecks before returning to a construction job. Direct deposit wasn't too common in 1990. People still routinely did their banking in person. I smiled at this. It was always nice to be in the past with nothing to do but contemplate the scene. Even if it was only for a little while.

"All right, Cal?" Lionel asked from the passenger seat.

"Sure."

"It is a bit nerve-racking, isn't it? Knowing something significant is in the offing, and yet having little idea what it is."

I frowned. "Every time I think we're at the end of this damn thing, someone moves the goal posts. Sometimes I think we should just forget the whole affair."

"I've started questioning things myself, you know." He smiled sheepishly. "Time travel was never going to be as neat and elegant as the problems in a physics textbook. However, I do find myself having less patience for the not-always-happy accidents that accompany our enterprise."

"That makes two of us."

"Rather ironic of you to say that."

"What?"

"Don't forget, Cal, you yourself were one of those accidents; the night we encountered one another in the fire, our temporal telemetries each slightly askew. Granted, you turned out to be a happy accident in the end. Though I didn't think so at first."

"Is that right?" Lionel hadn't spoken of this encounter since shortly after it happened.

"Well, I resented being followed," he said with a laugh. "Put yourself in my place. If you had a working time machine near your office, and some bloke kept turning up outside the Philosophy Department, you'd be a bit put out too. Roger and I thought you were some university bean-counter who'd gotten wise to our accounting shenanigans. We rather worried we'd have to shut things down, something neither of us wanted. If what we're really doing ever came to light…" a frown briefly came over Lionel's face. "But then Roger decided to follow *you*. It came as quite a surprise when you led him to the Philosophy Department, of all places."

I looked out the front window again. "It is strange being here in this time."

"I can appreciate your uneasiness. I'm a little unsure at—"

"No, that's not what I meant. We've already watched nearby events unfold on that tape," I said pointing to the bank branch, just as the four brick masons came out. The second one smiled and hit the mason in front of him on the shoulder, apparently over some joke they were both in on. "We can't change anything that happens—the First Law has seen to that. Yet we're here. We're actually *able* to be here. If someone had been filming us right now and showed it to us… we'd be caught just as tightly in the grip of fate as everyone on the video that brought us here. It's not that I wonder *why* we're here, as though I expect some divine voice to answer. I just wonder what, if anything, we'll be able to do."

"See what really happened at the bank, I expect, during the moments not seen on the video."

"Sometimes it feels like we're poking and prodding the First Law, just to see what we can get away with. Are we actually getting away with anything? This is just another of the infinite rooms within the past whose furniture we can't rearrange. When I'm back in 2016, fate—which, I'm beginning to think is just another name for the First Law—seems like an illusion whenever I'm deciding between alternative actions. Then when I'm in the past, fate is something I'm drowning in."

"Don't forget, Cal, the First Law is your doing. At least, coining that name for it and sussing out many of its idiosyncrasies."

It was true enough. In more ways than one.

Isaac Newton surely never foresaw rockets taking off for the moon when he deduced that a force equaled the product of mass and acceleration. Gordon Moore had not foreseen smartphones and wi-fi when he observed that the number of transistors per square inch on an integrated circuit would double each year. I knew the past couldn't be altered by a time traveler even before encountering Lionel and his time machine. Yet I never imagined sitting outside of a bank in early 1990 waiting to see the outcome of the events on a surveillance tape.

"Whatever we find out," Lionel continued, "remember that it's already happened, completely independently of us. There's nothing we can do to change it, no matter how much you might wish to."

It was his way of trying to settle me down, but it didn't have much effect. Knowing a person is right and actually believing he's right are two different things. I shifted uncomfortably in the driver's seat, and gave the key a half-turn to play the radio. The first station I came to was playing some forgettable synth-pop tune you'd hear in a shopping mall, accompanied by what counted for a rocking guitar during this time. I imagined the guitarist as a guy with long feathered blonde-hair, wearing a white shirt and white pants held up by suspenders. I quickly tuned to another station and was relieved to hear Robert Smith pouring out the vocals on The Cure's *In Between Days*. It was a song about a breakup, but it also referenced a choice made that couldn't be undone. Hearing the song made the world outside come together in the most natural way.

As if on cue, a twenty-something girl exited a red hatchback by the bank's front door. She wore a long black dress that fell loosely around her legs, ankle boots, and a denim jacket. Her hair was pulled back in a ponytail, and she wore black eyeliner. While the song continued, I forced myself to focus on just her, the way I sometimes squinted at an antique car rolling by in 2016, as though I could transform the present day into the past simply by concentrating on that car. The girl reminded me of when I was in high school and how all the cool kids dressed this way. Was she in college? An artist? What sort of music was she into? Whatever the case, the Cure made the perfect soundtrack for this moment. I watched her disappear through the front door of the bank. As I did, my gaze drifted by the dashboard clock. It read '10:31.'

149

"It's 10:31," I involuntarily said aloud, sitting up straight in the car seat. The footage on the tape started around 10:30.

And that girl wasn't on the tape.

"Lionel! We're at the wrong branch," I said, starting the engine. Lionel turned and gave me a skeptical look. Just as he did, the pay phone outside rang.

"Just go," Lionel said. "There's only one reason Roger would be calling." I pulled out onto the main road and made a left across two lanes of traffic, drawing a horn from a passing car. Less than a hundred yards away, we got stuck behind two cars at a red light.

"C'mon damn it," I growled. Out of the corner of my eye, I saw Lionel giving me a long look.

"Don't forget the First Law, old man. Whatever happens today, Laura *does* survive."

I took a deep breath as the light changed. "I know," I said quietly. Finally, the cars began moving, too slowly for my taste, but there was nothing I could do. There wasn't much traffic at this time of day, but I was stuck in a pack of slow moving cars. The clock now read '10:34.' We continued to crawl along. It might as well have been a funeral procession.

"There's Van Buren Avenue," Lionel said as we approached the next intersection. I made a right onto Van Buren and saw a clear street ahead, so I accelerated. We passed into an urban area with cars parked on both sides of a narrow street. We were speeding, but I didn't care.

A couple of blocks down, we made a left onto Halstead Drive moments after the light turned red. The second branch of Bruhl and Anderson Savings & Loan was about a half mile further down this street. To my left the sun began to show through the clouds. You could even see those rays of light that illustrators often used to convey something divine.

I could make out the bank just up ahead on the left. As we got closer, I slowed down and found a parking space on the opposite corner just in from the intersection. I slid the car crookedly next to the curb and turned the engine off as I got out.

The bank was in a brown brick building on the opposite corner. It was an older building with a rounded front. The entrance faced the diagonal of the intersection. Even though it had a glass front door, I couldn't see anything inside due to the reflecting light. The right-hand door had a large 'A' on it and looked to open inwardly. It must have been the door Jack noticed on the tape. If that wasn't enough evidence, a short yellow bus was parked near the entrance to the bank.

We waited for a car to pass on Halstead and crossed. Jack ran over from the direction of the bank. He was alone.

"Where's Roger?" I asked breathlessly.

"He went inside, like a minute ago," Jack said. "Wanted to see if he could find out anything. He said the tape had cut off by then so it would be okay."

"How long ago?" Lionel asked.

"Less than a minute before you got here, Doctor Bradshaw." We all turned back to the bank. Everything was still. At least it looked that way. I felt like the place was mocking us, and me in particular. It was maddening. We're here, right here, and Laura is inside! Why had we come this far only to stand around now?

A few more anxious moments passed with nothing happening—at least nothing that we could see. My watch now read '10:38,' which was a couple of minutes after the tape cut off. Whatever was going on, it was happening right now. Roger was in there, so I suppose he could tell us later what he saw, but that wasn't good enough for me.

"I'm going in there," I said firmly, taking a step toward the door.

"No, Cal," Lionel said. "That's not a good idea."

"Not a good idea to go in there or not a good idea for *me* to go in there?"

"Both," he said flatly. He placed his hand on my shoulder in an attempt to reassure me. "We're here. Roger's inside. Everything will be f…" he stared to say 'fine' but changed it to, "whatever it will be."

A pressure centered in my chest and simmered up toward my jaw. A middle-aged couple passed by on the sidewalk, and cars continued to move along Halstead Drive as though nothing important was happening.

"Fuck it," I said, brushing Lionel aside. I was just about to step toward the bank, and I felt Lionel behind me about to protest. However, just before anyone said anything, a loud ringing erupted in front of us, in the direction of the bank. It caught all of us off guard.

"The burglar alarm?" Lionel said, phrasing it as a question.

"The burglar alarm would be silent, wouldn't it?" Jack said. He was probably right. Even in 1990, most banks had silent alarms that a teller could press in the event of a robbery. Which meant…

"It's the fire alarm," Lionel and I said nearly simultaneously. I looked at the roof of the bank. The sun shone brightly over it, and I didn't see any smoke coming from the roof or any of the second floor windows. I took a step into the street just as a van rolled past. At that moment, the front door of the bank opened. I stopped, expecting to see Roger coming out and motioning us inside.

Instead, I was staring at Nick Murdoch.

He was younger and thinner, but there was no mistaking the narrow, beady eyes and foul expression on his face that seemed to be a mixture of anger and annoyance.

"Good Lord," Lionel said just above a gasp. I didn't say anything. Too many things in my mind were sorting themselves out and falling into place. As Murdoch exited the bank, he seemed to stare at us for a second and abruptly turned around to pull someone else through the doorway.

It was Laura. She wore a denim dress and a light brown jacket. She was crying and hysterically gesturing back toward the bank. I had never seen her this way, nor saw that look in her eyes. She was clearly in pain and wanted desperately to go back inside. But why? I hated the indecision welling up within me. She never said anything to me in 1992 about having seen me here today, so maybe I never intervened.

"Laura," I said futilely. What kind of a person would just stand around watching all this?

Murdoch was trying to pull her toward the street. He had a duffle bag in his left hand and held her forearm with his right hand. Laura was resisting as best she could. Her back arched toward the bank as he moved toward the street, looking around.

"How could you do this?" I heard her wail. "We can't leave them there. We have to go back. Goddamn it, we have to go back!"

"Shut up!" Murdoch hissed at her. He seemed as wide-eyed and as desperate as she was, but for different reasons. "Come on," he growled, giving her a hard tug. Laura dug in her heels and stayed planted to one spot. What happened next seemed to happen both instantaneously and as an event drawn out over a long duration. Murdoch threw aside her wrist, stepped toward her, and slapped her across the face loud enough that I could hear it across the street. As she recoiled, he did it again. I gasped.

"Get in the car, you bitch," I heard Murdoch say. "Get in the fucking car, now!" As his jacket came open, I saw he had a gun in his belt. She was sobbing now and looking around as though expecting someone to materialize and shepherd her away to safety.

Murdoch dragged her to the passenger side of the car, pulled open the door, and threw her inside. As he went back around to the driver's side, Laura's door opened as she tried to climb out. It quickly closed again. Through the back window I could see them struggling, even rocking the car back and forth. He must have pointed the gun at her, because all at once she was still.

As the car started, I thought of the First Law and my conversation with Lionel outside the other bank branch. *The past cannot be altered*. It happens this way and no other, regardless of who's witnessing it. Our being here is only a subjective trick, like a spectator believing that by watching his team play—or deliberately not watching them—he somehow affects the outcome. Nothing can be done. Nothing *was* done. Isn't that what I wrote in my article? Don't I always tell my metaphysics students that?

And yet....

"No," I said weakly, taking a step toward the car and into the street.

It was futile. I knew it was futile.

"No," I said louder and more confidently. Murdoch backed the car up a couple feet so he could pull away from the curb.

"*No!*" I yelled, as though I could hold back the car by force of will. Some chunks of asphalt were loose near the curb. They would probably be repaving this road during the summer construction season. I heard the car's transmission click into drive and the engine rev. The car skidded and fishtailed as it hastily pulled away from the curb.

I bent down and grabbed a piece of asphalt about the size of my fist. As the car pulled into the lane of traffic, I ran a few steps after it. Everything went quiet and slowed down. I focused on Laura's head over the top of the passenger seat and threw the chunk of asphalt as I ran.

I was never much of an athlete—I never played catch with my dad or any of the kids in the neighborhood—but as soon as the rock left my hand, I knew I had thrown it perfectly. It arced about twenty feet above the roadway, and came down in the center of the back window. Most of the window shattered, reigniting the sounds of the world around me. The car skidded to a stop.

"Jesus," I said in disbelief.

Murdoch turned around to look at the backseat. At the same time, the passenger door opened. Laura started to climb out, but he grabbed her and tried to pull her back inside as the car rolled forward. Somehow, she managed to get free and tumbled out into the street along with her purse as an oncoming car swerved to avoid her. The car stopped again and Murdoch got out. He looked over the top of the car at her. Lionel and Jack rushed by me, reaching her just as Murdoch pounded his fist on the roof of the car and got back inside. He squealed the tires, and the car sped away as I stood there with my mouth agape.

What the hell just happened?

Jack helped Laura up from the pavement, and Lionel pointed them to a café across the street. He looked back at me and nodded as if to say she would be all right. She was hysterical. I wanted to go with them. There was at least the chance that I could be nearby, maybe even talk to her.

"Cal!" Roger called out from the entrance to the bank.

He waved his arms furiously, motioning me over. When I got to Roger, he grabbed my arm and took me inside the bank. "It's bad," he said.

He led me through the lobby to the far side of the counter where we made our way behind the teller windows. The bank was somewhat familiar to me from having seen it on the surveillance tape, but actually being inside was another thing. The counters were an ugly maroon color, probably installed during the late 70's. There wasn't the thick, bulletproof glass at the teller windows that would be common in many banks ten to fifteen years later.

Something about this place made me uneasy as Roger and I rushed through the lobby. The alarm still rang loudly, making it difficult to focus, but there was something else. It was vague and ill-formed, but a feeling of dread permeated the bank.

There was no one in the lobby.

As we got behind the teller windows, I began to hear sounds coming from the rear of the bank, which was still out of sight from where we were. There was something frantic about the noise.

"Roger, what the hell's going on?" I noticed some of the teller drawers hanging open even though no one was there. There were a few bills scattered on the counter and floor as though someone had been in a hurry and dropped them. Roger didn't seem to be paying attention to me.

"Roger!" I yelled, jerking my arm out of his grip. This seemed to snap him out of his daze.

"It was a robbery, Cal," he said solemnly. "Look, we have to—"

"Please hurry," I heard a desperate voice call out from around the corner.

Roger frowned and shook his head despondently. "C'mon," he said, "we have to see if there's anything we can do."

Do about what?

I followed Roger down the hallway, which opened up into a larger area. At the far end was an enormous polished metal door that led to the vault. A few other people stood there facing the vault. They glanced back at Roger and me as we came around the corner. A woman in a red dress with tears in her eyes and runny mascara stood off to the left holding a phone. She was giving directions to a man standing at the vault door. He was turning the knob this way and that, according to what the woman on the phone was telling him.

"Can't they turn off this goddamn alarm? I can barely hear myself think," one of the men shouted.

Roger turned to me and said something I couldn't understand. I yelled at him to repeat it. He leaned in closer and said, "They're trapped in the vault."

"Who?" I yelled back. I could barely make out what he was saying. He mentioned a robbery again, and something I didn't understand about the fire alarm and the vault. That at least answered Jack's question about whether or not the burglar alarm would be silent. Then I noticed something else, looking around at this tense group of people in this small hallway. I leaned in close to Roger's ear and shouted. "Where are the kids from the field trip?"

He didn't answer, but instead looked at me with a strange expression. I understood instantly and turned back to the bank vault. Just as I did, the man at the vault door stopped turning the knob and grabbed hold of the large wheel that opened the door. It spun around several times until it came to a stop. Roger and another man rushed forward and helped pull the heavy vault door open.

A woman with dark, curly hair slid down the inside face of vault door as it opened. She fell limply to the tile floor with a thud. Instinctively, I rushed over and picked up her head. She was nearly unconscious and coughed weakly. I recognized her from the surveillance tape. She was the other teacher that accompanied the class on the field trip. A white cloud billowed out of the vault as the door opened. She seemed to be breathing, but very shallowly. As I sat her up, I got a look inside the vault for the first time. It was still dark, but I could see people sprawled about the floor in unnatural positions. A few of them moved slowly. Many others were still.

Several were too small to be adults.

I began to hear the most awful whimpering sounds.

"Oh my good God," gasped the man who opened the vault door. I stood there for a moment, breathless and stunned.

Finally, I took hold of the woman under her shoulders and slid her down the hallway and out into the lobby. Since she was clearly still alive, I laid her down gently in the lobby and returned to the vault. One of the men passed me in the hallway going in the opposite direction. He was carrying a little girl with blond hair wearing a pink dress and tights. The color had completely drained from his face. I tried not to look too closely so I might convince myself the girl was still alive.

When I got back, Roger was inside the vault. In between his coughs, I heard him imploring anyone who could to get to their feet and get outside into the fresh air. Uneasily, I joined him inside the vault. Taking a breath in the vault was more difficult than it should have been. There were a few adults lying on the floor that had yet to move. Even worse, several children lay motionless or slumped against the side of the vault. A dark-haired boy and a girl with pigtails had collapsed onto each other's shoulders, like a brother and sister who had fallen asleep together on the couch waiting for their parents to come home. As I saw this, the crying, the whimpering, and sounds of swallowing desperation echoed off the walls as if it were some cruel soundtrack to the scene.

At that moment, a little girl stepped in front of me. She had short brown hair and stared up at me as though she was working out the answer to a question that I'd asked her.

"Can you help my friend and me?" she asked matter-of-factly, even though there were tears on her cheeks. She looked at me so seriously and so calmly, everything else went quiet for a moment.

"Yes," I nodded, wanting to say more.

"He's right there," she said, pointing to a blond-haired boy lying on his side, wearing a gold San Francisco 49ers jacket. I could tell he wasn't conscious, so I didn't try talking to him. I bent down and threw him over my left shoulder. Without another word, the little girl grabbed my right hand tightly, and we started down the hallway, as if we were the only ones here.

The alarm, I now realized, had been turned off, and there were emergency vehicles out front. A group of firefighters in full turnout gear burst through the entrance to the bank. One of them saw the boy I was carrying on my shoulder and took him from me. He asked us if we were all right and told us to get outside into the fresh air.

There was a hive of activity outside. Two fire trucks blocked traffic in front of the bank, along with several police cars and an ambulance. EMS radios crackled all around me. I heard a firefighter in a white shirt mention something about the halon system, dispatching an extra ambulance and canceling a heavy rescue truck since the vault had been opened.

"Is Miss D. all right?" the little girl asked softly, still holding my hand. In the swirl of activity, I'd forgotten she was even there.

"Miss D?" I asked, at once realizing who she was referring to. "Yeah, I think she is," I said, looking across to the café.

The girl sighed. "She was crying and telling that man 'no.' He had a gun."

"So it *was* a rob..." I stared to say before remembering I was talking to a little girl. I wasn't used to children; I didn't have much experience with them. "Do you think that man was trying to steal some money?" I asked.

"Yeah," she said. Her tone of voice was flat.

"Did he, uh, did he hurt any of you."

"Unh-uh." She paused and turned to look at a bright red fire truck parked across Halstead Drive. "He was bad, though."

"I know."

"He told us to go inside that safe. He said it was going to be like hide and seek. But I knew he was lying." She looked up at me. "It was dark in there when he closed the door. Some of the boys were trying to scare us. And then it got hard to breathe." Here she was, a seven or eight year-old kid, who now had this terrible thing permanently etched onto her life. Yet she acted as though she was telling me about events that had happened to someone else. I smiled sympathetically at her.

"What's your name?"

"Jessica."

"My name's Cal." As I said this, I felt her squeeze my hand a little and sigh.

"Are my mommy and daddy going to come get me?"

"I'm sure they will," I said, looking around at all the police and firefighters running around. Jessica and I moved away from the entrance to the bank. I didn't want her to see any of her classmates being carried out, especially if—

"That man gave Miss D. something," she said.

"He what?" I asked.

"I think it was a tape," she said. "Were they gonna watch a movie together? She didn't like him. She didn't want us to go into the safe." *That* was how Laura got the tape. Now some things began to make sense.

"Cal?" Jessica said, interrupting my train of thought. "Is Heather okay?" Her eyes were wide, like she was working up the courage to apologize for doing something her parents had asked her not to do.

"I'm afraid I don't know who that is, kiddo."

"She's my friend," Jessica said, with a faraway look. "It was dark in there. Everyone kept coughing and bumping into me."

I looked at her blankly. I couldn't help thinking of all the abstract ethical problems I'd discussed with students over the years; runaway trolleys, killing a certain number of people to save many more, telling a lie to save a friend from a murderer. It now seemed so futile and disrespectful to talk that flippantly about life and death, no matter how many moral principles we might unearth.

For the first time in a while, I was conscious of exactly where I was. My younger self was somewhere in the world right now, too—probably in some classroom, half-asleep with a crush on the wrong girl, trying to tune out a sociopathic chemistry teacher. And all the while, this was happening inside a bank vault in a town I'd never even heard of until a little while ago.

"Can I have something to drink? My throat's kinda sore." Jessica said. I smiled at her. I wished I could take her to lunch and buy her a grilled cheese sandwich and a giant ice cream sundae. Even spend the rest of the day with her, just talking about…whatever she wanted to talk about, as long as it wasn't this. Anything to make up for not giving her a thought the first time I'd lived through this part of 1990. Anything to fill the time today with…something else, *someone* else, who didn't leave a class full of children to die during a bank robbery.

Before I could answer, a firefighter came over and asked if I was her father. I told him I wasn't. He said he wanted to take her to an ambulance to check her over. I automatically let go of her hand, and she went with him in a daze. As he led her away, she turned slowly back to look at me. She gave me a short wave, her hand looking very tiny. I waved back, my heart breaking as I did. I leaned against the outside wall of the bank for what seemed like hours. I was aware of the activity going on around me, but I didn't watch any of it.

After a time, Roger came out front and joined me. He didn't say anything at first. He just leaned over with his hands on his thighs, catching his breath. "Where are Lionel and Jack?" he finally asked without looking up.

"Here comes Lionel now," I said as he jogged over to us from the café . We walked a couple of doors down from the bank to a nearby storefront, out of the way of the emergency personnel and the multiplying bystanders. Lionel stared wide-eyed at everything going on in front of the bank.

"What on Earth happened in there?" Lionel asked.

Roger took a deep breath. "I got inside just before the alarm went off. There was no one around at first. No customers, tellers, or anyone. Then another man came in. He was back at the vault, Cal. You may have seen him." He must have been talking about the man who was trying to open the vault door. "He seemed obnoxious at first, asking me where everyone was and making a crack about robbing the place. Probably an instant later the alarm went off. He and I were contemplating what to do when…our friend," he said derisively, "came out from behind the counter. He was dragging Laura along with him. She kept telling him 'no' and 'not to leave them there.'"

"Did he see you?" Lionel asked.

"Not really," Roger said. "He gave us a quick glance before heading to the door. We both figured he had a gun so we stayed put. And then he dragged Laura outside."

"So you saw Laura," I said with a sense of wonder that didn't fit the occasion. Roger gave a low chuckle. He knew I was curious whether she might have recognized him three years later on the night she died. It was one of many things we'd never know for sure.

"Anyway," Roger continued, "we ran back behind the counter and found a teller standing outside the vault. She called another branch. It took a bit of convincing, as you might expect, but she got the manager at the other branch to tell her how to open the vault. Fortunately for us, he knew the teller who was on the phone with him. The ringing fire alarm probably helped our case, too."

"Who pulled the fire alarm?" Lionel asked.

"Murdoch, from what I gather," Roger said.

"Why would he do that?" I asked.

"A distraction, I should think," Roger said. "You have all these emergency workers converging on a bank instead of being deployed to chase down the robbers. Then they arrive to find out there are children trapped inside a vault. That there was a robbery almost gets lost in it all for a few critical moments. Gives him a little extra time to get away, doesn't it?"

"What was that white gas in the vault?" I asked.

"Probably the halon system," Roger said.

"Halon," I repeated. "I heard one of the firefighters say something about it."

"It's a fire-retardant gas that was sometimes used during this time period. It was later found to be environmentally unsound," Lionel said. "A fire needs oxygen to burn. Halon consumes the oxygen in the air and suppresses the flame. Unlike water, it doesn't damage electronic equipment or money or whatever may be stored in a bank vault."

I shook my head disgustedly. "He just left them there to die."

"A couple people—even three of the children—came to after you went out, Cal," Roger said.

"Yeah, but a few more didn't," I said more harshly than I'd intended. Roger looked down at the ground. "Sorry, Roger. I didn't mean anything by that." I turned to Lionel. "What about Laura. How is she?"

"She's rather badly off," Lionel said. "Physically she's fine, of course, but emotionally tattered. I don't think she knows about the halon being released. Jack's sitting with her. He should be here in a few moments."

I looked back over at the bank. Just as I did, three children walked out with two of the firefighters. That was a relief. Then I remembered the two kids I had seen slumped over on one another inside the vault. Where were they? Without intending to, I contemplated what their final moments had been like, inside a dark vault, with their classmates crying and frightened, and everyone struggling to breathe. I kicked the trashcan in front of me.

"Nick Murdoch was *here*," I spat. "He was even on that goddamn tape we watched!" The others looked at me with confused expressions. "Remember the guy who came in with Laura we thought was a chaperone? It was Murdoch."

"Good Lord," Lionel said.

"He was on that surveillance tape, and we didn't recognize him." I paused for a moment and pressed my lips together. "He was probably the one who…" I pressed my lips together. "In May of '93. He killed her. He murdered Laura." Lionel and Roger stood there silently. "How the hell didn't we figure this out? He wanted that tape because he was *on* it! Laura was dead. That tape was all that was left that would've tied him to this." I waved my hand at the scene around me.

"Don't forget," Lionel said. "Now *we* have that tape. Along with a first-hand account of what happened here today."

"How did Laura end up with the tape?" Roger asked. "She clearly wasn't in on any of this."

I looked over at the fire truck where I last saw Jessica. She wasn't there now. I hoped her parents would get here soon and wondered how they would handle this. Maybe I can check up on her in 2016. I could even dye my hair gray so she'd think I aged.

"Cal?" Lionel said, snapping me out of it.

"He gave it to her," I said flatly.

"Murdoch did? How do you know that?"

"One of the kids told me."

"Oh," Lionel said softly. He looked back and forth between Roger and me, likely realizing what each of us was thinking.

I was about to say something when Jack joined us. "Laura's all right. There are a couple of paramedics checking her over right now. I didn't want to hang around too long and risk getting questioned."

"Fine, Jack, fine," Lionel said, "no use turning up on the official records if it can be avoided."

Jack turned to me. "She kept saying that you saved her life, or whoever threw that rock and broke the car window. I made out like I didn't know what she was talking about."

I rubbed the bridge of my nose, trying to process the tangled timeline I had with Laura. "Saved her life," I repeated, shaking my head. "*I* picked up that block of asphalt, Lionel! *I* threw it at the car and broke the window." The three of them looked at me blankly, unsure of what to say. "*How* did I do that? We were just talking about the First Law, fate, and all that crap not more than an hour ago. I grasped it *all* in the moment I bent down to pick up that hunk of street. Yet I could *feel* myself striking back against it. The First Law was there, Lionel. I pushed back against it, and it rippled. I felt it."

Lionel gave me the smile I had grown so used to these last couple of months—the odd mixture of understanding and sympathy, yet without a trace of condescension. "Part of the narrative, old man. It had already happened, just like the terrible scene inside the vault. Even us being here is part of that narrative and always has been." He leaned in closer to emphasize his next point. "The one and only narrative of this time and place. You heard what Jack said. You saved her life. You actually did that."

"Saved her only to have her be murdered by the same man three years later," I said.

"It's merely the way it happened, Cal. Our being here only changes what we happen to know about the situation, not how it occurred."

I looked across the street to the café. Laura was inside. All that stood between us was a street to cross and an unlocked front door. She was right there! I'd hurled that piece of roadway; why couldn't I just walk across the street? It was merely a matter of putting one foot in front of the other. I stiffened for a moment and felt the muscles in my right leg twitch as I began to move.

As my foot left the sidewalk, the door to the café opened. Two paramedics ushered Laura outside. One of the paramedics held her arm and seemed to be leading her along. She'd calmed down considerably since I saw her earlier. She was sniffling a little bit, and her hair was disheveled. She stared straight ahead with a dazed look, not turning her head toward the bank, even though

I knew it must be at the forefront of her mind. A police officer walked over and led her to the back of a patrol car. He opened the front passenger door, sat her on the seat, and bent down to talk with her.

"It's time for us to depart," I heard Roger say with the cold, unsympathetic tone I was more used to. "It's only a matter of time before someone in the bank points us out to the authorities."

"First order of business when we get back," Lionel said, "is to figure out just how to make use of what's on that tape."

I lingered for a moment as the others walked away, staring at Laura sitting in the front of that patrol car. She wasn't saying much, occasionally nodding at something the officer asked her. I knew I was seeing her for the last time. I felt the moment crying out for me to do…something. But what? What do you say to someone who won't meet you for another two years?

"Cal?" a voice said behind me. It was Roger.

"I'm coming," I said, not wanting to rush.

He stared past me toward Laura. "There she is," he said with a faraway look. "Mentioning that this has already happened doesn't help much when she's sitting right over there." With a soft tone I wasn't accustomed to hearing from him, he added, "Or walking along the sidewalk a few houses away."

I recalled the story Lionel told me about Roger traveling back in time, trying futilely to save his late wife. I frowned. "I didn't know who she was talking about at the time, but she told me that Murdoch used her. He used her to get inside the bank and rob it. But I used her too, didn't I?"

"She didn't see it that way," Roger said.

"That's because she didn't know who I really was."

Roger smiled sadly and stared at Laura. "The night she died, when she told me about the safe deposit box, she was very worried what *you'd* think of all this." He waved his hand at the scene around us. "She even asked me if there was some way to avoid showing you the tape. I told her there wasn't, but that I was sure you wouldn't blame her."

I appreciated Roger telling me this. I closed my eyes and took a deep breath, trying to compose myself. "Did she say anything else?" I asked stiffly.

Roger furrowed his brow. "Something about… oh, what were the names she used? Jake and…damn, what was the other one?"

"Brett."

"Right. She was sorry you two were going to end up like Jake and Brett." He turned to look at me. "I take it you know who she means."

"I do," I said, picturing a sunny summer evening in Laura's living room.

"The word 'closure' is little more than an empty bromide," Roger said, using the more authoritative tone I was used to. "Doors close, chapters end, but there's no closure. You're still alive and she isn't, at least not in 2016. There's always loss, but there needn't be guilt. Her last thoughts *will be* of you. And she'll remember you fondly."

"Thank you, Roger."

He nodded in acknowledgment and glanced over to the entrance of the bank. Some people were looking over at us while talking to a couple of police officers. "I rather think it's time for us to go."

We walked briskly down the block, away from the bank, occasionally pushing our way through some of the bystanders that had gathered. As we got near the end of the block, I heard a voice call out to us from behind. We darted around the corner and into an open doorway that led to some upstairs apartments. Without another word, Roger and I activated our temporal return initiators. I watched a uniformed police officer rush by the doorway just as 1990 faded into the past for the second time during my life.

CHAPTER 18

Friday November 11, 2016

AS I RETURNED from 1990, I felt claustrophobic as the cylinders opened. When traveling back in time, we always emerged in a different setting, yet we always returned to this same place. This lab was always where my re-acclimation to the present took its awkward first steps.

Images of the bank, the vault, those children, and Laura flashed through my mind like the pictures on a television that someone left on in the background of a dinner party. I just let them play out as I made my way into the lab. Business would go on as usual, as the phrase goes. Jack hunched over the instrument panel checking over the settings. He mentioned something to Roger about the automatic start sequence working more efficiently this time around. Just as Lionel took off his jacket, the phone in his office rang.

"Nothing like coming home to a ringing phone," he said, going off to answer it. I didn't feel like discussing our latest trip. It always took me longer to fully adjust to the present, just as it took some people longer to get out of bed in the morning following a rough night's sleep. Now that we had a first-hand account of what happened at the bank, along with the surveillance tape, we could probably go to the police. It'd be difficult to explain how we acquired this information, but we could work that out. Lionel and Roger had plenty of experience with that sort of thing.

"Oh yes, yes I remember you. How are you?" I heard Lionel saying into the phone in his office. "He is, as a matter of fact. Just a moment, I'll put him on the line." Roger must have overheard this too because he started walking over to the office to take the call.

"Cal? Telephone," Lionel said, taking both Roger and me by surprise. Lionel had an amused smile on his face.

Who would be calling me here?

As seemed to happen in every movie when someone receives a mysterious phone call, I stood there staring at the receiver for a moment instead of just picking it up. "Hello?" I finally said into the phone.

"Cal!" Margo's voice said. She seemed to be trying to whisper and shout at the same time.

"Hi ya' Margo. How'd you know I was here?"

"What the hell's going on with you?" she hissed.

I'd only ever heard her use that tone when discussing some pain-in-the-ass university administrator. "Nothing's going on with me," I lied, thinking of where I'd just been.

"The police are here! They're hanging around outside the building right now, and I don't think they're leaving any time soon."

"What do they want?"

"You, for Christ's sake!"

I shook my head. "Oh, for crying out loud. I already told you, and them, I didn't steal anything."

"If only you *had*."

"What's that supposed to mean?"

There was a pause on the other end of the phone that seemed to go on for several minutes. "Cal, the police want to talk to you about a...murder," she said just above a whisper.

Murder.

The word hung there in the silence. I pictured Danny in *The Shining* just as the camera zooms in on the bathroom door with 'Redrum' written in lipstick. "They want to talk to me about a murder? Well, I..." I managed to stammer.

"What the hell have you *done*, Cal?"

None of this made sense. "Well, I didn't kill anyone, Margo—accidentally, on purpose, or in self-defense."

"I didn't think you did," she said before adding, "not really, at any rate."

"Jesus. Are the police still there?"

"*Yes*. Two detectives are standing by the entrance to the building."

"Well, didn't you tell them you hadn't seen me?"

"I told them I was worried you might bump me off next," she said flippantly. "Of course I told them I hadn't seen you! But your car's in the parking lot, so they know you're here somewhere."

"Shit," I said.

"Why would they think...damn it, I gotta go. They're coming back. I guess... good luck Cal. Try and stay in touch." Then the line went dead.

I stood in Lionel's office holding the phone up to my ear, wondering what to do next. The police had already been to Spalding once to question me, and they'd even arrested Lionel another time. It was only a matter of time before they started poking around Dancy Hall. I set the phone down and jogged back into the lab. Lionel was sitting at one of the work tables with his sleeves rolled up, looking over some papers. He must have noticed the expression on my face.

"What on Earth's the matter?" he asked.

"The police are at the Philosophy Department. They want to ask me about a murder."

"What!" He said this loud enough that it drew Roger and Jack over to our conversation.

"You've gotta get me out of here."

"What exactly do you mean, the police want to 'ask you' about a murder?" Roger asked.

"Well, I assume they think I killed someone."

"Who?" Lionel asked.

"I don't know. Margo had to get off the phone before she could tell me. We can figure all that out later. Right now I've gotta get out of here before they come looking for me. And you know damn well they will," I said, frantically running my hands through my hair.

"You know what this is, don't you?" Roger said gravely, looking at each of us in turn.

"Murdoch," Lionel said. "Has to be."

That conclusion seemed true the instant Lionel said it. "How the hell did he do that?" I asked. "You can't just tell the police you think someone committed a murder and have them rush out to arrest the guy."

"Well, I suppose we've all *thought about* framing you for a murder, Cal," Roger said laconically. The room came to a halt. Even I forgot my predicament for a moment as it broke the tension. "Sorry. Inappropriate joke."

"No. Just a bit ill-timed," Lionel said. "Regardless, Cal's right. He can't stay here."

"Maybe I could drive him home," Jack offered. "We've got all those period clothes in the wardrobe room. We've never used them for a disguise in the present before. It might work."

"There is some wisdom in that," Lionel said.

I shook my head. "I might make it out of here all right, but they're probably watching my apartment." Suddenly the solution struck me. I snapped my fingers and pointed to the time machine. "There! They sure as hell can't follow me to the past. Send me back to the 1950s or something, before anyone we're dealing with was even around."

Lionel bit his lip as he and Roger looked at each other. "Afraid not," Lionel said. "Remember, you'd be right back here 15 minutes later. And we're not sending you back in time without a Temporal Return Initiator." Lionel gave me a strange, almost sentimental look. "It's not a risk I wish to take."

"What about a motel?" Roger said.

"That could work," I said. "I'd have to check in under a fake name though."

"Well, that's easy enough," Lionel said, turning to look at Jack.

"It's all right with me," Jack said casually. "But how do we get him out of the building?"

"What about the loading dock at the end of the hallway?" Lionel said. "If there are any police around, they'd be watching the front entrance to the building most likely. Cal?"

I turned to Jack. "Is the trunk of your car clean?"

Sunday November 13, 2016

The Suter Road Arms was east of downtown, about a mile from the city's industrial wastelands. Despite the English-looking coat of arms on the sign, the place had seen better days, just like the Bates Motel before they moved the main highway. It was one of those two-story, block buildings with ten rooms on each floor that you accessed via an outdoor walkway. It looked like the exterior had been repainted ivy green within the last couple of years. At least it was clean, and only one other room was currently occupied. I had a room on the second floor, on the side of the building away from the front desk and the other occupied room. There was a diner called Jerry's across the street. The food was average overall, but they inexplicably made a delicious Manhattan clam chowder.

Along with buying me a change of underwear, T-shirts, and toiletries at a local big-box store—for which I'd reimburse them as soon as I could get to my check book—Jack had the ingenious idea to get me one of those disposable prepaid cell phones to make calls. At least the idea seemed ingenious to me. I complained about how cold it was standing outside Jerry's using the payphone; Jack guffawed and suggested the disposable cell phone idea. As often happened, it was a solution obvious to everyone but me.

I used the cell phone to call Margo and my attorney, Stacy Baab. The call to Margo hadn't gone well. The police tried pressuring her, not believing her when she told them she didn't know where I was. Margo resented this, but she knew how to handle herself. She dealt with officious bureaucrats on a daily basis, so this wasn't completely new. She even told the police to follow her home just in case they might catch me sneaking out the back door before her husband walked in on us.

She didn't say it over the phone, but I could tell she was disappointed with me. She agreed to cancel my classes Monday, but anything beyond this week and she'd have to place me on administrative leave. That wouldn't exactly be a feather in my cap when tenure review came around in the spring. I hadn't murdered anyone, but I felt like I'd let her down.

On the other hand, the call to my attorney was a bit more fruitful, albeit disheartening. She strongly advised me to turn myself in to the police and let the legal process sort everything out. I had the feeling she was just going through the motions in saying this, because she never actually asked me where I was. In any case, I had no intention of playing nice with the police. Stacy informed me of several facts concerning why I ended up in this predicament. I was playing against a stacked deck.

Lionel knocked on my door around seven o'clock. We shook hands and he came inside. He removed a pint of Scotch from his inside jacket pocket and smiled as he set it on the round table next to the door.

"Johnnie Walker Black," I said, unwrapping a couple of plastic cups at the bathroom sink. "You're really padding my room service bill."

"This one's on me," he said. "Rather a long couple of days I should think."

"The police haven't been by to talk with you, have they?"

"No, they haven't as a matter of fact. Ah, thanks," he said, pouring the brown liquid into each of the paper cups. "I guess we'll have to drink it neat." I took a long pull from the cup. "So, how are you holding up, Cal?"

I frowned. "Beats being in jail."

"Yes, I suppose it does. I am sorry about this, you know."

"Forget it, Lionel, it's not your fault. I just hope jail isn't my next stop after departing this five-star country inn."

Lionel looked at me uneasily. "Oh dear."

I drained my cup and poured another. I flopped back down on the bed and stared up at the ceiling for a moment. "I spoke with my attorney earlier."

"And?"

"Her sage advice was that I turn myself in and let the legal process take care of things."

Lionel chuckled. "Well, if they didn't tell you that, they wouldn't be earning their fee."

"She felt that was the only course of action available to me." I took another sip. The Scotch began tingling in my brain, but I didn't feel any better. "I'm starting to see her side of it."

"It isn't as black as that I should hope."

"Well, I can't just hide out in this motel room forever. I have classes to teach. At least I used to. Margo tells me she'll have to place me on administrative leave by the middle of the week. I can't very well walk into my classroom Tuesday morning like nothing's happening, even if watching me get arrested would give my students a hell of a story."

"What did you find out, Cal? Is Murdoch the one behind this?"

"Almost definitely," I said. "Steve Millard was the victim. They found him dead in his apartment early Friday morning."

"My word," Lionel said, just above a whisper. "How was he killed?"

"Strangled," I said flatly. "If he'd been shot, at least I could've pointed out that I don't own a gun and hadn't recently fired one."

"Did your attorney have any idea why the police are after you?"

I took another long sip. "They found my business card next to the body."

"Oh God," Lionel said aghast.

"That night I confronted Murdoch, he went through my wallet before I got away. He must've taken the card and planted it at the crime scene."

"Bloody brilliant," Lionel said. "I suppose we have to give him that."

"Now you see what I'm up against here." Lionel nodded silently. "I can't bear the thought that my life is over."

"It won't come to that, old man. Not if I have anything to say about it." For just a second, Lionel's assertion made me feel confident.

"I still can't figure why Murdoch is even doing this."

"He's scared of what we might know, I suspect."

"Then why not just kill one of us? That would take us out of the picture, literally. Why nibble around the edges like this, trying to frame us for crimes?"

"Perhaps he's trying to discredit us if we should come forward. The police are less likely to believe a petty thief, as I was accused of being. And they're especially unlikely to believe...well."

"A cold-blooded killer like me," I said, finishing his sentence. "Lionel, I can't go to jail. I won't." I hesitated for a moment, giving him a long look. I had the feeling he knew what I was going to say next. "You may have to send me back in time. Permanently."

"There are risks involved with that, too."

"Like what?"

"The longer one is in the past, the more it becomes like the present. You discovered that during your trip to 1992."

"This would be *different*. Send me back to 1947. Just after the war. No email, barely any television. People weren't in such a hurry all the time. We'd won the war—a *just* war. We haven't had one of those for a while, have we? People could actually feel good about themselves, truly feel good about what they'd done, without anyone trying to talk them out of it or mock them for feeling that way. I could even be there for the fifties, maybe hang out with some beatniks, just to see if it was really all it was cracked up to be. I could watch history unfold along with everyone else."

I saw it all in my mind, too. Tall art-deco buildings. Me in a long overcoat and fedora, hustling into a basement bar for a cocktail and meeting a dark-haired woman in a pink dress who was a docent at a downtown art museum. It was all right there!

Then it faded, the way dreams do. I was back in a drab hotel room, sipping Scotch from a plastic cup while Lionel looked on, sympathy in his tired eyes. I wanted to apologize for being so sentimental, but it didn't seem necessary. Lionel understood.

"We've all had that same urge to hide out in the past," Lionel said. "It seems every trying day that comes along, I envision myself as a country doctor in the Yorkshire Dales during the 1930's. I'd even have a dog that would accompany me on long walks in the countryside and wait patiently for me outside the local pub while I went in for a swift half." He smiled for a moment before turning serious again. "The past doesn't belong to us, Cal. It never will. We can visit there, certainly, but we can't truly inhabit the place. Not in the manner we sometimes imagine. Plus, there's the First Law to consider."

"What does the First Law have to do with idle fantasies?"

"Well, especially since you came along, Roger and I have been doing more thinking about the First Law and its implications for longer duration time travel. Of course, we know it prevents us from making all those grand changes to the past, like killing Hitler when he was just a tyke and so forth. However, for a longer duration trip, we worry about what might happen. Since it isn't our native time, the mere fact that we're there at all is a "change" of sorts. Remember when I told you about Roger getting arrested the second time he went back in time to try and save his wife?"

"Yeah, I do."

"Well, that was a manifestation of the First Law. Rather a gentle one, of course, but it was nonetheless a case of the universe keeping itself on track—ensuring the narrative continues to make sense. We have to believe that those manifestations would become more pronounced the longer one is there and the more one does."

"More pronounced?" I asked.

"More dangerous," he said. "Just as the forces opposing a moving object become proportionally stronger the faster it's moving, the forces of time itself become stronger the longer one pushes against them. Instead of merely being waylaid, one might actually be killed to keep the narrative sorted out."

It was a stunning revelation. "I never thought about that, but it makes perfect sense."

"I'm rather sorry that it does, Cal," Lionel said. "Anyway, getting back to present matters."

"Yeah," I grumbled, "getting back to that."

"Well, surely there's some way to get you out of the ringer on this."

"I'm all ears," I said.

Lionel looked down at his nearly empty glass. "I don't suppose you were making a speech to the downtown chamber of commerce when poor Millard was killed," he said.

"Nope. I was alone in my apartment, either asleep or falling asleep."

"Damn it," Lionel said, setting his cup down on the table in frustration. Then he paused, awkwardly leaning forward. I could tell he was thinking something over very carefully. "Cal," he finally said, "do you know when Millard was killed?"

"Overnight Thursday."

"Yes, yes, you said that. Can you nail it down a bit more precisely?"

I wondered what he was driving at. "I could call my attorney again. She might be able to find out."

"Well," he said, rubbing his hands together expectantly, "that would be just the thing we need."

"What're you talking about?"

Lionel stood up. "You call your attorney and find out the time of death. I'll get in touch with Roger and Jack. We'll see about getting you to the lab as quickly as possible."

"The lab?"

"Oh, one other thing," Lionel said, fetching his jacket. "Are you familiar with any bars on the other side of town? Preferably one that has a surveillance camera and a bartender with a good memory."

§ § §

It was weird being here.

The occasion may have demanded a better description, but 'weird' was the best he could come up with. He was pleased they thought enough of him to give him this task but anxious every time he glanced at the two men in the booth ahead of him and to the right.

The bar was long, and he sat at the end farthest from the door. A few other patrons were scattered along the bar, including a gruff looking man and a scrawny kid sitting several seats away. He kept an eye on them too, pulling the borrowed Pittsburgh Steelers cap lower over his face. The pair at the bar didn't know him, but it didn't hurt to be careful. The pair at the booth made him the most nervous. They would recognize him for sure.

He slipped a cigarette out of the box in his coat pocket. He was part of a largely defunct species known as the "social smoker." That is, someone who could smoke half a pack one night, then not give cigarettes another thought for months afterward. That was another reason he was here now. He watched the gruff-looking man at the bar light another cigarette. That's his third cigarette of the night, he thought, reaching into his pocket for a plastic bag. He slipped the bag open under the bar and set it on his lap. As he did this, he saw the guff man turn angrily to the kid and say something he couldn't make out. The man in the booth seemed to notice this too, though he only turned his head ever so slightly.

He risked a long look at the booth now, pausing to consider the younger of the two men in the booth who sat facing him. He suppressed a smile as he watched the young man in the booth. In his mind, he heard the lyrics to **Vapour Trail** by *Ride*, about people moving in and out of one's life, and how time passing away seems to belong to all of us. Cal had turned him on to Ride.

If memory served, Cal was talking about music over in the booth right now.

It was hard for Jack Greenwood not to smile at seeing himself seated in a booth a few feet away, hearing about a band called Ride for the first time — the same band that he happened to be thinking about at this very moment. What had Cal told him before he left? Something about one person being in two different places at the same time. A strange loophole in the law of non-contradiction.

Jack could tell that Cal wanted to accompany him on this trip back in time. It may have had something to do with probing the boundaries of the First Law. Everyone seemed to be talking about that more often lately, and they seemed more grave about it. But mainly, Cal seemed to want in on the "joke" that Jack was in the midst of now, to put one over on himself by seeing himself somewhere in the past. Cal was that kind of person: outwardly cynical, but with an odd, playful sense of inner sentimentality.

Jack turned his attention back to Nick Murdoch and Steve Millard at the bar. Steve stood up to leave, giving Murdoch an awkward smile he barely acknowledged. Over at the booth Cal seemed to notice this too. Murdoch leaves second, Jack reminded himself. Then we get up to follow him a moment later. The timing of what Jack was about to attempt was going to be difficult. He had to make it to Murdoch's seat just in time, but without being seen by either Cal or himself.

Jack tensed as Murdoch stood up to leave. His eyes darted back and forth between the bar and the booth where he — the "other" him — and Cal were preparing to leave. Before he'd departed the lab, Dr. Blanchard had reminded him that he and Cal would be watching Murdoch, so he could probably move in behind himself and Cal without being noticed. At present, Jack hoped that was true. He ashed his cigarette, noticing that it still had a little ways to burn. That was good. Just as they planned.

Murdoch pulled on his coat and started for the door. Jack sat up and watched him. He and Cal were at the booth pulling on their own coats. At the bar, Jack swallowed the last of his beer and prepared to move. The instant the front door of the bar closed, he and Cal stood up from the booth and started to move toward the door. Jack slipped off his own stool and followed a few feet behind. It seemed a foregone conclusion that neither he nor Cal would turn around as they walked out — neither of them remembered seeing another version of Jack at the bar during their initial trip here — but he was edgy about it anyway.

Still, it didn't matter now. Jack made it to where Nick Murdoch had been sitting just as the bartender was reaching for Murdoch's glass and ashtray. Jack got to the ashtray a moment before the bartender did. The bartender started at this, but Jack held up his cigarette with an apologetic grin. The bartender shrugged, removed the empty glass, and went a few feet away to wash it. Jack stubbed out his cigarette in the ashtray. As he did, he grabbed one of the butts Murdoch had left behind. He deposited it in the Ziploc bag, turned, and walked out of the bar for the second time in the last few moments.

CHAPTER 19

Tuesday November 15, 2016

A S I WALKED into Noll Hall, I was fully prepared for the reactions I was bound to get. In fact, I did my best not to smile about it as people saw me, stopped what they were doing to stare, and then quickly returned to their task to cover themselves. News travels through an academic department as if it were a sewing circle. I hadn't been here in a few days, so I went straight into the department office to check my mail. One of my colleagues, Carl Pynes, who specialized in philosophy of science, was at the photocopier. I saw him give me a furtive look, then concentrate intently on the copy machine as if he were operating it with some kind of telepathic link.

"Hi ya' Carl," I said in an overly jovial voice. "How are you?" He frowned but didn't turn around. An outright snub. That was unusual. Academics are typically more passive aggressive than that. I went over to my mailbox and sifted through some unwanted pamphlets from academic presses. As I tossed them in the trash, Pynes hurried out of the office and down the hall. Kaitlin Finch, our student assistant, was sitting at a nearby table pretending to do some work for another class. "Afternoon, Kaitlin," I said. She looked up at me, wide-eyed.

"Hi," she managed to say, barely above a whisper. I started into the hallway just as Bruce Hardwick entered the office. He had no trouble openly looking me up and down and smirking. Moral superiority was his specialty.

"Cal," he said condescendingly by way of a greeting.

"Bruce," I replied flatly.

"I figured if you turned up here at all, it would be in a pair of handcuffs."

"Why, did you lose a set?" His smug smile vanished and his lips tightened noticeably.

"You pathetic son of a—"

"Uh-uh. Careful Bruce. I already killed one guy with my bare hands. You might be next." I could tell he was mulling over whether or not I was serious. I brushed past him into the hallway.

As I did, Margo emerged from her office. She hurried over to me shaking her head. "Cal, Jesus Christ! What the hell are you doing here?" she hissed, looking to see whether anyone else was around.

"It's Tuesday. I've got my philosophy of time seminar coming up in..." I looked at my watch. "Damn, just under an hour."

She rolled her eyes at me and huffed. "Get in here," she said, pulling me into her office. She closed the door behind us. She stood next to her desk with her hands on her hips. "You can't just turn up here like this."

"What are you talking about? I work here."

"*Are you insane!*"

"Opinions vary."

She leaned in closer and spoke in a stage whisper. "I don't know what you're trying to pull by being here today, but you can't do this. Don't you realize the position you're putting me in?"

I slowly leaned closer so my face was about six inches from her ear. "Why are you whispering?" I said in a normal tone of voice.

"The police were here again yesterday morning! They even called me at home this weekend," she stammered, trying to get out what she was going to say next. "Now I have to tell them you've been here. Do you see what you've done? If I don't call them, I'm aiding and abetting a fugitive."

I shrugged. "I'm no fugitive."

She threw up her hands and dropped all pretense of trying to be quiet. "This isn't some clever game that ends with the police elbowing you in the ribs and admiring you for your boundless confidence and ironic wit. You're wanted for a murder, Cal! And frankly, I think you *did* do it."

I slapped my hand on her desk triumphantly. "I knew it! I knew you thought I really killed that kid. I even said so on the phone the other day, remember?" She put her hand to her head, about to really let me have it. I decided I'd had enough fun. "Before I give you more rope to hang yourself, Margo, you'll be relieved to hear that I'm no longer wanted for murder or any other crime."

She looked at me sharply. There was an even chance that she would smack me in the face for having a go at her—completely justified—or that she was going to ask me what was going on.

"What, just like that they dropped the charges?" she asked skeptically. "You'll have to introduce me to your lawyer."

"It's a deal. But in this case we'll have to put it down to good fortune."

"I don't know whether to believe you or not, Cal," she said, looking at me sideways.

"First off, I'm sorry for having a little fun at your expense just now. I'm sure you'll respond tenfold somewhere down the line."

"You better believe it."

"Fair enough. Anyway, the whole thing's simple. I was in a bar clear across town when the murder took place."

"Are you serious?" she asked, trying to hide a smile of relief.

"Mm-hmm. You can even check with the police if you want. There's surveillance footage of me at the bar and everything."

"My gosh, Cal, that's wonderful!" she said.

"I figured you'd give me the benefit of the doubt eventually."

She narrowed her eyes at me and leaned forward on her elbows. "How come you didn't say anything Saturday about having an alibi? When we spoke on the phone, you sounded at your wit's end."

Because on Saturday I hadn't yet been to the bar the previous Thursday, I thought. It was Sunday night when Lionel had come up with his 'alibi solution' to my quandary. It was simple: travel back to the time when Steve Millard was murdered and turn up some place else where people would remember me. My attorney had to call in a couple favors with her police contacts to get a more precise time of death, but I promised her that she could take full credit for unearthing any evidence that would lead to my exoneration.

We found a bar called Elmo's on the other side of town, about five miles from Millard's apartment. Apart from being a country and western bar blasting shit kicker music, the place worked splendidly for our purposes. The bartender, incongruously named Sully, was only working there on his night off from another local establishment. He didn't seem much of a fan of the atmosphere either. My choice of bourbon rather than light beer piqued his curiosity, and we got to talking a bit while trying to ignore the karaoke and line-dancing going on in the background. That was a plus too, because in addition to showing up on the surveillance tape, Sully remembered me when the police contacted him yesterday afternoon. Even the homicide detectives apologized for inconveniencing me.

"Well, I had a lot on my mind Margo," I said, answering her question. "And besides, who knew if the police would believe my story about being somewhere else when the murder took place. It was just fortunate that they had me on the surveillance tape. It all worked like a charm."

"Worked like a charm?"

I hadn't meant to say that. "My attorney getting hold of the tape, talking to other people at the bar who remembered me, you know," I added, trying to cover myself. "Innocent men have spent years in jail before being exonerated. Besides, on Saturday I didn't know exactly what time this kid was killed, which meant I also didn't know whether I had a provable alibi. Remember, Margo, I *didn't* murder him."

"There's still one thing I'm curious about. If you're so far in the clear on this, how is it that the police ever suspected you to begin with?"

"They found one of my business cards at the crime scene."

"Oh, good lord."

"It was just bad luck. I ran into the kid who was killed one night at the Green Friar, not too far from my apartment. We got to talking, and he told me he used to be enrolled here at Spalding and was thinking of coming back. He seemed nice enough, so I gave him my card and told him to give me a call if he ended up going through with it."

"That's one hell of an unfortunate coincidence," Margo said.

"If I had known he was going to turn up murdered, I never would've given him my card." I stood up to leave. "I'm a philosopher, for God's sake. Why do I even have business cards?"

"Remind me to bring that up at the next meeting with the dean," Margo said, getting up to open the door for me. "I'll have to tell the department gossips how everything turned out, though I should really make you do that yourself."

I turned and walked down the hall to my office. For the first time in what seemed like years, the only thing on my mind was my afternoon seminar. Time travel felt like a happily abstract problem again.

§ § §

"When did you say this picture was taken?" Cal asked.

"Nineteen fifty-nine," Lionel replied. "In early June."

"Looks like quite a mess at this theater," Cal said. "But I'm not seeing what this has to do with our present situation. I mean, Murdoch couldn't have been more than an infant in 1959."

"As I said, a man died in this accident, even if you can't make that out in the photo."

"All right," Cal said, waiting for more.

Lionel's hand trembled as he slid another photo towards Cal. "This photo was taken just before *the accident."*

Cal grabbed the photo. "Half dozen people gathered on the stage. Any idea what play they're getting..." he stopped talking suddenly as his face transformed into a mixture of fear and fury. He clutched the photo tightly, leaning in to look at it more closely. He slammed it down on the table and stood abruptly.

"That's impossible," Cal bellowed.

"Cal," Lionel started to say.

"That can't be!" Cal yelled, pounding his fist on the table.

Lionel had never seen Cal this upset. Cal paused at the far wall, clasped his hands behind his head, and remained silent for what seemed like several minutes. "There's just... there's no goddamn way this could've happened. What's he doing there!" Cal stammered. He closed his eyes and tried hard to calm himself. "What else do we know?"

"If you're referring to how the two of you ended up in that theater together, I haven't the foggiest idea."

176

"This doesn't make sense," Cal said as he returned to the table, shaking his head.

"I should think not. Nevertheless, the photograph is authentic. When you begin traveling back in time, there's no telling where you might turn up."

"June of '59," Cal said aloud, hoping it would somehow answer the myriad questions the photo raised. He pursed his lips as he looked back and forth between the two photos. "Who's the guy that was killed?" Lionel didn't say anything. Cal looked up to see Lionel staring intently at his shoes. "Lionel?"

Lionel frowned. "I don't know."

"What do you mean you don't know?"

"No one knows, it would seem. Jack and I searched through every newspaper archive we could find for a month after the accident. There's nothing in the public records either. The dead man couldn't be identified."

Cal shook his head. "How could a guy that was killed in front of half a dozen people go unidentified?" He noticed Lionel looking at him sadly. At first, Cal didn't understand. Then he realized what Lionel had already concluded. "Oh," Cal said softly. "He wasn't of that time."

"I suppose there could be a more innocent explanation, but…you're likely correct."

Cal went back to examining the photograph taken just before the fatal accident. "So, one of us doesn't return from this particular trip back in time." He and Lionel stood silently, not looking at each other.

Cal looked again at the expression on his face in the photo taken before the accident. He tried desperately to figure out what was going through his mind as he and Nick Murdoch stared at each other across a row of theater seats in 1959.

Thursday November 17, 2016

I ended my metaphysics class about fifteen minutes early and was in a hurry to get back to my office. Naturally, three students cornered me after class with questions. Ordinarily, they were the kind of questions I enjoyed addressing since they concerned the material rather than attempts to weasel out of doing work. Today, however, it seemed like the universe put these students here just to piss me off.

I finally extricated myself from my students and hurried downstairs to my office. I was anxious to get to Dancy Hall where Lionel was waiting for me. Now that I was off the hook with the police, our plan was to turn the tables on Murdoch. Since we'd used time travel to un-frame an innocent man for a murder—me—I reasoned we could just as easily use time travel to "frame" a guilty man for the same murder—Murdoch.

Yesterday, Jack traveled back in time to AJ's Bar on the same night he and I were originally there to follow Murdoch. We worried he might be a little unsettled at encountering himself in the past, but that wasn't the case at all. He found the whole thing delightfully intriguing. I probably would have, too, if I'd encountered a previous version of myself. Not that I ever expected to get the chance. Jack pilfered one of Murdoch's used cigarette butts, which I then planted outside the door to Steve Millard's apartment two weeks ago on the night he'd been murdered. The butt contained Murdoch's DNA.

Upon returning, I went straight to the phone to call the police. They weren't very forthcoming with details about the ongoing investigation into Millard's death, but I could tell from the oblique way the detective talked that they found the cigarette butt I'd planted. They just needed some help figuring out to whom it belonged. Hence, my phone call. The detective responded skeptically at first, even accusing me of planting the butt myself—which, ironically, was true. As I patiently explained how that wasn't possible, given my own alibi and the timeline of events, I sensed his doubts melting away.

Lionel and I also decided that I should go for broke and tell the police everything we knew about Murdoch's other crimes, including Laura's murder in 1993 and the ill-fated bank robbery in 1990. We had nothing to gain by parceling out the information in dribs and drabs, and in any case, we wanted Murdoch out of our lives. Permanently. The detective responded with an audible groan when I brought up the bank robbery, until I mentioned the surveillance tape that could corroborate my account. He told me he needed a little time to check into all this but to come down to the station the next afternoon to make a formal statement. I was on my way there now. My attorney would be meeting me there.

The police would match the DNA on that cigarette butt to Murdoch, and this would in turn match the physical evidence from the scene of Laura's murder. Even if the surveillance tape didn't actually show the robbery taking place, let Murdoch try to explain why he was there minutes before a robbery, alongside a women he'd later kill.

We had Murdoch now. There was no question.

I double-checked whether the surveillance tape was in my shoulder bag and started to walk out. As I opened the door, I could hear Margo's voice further down the hall. She seemed to be heading in my direction. The last thing I wanted was to be caught up making small talk, even if it was Margo.

"Yes, it's right over here," I heard her say as I opened my office door. I came outside and was facing away from her as I closed the door behind me. "Oh, here he is now, probably trying to slink out without saying 'good-bye.' I turned around to deliver a rejoinder to Margo. Whatever I decided to say evaporated.

She stood next to Nick Murdoch.

CHAPTER 20

"ET'S GO SEE your friend," Murdoch said after Margo disappeared down the hall. He held his jacket open for a moment, revealing a gun tucked into his belt.

"What do you want to go there for?" I asked.

"You piece of shit!" Murdoch hissed in my ear. "The cops are at my place right now, waiting for me."

"Oh?" I said flatly. It seemed the police believed my story after all. When we got outside Noll Hall, Murdoch yanked me back by the jacket. I thought he might shoot me right then and there.

"You're supposed to be in jail right now." I just looked at him without saying anything. "How did you do it?"

"Do what?"

"How the fuck did you get the cops to think I killed that kid? They found that card I planted there. So why are they after me and not you?" He scowled at me for a moment and then pushed me away in the direction of Dancy Hall. "We'll see what Bradshaw has to say when we get there. I'm sure you two pricks are in it together."

I couldn't help noticing the contrast between how Murdoch looked on the tape from twenty years ago and how he currently looked. His forehead was larger as more hair had receded. He was also working on a spare tire, the kind common to men entering middle age. His narrow, black eyes bothered me the most. There was something behind them that one didn't often see in another person. They betrayed a total disinterest in human dignity.

"We're here," I said once we got to Dancy Hall. "Do you still want to go in?"

He pointed to the door. "I'll find out what you did."

Lab 7 was around the next corner. I told myself that Murdoch was now on our turf and tried to recall all that I'd learned about his background and the overall situation. We knew this might happen, I said repeatedly in my mind, trying to strengthen my resolve. Yet when we reached the double doors to the lab, my heart sank when I saw Lionel through the window, puttering around inside. All at once, I realized the prominent role he played in my life during the last couple of months. He was absorbed in some task, completely unaware of how the next few moments would unfold, and this left me with a solemn feeling. As ever was, our fates were intertwined. Straight down the line, just as Walter Neff had warned in *Double Indemnity*.

I knocked on the door halfheartedly, watching Lionel turn around and meet me with a pleasant, expectant look. He took a step toward the door and stopped suddenly. He seemed to grasp the situation immediately, knowing there could only be one reason I'd have brought Nick Murdoch here. He opened the lab door slowly. "Are you all right, Cal?" he asked.

"As well as can be expected," I said without much feeling. Murdoch brushed past me and into the lab. He pushed Lionel aside, and for the first time he took the gun out of his belt as the door closed behind us.

"Who else is here?" Murdoch asked Lionel.

"Only the three of us," Lionel said.

"Really?"

"Take a look round, if you like," Lionel said with a frown. Murdoch looked back and forth between the two of us.

"You two, move over there," he said, pointing to the far corner of the lab. "Don't try for the door. You'll never make it." Lionel and I walked over toward the wardrobe room. Murdoch pointed his gun at us as he walked backward toward the hallway where Lionel's office was. He passed by the Nora Pads but only gave the time machine a cursory glance.

"He just turned up at my office as I was leaving to come here," I said. "I guess it doesn't really matter now. It's killing him that his little stunt with my business card didn't work."

"Yes," Lionel said, "I suppose it would be."

"This could be..." I started to say as Murdoch reappeared. He took a long look at us, and then he did something I didn't expect. He chuckled.

"I don't even know where to begin with you two assholes," he finally said. Lionel and I exchanged glances. "All I wanted you to do was find something."

"You mean *not* find it," I said.

"Come again?" Murdoch said.

"You didn't want us to find that stuffed bird. You just wanted to make sure that it *couldn't* be found. Because if Lionel couldn't find it, then no one could."

"I guess you're right, Sutherland," Murdoch said, his voice rising. "But your other pal there, Blanchard, couldn't leave it the hell alone. He just had to see if there was something inside. Like I wouldn't notice."

"Well to be fair, it was Cal here who cut open your bird and found the key," Lionel said nonchalantly. I shot him a look of disbelief, which he returned with a casual shrug.

"So I shoulda turned up at your place and kicked your ass then," Murdoch said. "Just tell me this. Where the hell did you find that bird anyway?"

"It's what we do," Lionel said. "Dogged research. Like I told you, the bird turned up in—"

"Aw, bullshit! It wasn't in some goddamn police evidence warehouse."

"Oh?" Lionel said. "What makes you so sure?"

Murdoch fixed Lionel with a glare. "Never mind." Murdoch looked around at the lab. "What the hell is all this stuff, anyway?" I shifted uncomfortably, instinctively aware that the time machine was hiding in plain sight.

"Just some equipment I use for my scientific research," Lionel said. Murdoch turned around to look at the Nora Pads. He walked over to the instrument desk where I'd grown used to seeing Jack preparing to send one of us back in time.

"Temporal wave tuner," Murdoch said aloud, reading one of the labels next to the dials. I stiffened. Could he figure out what he was looking at? "Return pathway capture? Spatial origination?" Murdoch looked at Lionel, who didn't say anything. "Sounds pretty scientific."

"A brilliant deduction," Lionel replied dryly.

"How did you find that bird?" Murdoch asked again.

"What's the difference? You have it now. You got what you wanted."

"I want to know how you found it!" Murdoch shouted, pointing the gun at me. "I want to know why the police were waiting at my apartment right now. And I still want to know how you're not in police custody." He stepped close to Lionel, looked him in the eyes, and placed the gun barrel in the middle of his chest. "Tell me!" I could see Lionel stiffen with alarm, looking truly petrified for the first time.

"Don't!" I yelled involuntarily. Murdoch instantly slid in front of me, the gun barrel now pressing against my chest.

"Then you tell me, Sutherland."

I fixed him with a hard stare. "Okay, I'll tell you something. March 7th, 1990. Bruhl and Anderson Savings & Loan." Murdoch's eyes widened, and he even took a step back from Lionel and me.

"No, no, no, no," he muttered, shaking his head as though he just saw me perform a magic trick and was convinced it couldn't be as it appeared. "This isn't…this doesn't make any sense."

I patted my shoulder bag. "I've got the tape right here in my bag." Murdoch lunged for me and grabbed the bag off my shoulder. He turned it upside down and made a mess on the floor as my lecture notes spilled everywhere. The tape tumbled out last. Murdoch stared at it for a moment as he tossed my now-empty bag aside. "That's not the only copy either," I said.

"It's what you were hoping no one would find, wasn't it?" Lionel said. "Yet we found it. Now can you see what will happen to you if you try and harm us?" It felt like the moment in a film where the tide turns suddenly, and the police come swooping in to arrest the bad guys. Yet as soon as this feeling overcame me it faded. Murdoch looked down at the tape and then at Lionel and I. He didn't look troubled by it anymore. I suddenly realized why. He'd already decided to disappear again, probably even had his new identity all worked out. He moved the slide back and forth on the gun and pointed it at me.

As I tried to think of something to say, Lionel looked back and forth between me and the time machine. His eyes came to rest on me. They had that oddly sympathetic look I'd come to know so well. I knew exactly what he was thinking as though his thoughts were my own.

"No, Lionel. Don't do it." Murdoch started at this, probably figuring Lionel was reaching for a gun.

"It's still bedeviling you, isn't it?" Lionel said, taking a step forward.

"What?"

"Trying to figure out how we did it."

"Did what?"

"Lionel, no!" I said again, knowing it was futile.

"The tape. Cal's alibi. Even finding that silly bird."

"This better be good," Murdoch said.

"Time travel," Lionel said. My heart sank. "I'm sorry, Cal, but it's the only way." Murdoch stared at us for a moment. He didn't believe Lionel. Lionel waved his hand at the equipment in the lab. "What do think all this stuff is then?"

"How the fuck should I know?" Murdoch said. I caught him glancing around at some of the equipment.

"All right, never mind the equipment. Think though everything that's happened recently. You said yourself there was no way we could've got a hold of that bird, right? The stuffed bird that Laura Dietrichson, who isn't your sister by the way, kept on a bookcase in the second bedroom upstairs in her house." I watched Murdoch's eyes grow large as Lionel said this. "There was no way we could have done it, unless we traveled back in time to the morning after she was killed and grabbed it before it was packed up with the rest of her personal effects. And don't forget: *we did get the bird.*"

"This is some kind of trick," Murdoch said, once again raising the gun to Lionel's chest. It now seemed absolutely necessary that Murdoch believe the apparatus behind him was a working time machine.

"The rock outside the bank in 1990," I said.

"What are you babbling about?" Murdoch said.

"You remember. You were driving away from the bank with Laura in the passenger seat. All of a sudden, something broke the back window of your car. It was a chunk of asphalt, right?"

Murdoch's mouth hung open, and his eyes seemed to glaze over. He looked at me intently as I continued. "A thing like that never showed up in any of the police reports or on the news." The gun dropped to his side, and he took a step backwards. "*I threw it.*"

Murdoch turned to look at the Nora Pads but kept one eye on us. He flinched as Lionel approached him. Lionel stopped and put his palms out in front of him. "They're called Nora Pads, and as you can see, there are six of them. Each one wide enough for a person to stand on while awaiting the machine to activate and send him back in time." It was obvious Murdoch was beginning to believe all this in spite of himself. "This can't be explained any other way, can it?"

"Look in that room over there," I said pointing to the room that housed our wardrobe of past clothing attire. Lionel opened the door and turned on the light. Murdoch peered at the rows of vintage clothing. He stopped to examine a few items of attire from the early 1900s.

"Now why else would that be there?" Lionel asked. "This is a physics lab. It's not like the theater students clear across campus are going to store all their costumes here."

Murdoch looked back and forth between Lionel and me and then turned to the time machine. He pointed the gun at Lionel. "Prove it, Bradshaw." I saw Lionel trying to hide a smile.

"Indeed," Lionel said, "but first we'll need to get changed. Yourself as well." Murdoch frowned at this and seemed to snap out of believing our story. "Look at you. There were no Skechers shoes or hooded sweatshirts where we're going. Now, Cal and I can change first. As you can see, there's no way out of that room."

"Leave the door open," Murdoch said.

Lionel and I went into the wardrobe room. "Rack 5," he said. When we had our backs to Murdoch, Lionel whispered to me. "Back in time, is *our* time."

Lionel as usual selected a suit, navy blue with a white shirt and a red and blue striped tie. I grabbed a white dress shirt, tan suit jacket, and dark high-water pants. Every time I took a step, you could see my socks above the loafers. We walked back out into the lab. Murdoch just stood there looking at us. I finished tucking in my shirt and adjusted my pants.

"What's that?" Murdoch asked.

"What's what?"

"That thing on your belt. You both have them," he said, nodding to the small black box that contained the TRI.

"Oh, that's a temporal return initiator," I said casually, attempting to sound like it wasn't really important. I could feel Lionel tense up next to me. "It's not really anything. It's just so…"

"I don't give a shit what it is. You've both got 'em, so give me one too." Lionel frowned at this and went back into the wardrobe room, returning with a belt. Murdoch took a step back, keeping his gun pointed at us while he awkwardly switched out his belt using one hand at a time.

"Aren't you going to change clothes?" Lionel asked when he was done.

"Nope."

"But you can't go back looking like that. You'll stick out like a sore thumb. We have to blend in when we travel back in time."

"I still haven't decided if I believe you yet, Bradshaw."

"Well at least change your shoes. How about a pair of black loafers. What's your size?"

"Nine," Murdoch said reluctantly. Lionel quickly got Murdoch a pair of black dress shoes to replace his gray walking shoes that would have drawn looks in the past.

"Now, if you'll just stand over on one of the Nora Pads, we'll get started."

"Uh-uh," Murdoch said.

"But that's the time machine," Lionel said. "If you truly want to do this, that's where it all happens."

"We all go over and stand on them at the same time. Fix it so we can do that. And I want to see what you're doing, too."

"Very well," Lionel said. He and Murdoch walked over to the instrument desk as Lionel adjusted some switches and clicked through a few different on-screen menus. Occasionally he stopped to say something to Murdoch to explain what he was doing. I don't think Murdoch understood what he was talking about. He just wanted to keep an eye on Lionel.

"All right," Lionel said as he finished. "When I start the wave manipulation, we'll have about 15 seconds to get onto the Nora Pads."

"Then what?" Murdoch asked.

"Some cylinders will close around the three of us, and we'll be on our way," Lionel said. I could tell Murdoch didn't like the idea of being closed in like this. "Look, you saw what I was just doing," Lionel told him. "I set the machine for the three of us, didn't I? Whatever happens to one of us happens to all of us. Now, are you ready?"

Murdoch frowned at both of us. "You two go up there first, I'll walk behind you."

"Cal, are you ready?" Lionel said with a trace of intensity.

"Oh yeah."

"Right!" Lionel said. He pressed a button that activated the time machine. He and I walked quickly up to the Nora Pads. Murdoch followed closely behind and stood on a pad next to Lionel with me on the far end. Out of the corner of my eye, I saw Murdoch keep his gun pointed at Lionel. For a moment nothing happened, but then the mechanical whirring began. As the cylinders closed around us, I could see Murdoch looking around nervously and breathing more rapidly. Then the cylinders closed as I felt a tingling sensation. A moment before it was complete and the bright light surged all around me, I could've sworn I heard someone cry out as though terrified by something. Then the tingling sensation went away as the world came into focus again.

CHAPTER 21

Wednesday June 3, 1959

ALOUD FLUTTERING surrounded me as little black dots meandered everywhere. I couldn't make out what was going on at first because the sun was too bright. I leaned back and put my hands to my face as the scene around me slowly took shape. The fluttering bits turned into gray forms that I could now tell were birds.

There is always a period of disorientation during the initial manifestation in the past. It's as if my collective memory is briefly scattered into the wind. Sometimes a disembodied image would sluice through my mind, disassociated with my consciousness. I'd only realize after a moment that it was one of my own memories. As I absentmindedly watched the pigeons reform into a gaggle on a higher building off to my right, I heard a dull thud and a scraping sound.

Then I fully recalled where I was and who was with me.

"Steady on," I heard Lionel say. I looked over to see Nick Murdoch in a half-sitting position, trying to move away from Lionel and me.

"What is this? What the hell just happened!" he shouted, looking around.

"Why does everyone say that?" Lionel asked me laconically. Murdoch waved his gun wildly at both of us. Lionel put his hands up and took a couple steps back. "It's all right, we're—will you stop waving that around?" Murdoch pointed his gun at us with a desperate look in his eyes. I was afraid he'd panic and shoot both of us.

"We're on a roof, Murdoch," I said. "We can't just appear suddenly in the middle of the road for everyone to see. Take a look over the side."

"You'd fuckin' like that, wouldn't you," he said.

I rolled my eyes. "*Glance* over the side then." Murdoch slowly backed up to the low brick parapet, keeping an eye on us while stealing a look at what was below. Near the edge, he paused and stood transfixed by what he saw. I took a step toward him, scrapping my heel on the roof. He snapped out of his brief daydream and pointed his gun at me again.

"Either it's June of 1959, or the largest classic car show in the history of the world just happens to be going on nearby," I said.

Murdoch seemed to consider this for a moment. Then he did something I'd never seen him do: he smiled in a very innocent, childlike way.

"Goddamn," he said, slapping his leg. "Goddamn! We really *are* in the past." For a moment, it felt like we were three comrades in arms, delighting in the experience of existing in the past. Murdoch looked back over the side. "Where did you say we were again?"

"June 3rd of 1959," Lionel said.

Murdoch put his hand to his forehead. "Jesus, I haven't been born yet."

"Neither have I," I said flatly. I thought I saw Lionel smile at Murdoch's statement. I worried Lionel was letting his guard down a little. Now wasn't the time to relax. Murdoch's sense of awe and wonder would quickly fade, and we'd still be attached to a murdering criminal from 2016.

"So this is how you do your little tricks, huh?" Murdoch said with an edge in voice.

"Tricks?" Lionel said.

"Finding stuff for people and then making up some bullshit story about it. Taking their money. And you guys think I'm the freakin' crook here."

"Well, it doesn't work *exactly* like that," Lionel said.

"Oh yeah? You steal things from people, right? Just because you're doing it, like, in the past doesn't make it okay." Murdoch then nodded at me and spoke mockingly. "C'mon Sutherland, isn't this the kind of thing you get off on? Deep thoughts about right and wrong and shit like that."

I frowned. "We don't steal anything from anyone."

"It doesn't *work* like that," Lionel said again.

"Wait a minute. I really haven't been born yet, have I?" Murdoch said.

"Yes," I said. "Er, no. You haven't."

"You ever see that movie *Groundhog Day*?" Murdoch asked.

"Sure," I said.

"Well this is kinda like that."

"Not really," I said, but I could tell he was ignoring me.

"If I haven't been born yet, I can do whatever I want, right? No one can stop me." I saw his eyes get bigger, thinking through all the things he could do.

I put out my hand to try and slow him down. "We're in the past, Murdoch. Things are different here. You can't just—" I started.

He pointed the gun at me. "Bullshit! Now let's get off this roof. Single file. You first, Sutherland. And if you fuckin' try anything or think about running, your limey friend here will never know what hit him." I looked at Lionel uneasily.

"It's all right, Cal," Lionel said. "Just do as he says. We'll be all right."

I took a deep breath and headed for the stairwell off the roof. As I opened the door, I could hear faint sounds of machinery below. One flight down from the roof, the stairway ended at a door. I opened it and entered a large open area that took up the width of the building. There were rows of mostly middle-aged women in print dresses sitting at long tables with commercial sewing machines and large bins next to them. They all had blank expressions amid the hum. One or two of them looked up, seemed to consider us for a moment, and then went back to their work.

There was another door in an aging brick wall just to our right which led to the rest of the stairs. Just as I reached for the door, a male voice called out from behind me.

"Hey, who are you fellows? How did you get in here?" A small man with a black crew cut and short-sleeved button-down shirt walked up to us.

"Terribly sorry," Lionel said genially. "Afraid we lost our way. We'll just be going now."

The man seemed unfazed by this. "You're not supposed to be in here. No visitors are allowed up here without my say-so. Now, who are you and—"

Before he could continue, Murdoch took a fast step forward and shoved the man hard, nearly knocking him over. "Fuck off, gay boy!" He glared at the man who just stood there with a mixture of shock and hurt. *Could* he shoot this guy, here in the past?

"Let's just keep going," I said, moving quickly to the door, hoping that Murdoch would be forced to follow me before he could draw his gun. Without turning back, I pushed the door open and kept walking. To my relief I soon heard footsteps behind me. I moved as quickly down the stairs as I could, determined to get out of the building.

At the bottom was a small rectangular sign that read 'Exit' in dark lettering. It was easy to miss, and would have surely violated the fire code in 2016. I pushed the door open and exited into an alley. The alley ended at a brick wall to my left. There was a sidewalk and street about fifteen yards to my right. I felt hemmed in, the term 'dead end' suddenly taking on a literal meaning. I started for the street without waiting for Lionel and Murdoch to catch up.

"God dammit, stop a minute!" Murdoch yelled from behind. I took another step toward the end of the alley, hoping I was close enough to the street and any bystanders that Murdoch wouldn't think of firing a shot. "What the hell are you in such a hurry for, Sutherland?"

"You can't carry on like this here!" I admonished him.

"Please, Cal," Lionel said calmly. He took a step between us. "He's quite correct. You can't go around threatening people or trying to do any of the things I can tell you're thinking about doing."

"Oh Jesus, who gives a shit about that little pissant upstairs? Maybe we'll take a walk back up there. You guys wanna watch?"

"You can't," I said. Murdoch was about to interrupt, but I went on talking before he could. "You have to understand, this isn't a movie. We can't *change* the past. If that guy upstairs lived to the ripe old age of ninety and died in his sleep one night, then that's just the way it is and always will be, okay? So you can't just flail around doing whatever you want. You don't know what might happen." Murdoch narrowed his eyes at me as if I'd just given him a riddle to solve.

"He's telling the truth," Lionel said. "We call it the First Law. Well, that's Cal's name for it actually."

Murdoch smiled at this and shook his head. "I don't believe it," he said.

"But it's—"

"Aw shut up," he said, leaning in close to me. "You ever kill anyone, Sutherland? I have. I know what it feels like. I know what it's like the second before it happens and my mind's made up." He pointed up at the building we'd just exited. "*That's* what happened upstairs. So don't you try and tell me I wasn't gonna fuckin' do it."

"Think about what Cal's telling you," Lionel said.

He waved his hand dismissively. "Shut up."

There wasn't anything more to say. Murdoch was just like everyone else when it came to time travel. He figured you could do anything you wanted in the past—that because it felt like one's present, ordinary life it was just the same. No talk about logical laws or closed causal loops would persuade him otherwise.

"So, now what?" I asked, nodding toward the gun in Murdoch's waist. "You're driving this bus."

Murdoch smiled, clearly enjoying having the upper hand. "What's the deal with these things on our belts?"

"They're temporal return initiators. Or TRIs, as we call them," Lionel said.

"Go on," Murdoch said impatiently.

Lionel sighed. "You just press that button next to the red light, and that's how you return to the present."

"You mean back to that lab?"

"Mm-hmm."

"And it happens instantaneously?"

"More or less. There's a delay of a second or two while it activates. However, you can't just activate it in the middle of a crowd. Everyone would see you disappear into thin air."

Murdoch smiled again, this time in a way I didn't like. "So that was your plan all along."

"What're you talking about," Lionel said, glancing at me.

"You guys just disappearing suddenly in the middle of a crowd, hoping I'd follow you back to 2016. I bet you'd have the cops waiting there for me, too. I gotta hand it to you, Bradshaw, that's pretty good." The smile faded from Murdoch's face. "Take 'em off."

"What?"

"The belts. Take them off and drop 'em there." He pointed to next to some aluminum garbage cans.

"We can't do that!" Lionel protested. "It's our only means of returning. We'd be...we'd be stranded here."

"I don't give a shit," Murdoch shrugged. For a moment, I thought about running, just taking off and sprinting into 1959 and getting lost here. Maybe I'd get away before Murdoch could reach his gun and fire. But it was never truly a possibility, not with Lionel here too. My heart broke when I saw him look down—the stiff upper-lip the British are so well known for imprinted all over his face—and begin undoing his belt. Lionel tossed his belt next to one of the garbage cans. I took mine off quickly, wanting to rip it off and get the whole thing over with. I dropped it on top of Lionel's belt.

We were now stuck in the past, alongside a man with a gun who had no regard for the First Law or our lives.

"Now get going," Murdoch said.

As I moved along the sidewalk, my feet felt like they shuffled beneath a detached body. Nineteen fifty-nine happened all around me as if I were wandering through another person's dream. The pastel-colored automobiles with their delightfully gaudy lines, the women in flowered dresses, and the happy chatter all seemed to mock me. I half expected everyone to suddenly stop in their tracks, pointing and whispering at me like some gothic horror movie. Every step I took was a test of faith in the First Law. My faith was beginning to waver.

I glanced behind me every now and then to look at Lionel. He had a blank expression on his face, but he gave me a small nod. It was a reminder that we hadn't come to this date by accident. Yet everything was unraveling. We had counted on having our TRIs so that we could leave instantly if need be. Now, I felt like I was flying an experimental plane with no ejection seat and no parachute. Straight down the line, I heard in my mind again.

Murdoch looked around, taking in the sights. Then I saw the sour expression on his face. He wasn't marveling at anything. He was watching for something.

"Hold it," he called out suddenly, making me flinch. A couple of women carrying shopping bags turned to look at us, perhaps thinking he was talking to them. We needed some privacy. There was a shoe store to my right. Its entrance was set some ways back from the sidewalk with large display windows of men and women's footwear on either side. I ducked into the small doorway between the display windows. We were several feet away from the sidewalk, but still close enough that I felt safe. My mind raced in many different directions, but

I inevitably noticed a pair of white canvas P F Flyers in the display window. They were just like the ones Jonny Quest wore. Lionel moved up next to me.

Murdoch glared at us for a moment and then walked over to the front door, running his hand over the frame and examining it closely. If we only had our belts, we could just disappear right here, and nobody would even see us.

"Interested in doing a little shoe shopping?" I said sarcastically.

"Funny," he said, staring all around at the display enclosure. "You know Bradshaw, I've gotta admit, time travel is one fucked up thing."

"Splendid," Lionel said, rolling his eyes.

"I hate to sound like a little kid, but can we go now?" I said.

"What do you mean, go?" Murdoch asked.

"He means you got what we promised," Lionel said. "You know how we were able to do everything that we did. You're in on one of the greatest secrets in the history of humanity."

Murdoch stood within a few inches of Lionel's face. "And what the hell am I supposed to do with that?"

"Do with it?"

"Yeah. What are you gonna do, give me a free ride in your time machine every time I ask nicely? C'mon."

"Well, at any rate, you know how to get back. It's that button on your belt. We'll be going now." Lionel started to walk away. Murdoch scowled. He reached out, grabbed Lionel by the shoulder, and flung him back. I managed to catch him before he bumped into the display window. Every time he became angry like this, there was something less abstract and more fully formed about Murdoch. Our lives meant nothing to him.

"You're too smart to try something that stupid," Murdoch said. I let Lionel go. He smoothed out his suit jacket and ran his hands through his hair, but I could tell he was shaken up. "I'm not leaving here empty-handed," Murdoch said with a smile.

"What's that supposed to mean?" I asked.

"You guys aren't the only ones who can take stuff from the past." Lionel and I looked at each other uneasily. "Take a look at that door." We turned and gave the shoe store's entrance token glances. "No alarm. Even these windows aren't protected. If I had a hammer and a half-decent car waiting, I could clean this place out without breaking a sweat." He smiled at us.

"You're going to rob a shoe store?" I asked.

"Please," he grumbled, "what am I gonna do with a bunch of 50 year-old sneakers? Up on the next corner there's a bank." I flinched at the word 'bank.' It brought back memories of Bruhl & Anderson, those children trapped in the vault, and of Laura.

"I keep telling you," Lionel said, enunciating each word, "you can't do that here. We're not in the present. If no one robbed the bank in 1959, then—"

"Shut the fuck up, Bradshaw."

I turned to look at the passersby on the sidewalk, a pained expression on my face. I shook my head despondently.

"What the hell's your problem?" Murdoch said to me.

"We're in 1959, on a beautiful sunny day. Look at these people. How could you not want to walk out there and get lost in the scene? Just float along on it for a while." I turned back to face Murdoch. "*That's* something we can do. And all you want to do is rob a goddamn bank."

"Me?" Murdoch laughed. "I'm not gonna rob that bank." He stuck a finger in the center of my chest. "You are."

My gazey daydream evaporated as my mouth fell open. "What?" I said vapidly. "Uh, uh, I can't."

Murdoch reached inside his jacket and moved so he was right behind Lionel. I watched Lionel stiffen at this. "Oh, I think you can," Murdoch said.

I tried pleading again. "*No one* can. It's what we've been trying to tell you."

"Shut up with that bullshit," Murdoch said.

I looked at Murdoch in frustration, just as I would look at a student who simply refused to accept my explanation of things. Robbing that bank was wrong, and it had nothing to with stealing or theft. It felt wrong to do this to the people of 1959. It would be a crime against the past. I threw my hands up in the air.

"I can't rob a bank," I said despondently. "I wouldn't know how."

"It's not that hard," Murdoch said dismissively.

I looked at him fiercely. "I'm sure it isn't, Murdoch, but I don't have all the tools a seasoned pro like you once had. There aren't any grade-schoolers around that I can just let suffocate in a vault while I make my getaway."

Murdoch rolled his eyes. "Please."

"And I sure as hell don't have Laura, do I? *I* can't use her to get me in the front door and behind the counter. I can't shove the surveillance tape into her purse while I drag her out of the place crying as children lay dying in a goddamn bank vault!" I yelled. This drew a few stares from passersby, but I didn't care.

"Who gives a shit about Laur—" Murdoch started to say, but stopped. He gave me a strange look, turned to Lionel for a moment, and then turned back to me. He guffawed and shook his head. "Well I'll be goddamned," he drawled. "You met her somewhere, didn't you?"

I turned away. "Fuck off."

"Oh!" Murdoch said in morbid delight. "You knew her pretty well then. How about it, Sutherland? Were you the first guy she *had* after me?" He shook his head disgustedly. "You're pathetic."

I turned on my heel and took a step toward him. If I reached him, I could've snapped his neck. In that moment, I *could've* killed him. Murdoch casually stepped back and opened his jacket to reveal the gun in his waist.

"C'mon Sutherland. Go for it." Murdoch said. I stopped, and it wasn't fear that left me standing here. It was self-loathing. It shouldn't have mattered what Nick Murdoch, of all people, thought of Laura's and my affair, but it did. He saw right through me, into a place I'd barely spoken of, even to Lionel. I hated myself for revealing it. I felt thoroughly beaten and threw up my hands.

"What's the difference?" I wailed. "Even if I could do what you're asking, you're not just going to let Lionel and I go once I hand you have a sack with a dollar sign on it. We're dead no matter what."

"Cal," Lionel said, "you *must* do this. You have to go through with it."

I looked at him in disbelief. "I can't rob a bank—you know that. What about the First Law? What about everything else?"

"You have to give robbing that bank a go. It's apparently the only way… for this to get where it ends up." I could read the subtext of what he was saying.

"All right, enough of this shit," Murdoch said, breaking us up.

A woman suddenly walked up between the three of us on her way into the shoe store. She seemed disappointed that no one among the three men standing there thought to open the door for her. I had other things on my mind.

"If I had a gun or something it would make things easier," I finally said.

"Don't worry, Sutherland, guys less hard up than you have pulled off bank robberies before." He glanced at Lionel. "Just don't forget what's on the line here. If you crap out or try getting a hold of the police, bye-bye Bradshaw. You see that street we passed back there? There was a shuttered jewelry store near the corner. Meet us there when it's done."

"Then what? You'll let us both go?" I said dryly.

"Time will tell," he answered mockingly. "Oh, and take it from me. You're gonna want to hurry up inside that bank."

I looked from Murdoch to Lionel. We were out of options. I had to do it.

"Good luck, Cal," Lionel said. Murdoch nudged him forward, and they walked away from the shoe store entrance, turned left on the sidewalk, and disappeared around the corner.

I stared at the bank, wondering how in the hell I was going to rob it.

§§§

Another bank on another corner sometime in the past. It should've been called 'The First National Bank of Irony.' Instead it was 'Beiter and Wojcik Savings and Loan.'

The bank made up the ground floor of a five-story building on the corner of the main street. There were two large windows rounded off in half-circles just below the roof line. The entrance to the bank was a revolving door. My hand went to my side, instinctively feeling for the TRI I knew all the while was no longer there.

There was no way out of this.

I took a deep breath and briskly walked forward. Here I was, forced to rob a bank because my friend's life hung in the balance. I thought again of all the times I'd flippantly presented a scenario like this to an Ethics class, using it as an example of coercion wherein the person couldn't be blamed for his actions. Now I was living out a philosophical thought experiment. Surely I couldn't rob this bank. If it hadn't "already" been robbed on this date, I couldn't walk in and rob it now. Where the hell was the First Law in all this?

As I got near the entrance, I expected to see a 'Closed' sign hanging on the door, or a police patrol car slowly passing by, looking me over. However, there was none of that; not even a random pedestrian to delay me by asking for directions to some place I didn't know.

I pushed open the revolving door and went in. The lobby was very ornate, with marble floors and columns at each end of the row of teller windows. There were six teller windows along the rear wall with what looked like offices on either side of me. The bank was busy, or at least more crowded than I would've liked. Each of the teller windows was behind a set of bars.

How the hell do you rob a bank without a gun?

I noticed a long table in front of me with pens attached to it and several little slots for deposit and withdrawal slips. I could write a note! I'd seen bank robbers in movies slip a teller threatening notes lots of times. Maybe that would work here.

I went to one side of the table and took out a withdrawal slip, which seemed appropriate. A woman on the opposite side of the table filled out some papers with a small stack of bills next to her. She didn't look up from what she was writing. The front of the withdrawal slip was preprinted with lines and boxes to write in figures, so I turned it over to the back. I just started writing what I thought was a threatening note, explaining that I had a weapon, even that I had an associate elsewhere in the bank that would intervene if anyone gave me trouble. When I was halfway through writing the fourth complete sentence, I felt like a fool. I'd learned my first lesson of bank robbery: a short and sweet note is much more effective.

The woman on the opposite side of the table finished what she was doing and replaced her pen. As she walked away, I grabbed another withdrawal slip and went to work. I finished in a matter of moments. The note read:

I have a gun. I'll use it.Give me the money in your drawer.Small bills.Make it fast.

I replaced the pen and stepped away from the table. I could tell I was walking unnaturally slowly. It reminded me of Henry Fonda in *The Wrong Man*, when the police send him into the grocery store that had been robbed so that the owner could get a look at him.

Yet no one was looking at me.

There were two people in line ahead of me. This was the worst part. The counter was right there. It was only a matter of will at this point. My eyes darted around nervously. Something should happen. Something should stop this, and prevent me from going through with it. It could be anything. Maybe it'll—

"Excuse me, sir?" a female voice behind me said. "I think it's your turn." I lunged forward awkwardly as though I had been about to step forward without her saying anything to me.

The open teller window was ahead and to my left. Through the silver-colored bars, a female teller waited for me. She looked about 50 years-old and wore wire-rimmed glasses. She had the kind of pleasant face you'd find on an elementary school teacher. I wondered how this would affect her life.

"Good afternoon, sir," she said with a smile, "how may I help you today?"

I kept my eyes fixed on her. I wasn't taking it for granted that silent alarms weren't in use yet. My stare must have looked unnatural, because she flinched a little as the smile faded from her face. I slowly slipped the note under her cage. She took it and was about to ask me a question but stopped abruptly. Her eyes grew wide with terror. She stared at the note a moment and then looked up at me. I shook my head in an apologetic gesture, wanting to cry out there was no gun, that she really wasn't in any danger, and that I was being forced to do this because we had foolishly traveled back in time with a hardened sociopath.

My right hand was still in my jacket pocket. She must have interpreted my nod as a threatening gesture, because she glanced uneasily at the tellers on either side of her. Time seemed to dilate. It was now, *right now*, that the First Law should intervene. I could feel it. Every lecture on the philosophy of time, every word I'd ever written on time travel, cried out to me at this moment. This bank *hadn't* been robbed today, certainly not by one Calvin Sutherland, native to the temporal locale of 2016.

Would she scream? Will someone else come over to ask an unrelated question, realize what's happening, and sound an alarm? Will I sneeze suddenly and shift my coat in such a way that she'll realize there's no gun there?

Her hand moved down suddenly, causing me to flinch. Christ, was she was pressing the silent alarm?

Instead, she slipped open a drawer with one hand and reached for a small paper bag with her other hand. She kept looking down, not making eye contact with me. I realized the little toe on my right foot ached as I'd been tensely holding my foot in an awkward position for a while. The teller took money out of her drawer and crammed it haphazardly into the paper bag, her hands shaking all the while.

I exhaled with relief, still in disbelief that things had even gotten this far along. I looked around anxiously at the other tellers. No one paid attention to me. They were all waiting on other customers. The teller next to me was an attractive young blonde. The guy she waited on was actually trying to chat her up. He even said at one point that "he might need a little help counting it later if she's free." I wanted to groan. Guys like me were constantly living down that crap and gnashing our teeth at every inane take it spawned in feminist philosophy.

The bag was half-full now, and I could hear the teller's short, shallow breaths. I didn't want her passing out or hyperventilating on me.

"That's good," I said, which must have sounded chilling to the teller. She slid the bag toward me, spilling a couple bills as she did. I grabbed the bag quickly and crumpled it up at my side, not wanting anyone to see it. Her eyes were downcast, and she still seemed too afraid to look at me directly.

"I am truly sorry for this," I said, trying to match Lionel's familiar sympathetic tone. She didn't look up, but I hoped she heard me.

As I turned around, I saw an array of security guards and bank officials in my mind's eye. In reality, the only one there was the next customer in line, a woman dressed in a stylish green coat with a matching pillbox hat. She looked down at her deposit slip, reading it over to pass the time. She didn't notice me. There was nothing between the exit and me but sunlight. I walked as quickly as I dared, wondering how I could've pulled this off. I felt the paper bag full of money, a real, corporeal object in my right hand.

The sunlight seemed too bright when I first got outside. I walked down the sidewalk as quickly as I could without drawing attention to myself. I didn't dare look behind me, though I wanted to very much. It seemed like every time someone in a movie was caught robbing a place, it was because he acted suspiciously. If you look like you belong, people tend to assume that you do belong.

I rounded the next corner on my way to the shuttered jewelry store. I saw Lionel sitting on a bench. Murdoch stood behind him, watching for me. I slowed as I neared them and stopped several feet away, exchanging a glance with Lionel to make sure he was all right.

"Well?" Murdoch asked holding his hands up at his side. I lifted the bag in my right hand and opened it so Murdoch could see what was inside. His eyes widened, and he laughed in spite of himself. "I didn't think you had the stones to pull it off! Give it here."

"No."

"Aw shit," Murdoch said, rolling his eyes. "Let me guess. You want Bradshaw to start walking toward you, and when he gets a little past halfway, you're gonna toss the bag to me, right?"

He'd seen right through my plan. "I'm not just *giving* you the money."

"Says who?" he said, taking a step toward Lionel.

"If I do that, Lionel and I are both dead."

"How about I just shoot you guys right here and now and head back to 2016? What do you think this is, a negotiation? Give me that fuckin' bag." Murdoch walked over and snatched it out of my hand. Lionel stood up.

"All right you twat, you got everything you wanted and a great deal more. Cal and I are leaving."

"Correction. We're all leaving together," Murdoch said, putting his free hand inside his jacket. Lionel started to protest, but Murdoch cut him off. "Same as before. You walk a few steps ahead of us Sutherland, and don't try running off."

"Goddamn it," Lionel spat.

"Shut up," Murdoch replied, turning to me. "Get going." He was as close to killing us now as he had been back in the lab in 2016. I turned angrily on my heel and started walking. At the corner, I couldn't help looking to my left, in the direction of Beiter and Wojcik Savings. As I feared, there were two black and white police patrol cars in front of the bank, and a small crowd had gathered. I lowered my head and turned in the opposite direction. As I did so, another patrol car rolled past us on the street but didn't slow down. I glanced back and saw Lionel and Murdoch both look toward the bank. Murdoch smiled, clearly enjoying our predicament. He was also looking around suspiciously, taking careful note of the buildings and businesses that we passed.

Suddenly it occurred to me where we were going. I'd already pulled off one daring daylight bank robbery. Murdoch was looking around for another place to rob. He was probably going to have Lionel do it this time. The police, after all, were already occupied investigating the robbery at Beiter and Wojcik, so it would take them longer to respond to another robbery elsewhere. It was a diversion. Just like the fire alarm he pulled at Bruhl and Anderson in 1990. What's more, no one would be on the lookout for a white-haired Englishman. I looked back at Lionel to make sure he was okay. He gave me a despondent shrug. As I turned back around, I bumped into someone.

"Sorry," I said instinctively before noticing it was a police officer. Another taller police officer moved out from behind the first one and stood just to my left. I froze for a moment and then put my head down to keep moving.

"Wait a minute, buddy," I heard a gruff voice say. My heart sank.

"Sorry again about that, officer," I said, trying to sound sheepish. "I guess I just wasn't watching where I was going." The taller officer fixed me with a skeptical look and leaned in to say something to his partner. I thought I heard the words 'description' and 'jacket.' Out of the corner of my eye, I could see Murdoch and Lionel standing about ten yards behind. The police hadn't noticed them. Murdoch frowned and slowly shook his head 'no.' I tried walking away as if I didn't hear the officer.

"What're you, deaf? Stay put," he said, this time moving in front of me. "Where are you going?"

"Where am I going? Nowhere special," I said, trying to sound like Gene Wilder in *Blazing Saddles*.

"Nowhere special," the first patrol officer said with a mocking laugh. "That's swell. What's your name?"

"My name?" I hesitated, stupidly trying to think of a character from a movie that hadn't been released yet. "It's, uh, Michael Corleo—"

"Where you been for the last ten or fifteen minutes?" the tall officer asked.

"Just walking around." I couldn't get a good look at Murdoch and Lionel. Turning my head would've been too obvious, and I didn't want Lionel caught up in what was happening.

"Uh huh. You stop anywhere?"

"No, not really. Just a little window shopping," I tried to say brightly. The police officers each looked at one another.

"You happen to stop by any banks?" the officer said. The word 'bank' confirmed my worst fears.

"No," I said, trying to sound offended.

"Beiter and Wojcik Savings. You do a little window shopping in there?"

"I don't think you *can* window shop at a bank." This was an awful turn of events. Bumping into these two police officers was no mere coincidence. It was the First Law. There was no way I could travel back to 1959 and just get away with robbing a bank. Then things got even worse.

"All right, let's see some identification," the taller officer said. Naturally, I'd left it behind in 2016.

"I'm afraid I don't have it on me," I said downcast.

"Didn't think so. All right, get up against—"

"Look, I didn't rob that bank!" I shouted. I couldn't see for sure, but I sensed that Murdoch had taken a step closer to me.

"Who said anything about robbing a bank?" the first officer said with a knowing smile.

"See that guy there," I said, pointing to Murdoch. His eyes widened with alarm. "*He* made me do it. Why don't you ask him about it?"

The officer considered Murdoch for a moment and then turned back to me. "This guy over here made you do it, huh?"

"He's got a gun. He threatened to kill…" I was about to say 'Lionel,' but stopped, figuring it would be best to keep Lionel out of this as long as I could. "He threatened to kill me if I didn't do it." Maybe this was the way out. No way that Murdoch, even here in the past, would just shoot us in front of two police officers. He may have had a TRI belt and could simply escape back to the present, but Murdoch wasn't a time traveler. He wouldn't be thinking like one. He'd be thinking like a seasoned crook confronted by the police.

Murdoch walked over and scowled at me. "Who the hell are you talkin' to, man? I ain't never seen you before in my life."

"But it was him, I'm telling you," I repeated. I thought I saw Murdoch hide a smile.

"All right, enough of this garbage. Get up against the wall," the first officer said, putting his hand on my back.

I braced myself against his push for a moment. "Look in that bag he's got. The money from the bank is in there. Take a look inside!" I felt the officer hesitate and consider this. Murdoch seemed ready for it. He took a step back and pulled the bag away from us.

"Hey, this is medicine for my kid's fever. It's none of your business. You oughta lock this fruitcake up, officer."

"You son of a bitch!" I yelled at him. "Look in the bag!"

"We can't do that," the officer said. "It's private property, and we've got no probable cause. He doesn't fit the description of any bank robber. Whereas you, my friend, fit that description to a tee. Now get up against that wall." He shoved me hard against the brick wall, next to the entrance to a small diner. "You can go, if you want," I heard him say to Murdoch.

"No harm done, officer," Murdoch said. He leaned in close to me and winked. "There oughta be a law against guys like you." Then he walked away, looking like he didn't have a care in the world.

The officer holding me turned to his partner. "Go inside the diner and call it in. Try and get a black and white to take us over to the bank. We'll see if anyone there recognizes this bird."

"Right," the taller officer said, going inside the diner. I was pinned to the wall pretty good and couldn't move. I was trapped. Worse still, Murdoch had gotten away. He'd probably try to commit some other crime, beat a retreat back to the present, and we'd never see him again. In addition, God knows who he would tell about the time machine. How had everything gone so wrong?

I felt the officer patting me down. He certainly wasn't taking it easy. I'd probably have a few bruises once I got back to…shit! It wouldn't be the present and 2016. At least not yet. I'd probably rot away in a jail cell for decades until 2016 came around of its own accord.

Suddenly I felt the officer pull away from me.

"Hey goddammit, what the hell are you…" he started to say, and then he groaned. I turned around and saw Lionel holding the officer's baton, about to hit him again. It landed with a dull thwack at the base of the officer's skull, and the officer slumped to the ground.

"I'm terribly sorry about this," Lionel was saying to the unconscious officer, "but I'm afraid you had hold of the wrong end of the stick."

"Lionel!" I exclaimed.

"Lucky thing for us you ran into these two police officers," he said.

"Not the description I would've opted for."

"Oh, I dunno. It got us free of our friend, didn't it?" I wanted to laugh. It seemed like such a long time since Lionel and I had a light moment.

"I'm afraid I was too busy getting arrested just now to think it through."

"You know where he's going to end up, right?"

"The Towne Theater," I said after a deep breath.

"Parkside Drive is just another block down and then to the right. If we're correct about all this, he'll lead you straight there."

"Look out!" I yelled. Inside the diner, the other officer saw Lionel and me standing over his unconscious partner. He rushed for the door as I made a move to run. Lionel casually glanced at the baton and wedged it into the door handles, barring the doors shut.

"Good thinking, Lionel."

He turned to me with a grave expression. "It's time to finish this, Cal."

"Yeah."

"I'm going back for the TRI belts," Lionel said. "They should still be in the alley. I'll hustle over to the theater as soon as I get them."

"Are you sure this is going to work, Lionel?"

He smiled. "Of course I am, old man. So are you." He slapped me on the shoulder. "Now go get that bastard."

Lionel crossed the street and quickly walked back toward the alley where Murdoch had made us part with our TRI belts. Without meaning to, a picture of Laura rose up in my consciousness. It was just a random image of her sitting in a living room chair in 1992, reading a book and absentmindedly running her hand through her hair. As the image faded, I took off after Nick Murdoch.

CHAPTER 22

I WALKED QUICKLY, wanting to get closer to Nick Murdoch before letting him know I was behind him. There were a number of people on the sidewalk, and I worried he might take a shot at me and accidentally hit one of them.

He was about twenty yards ahead of me, but I could see him holding the bag of money close to his waist as if he was afraid someone might take it from him. In his mind, he probably felt the money was his fair and square, as though he'd withdrawn it from a personal checking account. It must have been how he slept at night following the bank robbery in 1990.

Murdoch came to an intersection where he had to stop alongside the other pedestrians and wait for the traffic to clear. At a causal glance, he looked the same as everyone else in 1959—as if he actually belonged here. As he turned to look up the street at the passing traffic, I saw the side of his face and one of the narrow eyes I'd come to know so well.

"Nick Murdoch!" I yelled. Several heads turned to look back, but I only noticed him. I stopped where I was and fixed him with a glare, daring him to make the next move. His eyes widened, wondering how I'd gotten away from the police and how I came to be here. He looked all around, probably scanning for the police. He snarled and slipped his hand inside his coat. He seemed to consider me for a moment and then turned to cross the street with everyone else. I followed, quickening my pace.

As he crossed the street, he kept looking back. It told me he didn't want to take a shot at me here on the street; he would try to lead me elsewhere. That was exactly what I wanted. Murdoch broke into a trot and I followed suit. A few people stared at me as I went by. I even bumped the shoulder of a well-dressed businessman who seemed offended.

Suddenly Murdoch ran into the street. A red and white Chevy Bel Air screeched to a stop just before running him down. I went into a flat-out run, cutting between the cars that had also come to a stop.

We ran down the sidewalk on the other side of the street. I had closed the gap between us to about fifteen yards. At the next intersection, Murdoch ducked around the corner. My heart skipped a beat when I saw a street sign that read Parkside Drive. I slowed at the corner, carefully peeking around the edge of the building to make sure Murdoch wasn't waiting to ambush me. I took off after him again. This was a side street, so there were very few cars and no pedestrians. Murdoch crossed Parkside Drive and I followed. He looked back at me quickly and ran toward a building. I didn't need to read the sign on the front of the building to know where we were.

The Towne Theater.

I sprinted across the street, reaching the entrance just as the door Murdoch entered swung shut. The lobby was cold and deserted. All the lights were off, but I could see a vacant coat check window to my right. There were three sets of double doors leading into the theater, with a staircase off to the left that led to the balcony. I walked to the set of doors on the far left and opened them cautiously. As I entered the theater, I accidentally bumped into a man pointing a camera toward the stage. He gave me a cross look, but I was too preoccupied to apologize. Someone from the stage called out to him to get plenty of candid photos for the program, and they would take the posed shots of the cast later on.

The theater itself was small but well-adorned, with dark wood molding and maroon seats whose upholstery was in good shape. There were about half a dozen people on the stage. Two men were unpacking some theater lights. Pieces of a used set stood behind them. It looked to be part of a kitchen with a farmhouse style window that looked out onto a matte painting of a setting sun.

Nick Murdoch was in the far aisle about forty feet away with the theater seats between us. He still held the bag of money at his side as he saw me. I glanced at the stage, vaguely aware of the man with the camera snapping pictures from the rear of the theater. None of the stage crew noticed us yet. Murdoch looked at me and lunged toward the stage. I moved in the same direction, just as he stopped. Then he made a move away from the stage, back toward the exit. I copied him again just as he stopped. It felt like the game where two children are chasing each other around the dining room table. He faked toward the exit again and then cut back toward the stage. I was wearing loafers and slipped as I moved to follow him.

"Hey, what're you guys doin' in here?" a male voice called out from the stage. As Murdoch got about five rows from the front of the theater, he drew his gun. A worried cry went up among the people on the stage. One of the men dropped a light while he and two others ran off just as Murdoch got onto the stage himself.

I ran toward the stage and jumped onto it, not even noticing the stairs next to me. I felt oddly protective of the people here in 1959. They reminded me of where I was, *when* I was.

Murdoch pointed his gun at me when I got to my feet. Seeing that he was focused on me, a man and woman standing next to the partial set slowly backed up until they were off-stage and could run away if need be. Unfortunately, one woman remained near me on the left side of the stage, opposite Murdoch. She seemed too petrified to move. She had chestnut-colored hair and looked to be in her early 30's. She didn't look anything like Laura, but reminded me of her anyway. I edged over toward her.

Open boxes and tools littered the stage. Someone had wheeled out a wooden ladder that stood a few feet behind Murdoch. The curtain was pulled all the way back so that I could see the ropes and pulleys used to raise and lower the lights and overhead props. The rope connected to one of the lighting rigs had been detached from its stay on the far side of the stage.

This was the right place. But how? *How* does it happen?

The woman next to me let out a small shriek. I moved so that I was standing partially in front of her. I took a step or two back, hoping to move her off the stage and out of danger.

"It ends here," I said.

"You got that right, Sutherland."

I looked out toward the seats. Some of the people that had been on the stage made their way to the rear of the theater and were nervously looking on. They stood near the exits in case they had to make a quick escape. Murdoch turned his gun toward them, drawing gasps. I took a step toward him. "No, don't!" I yelled reflexively. He immediately turned back to me. I could hear the woman next to me whimpering. "You can't shoot them," I said. He smiled, daring me to do something to stop him. "Remember where we are, Murdoch! You can't shoot them because you *didn't* shoot them. None of them die here."

"Shut up!" he yelled.

"Besides, the police are on their way. Too many people saw us running down the street. You can't get away this time."

"*I* can't get away?" he said with a laugh. With his other hand, he pulled his coat back. I saw the TRI attached to his belt. "I can get away any time I want to. You're the one who's gonna be stuck here trying to explain everything. You just tell the police all the same shit you've been telling me. Maybe they'll go for it. You can tell the cops how all these people I can't kill suddenly turned up shot." He pointed the gun toward the rear of the theater.

Maybe he actually *could* do it. I wasn't supposed to be able to rob a bank, but I had walked in and took the money as though I'd never left 2016. This theater was supposed to be the place where it ended. Lionel and I had been *sure* of that. Even the two people that inadvertently led us here were standing in the back of the theater right now.

Suddenly one of the rear doors burst open. Murdoch and I both jumped. It was Lionel. He had our TRI belts looped around his left arm. He looked back and forth between Murdoch and me, not knowing what to do next.

"You still think *all* of the people back there are safe, Sutherland?" Murdoch said. He was right. Like me, Lionel wasn't of this time. I was about to call out to Lionel, to tell him to run, to active the TRI and get the hell back to the present. As I turned back to Murdoch, I caught a glimpse of the rope dangling behind him on the far side of the stage.

In an instant, everything made sense.

"Shoot me!" I yelled fiercely, my voice seeming to come from somewhere else. Murdoch started at this as he turned back to me. To my own surprise, I was smiling. "Go on, do it! What have you got to lose?"

He narrowed his eyes, as if trying to figure something out. He moved a step back, brushing up against the free rope that was attached to the lighting rig. "C'mon Murdoch, where are your balls now? Were you pissing your pants like this when you killed Laura?" He glared at me, adjusting his grip on the gun.

My faith in the First Law wavered, but only for an instant.

"Do it, you son of a bitch!"

Murdoch locked his arm straight, and he leveled the gun at me. The world seemed to slow down. I saw the gun pointed at me and the front of Murdoch's hand flex as he was about to squeeze the trigger. It felt like I had hours to react. I even wondered whether I was about to die, and then had a moment to realize I wouldn't.

I ducked to my left, bumping into the frightened woman. At the same instant, a loud bang echoed throughout the theater. For a second, I felt enveloped within the sound of that gunshot. I recovered enough to realize the shot missed both of us, just as an ungodly rolling sound, like a mechanical conveyor going off track, came to life around us.

Someone at the back of the theater shrieked. Next to me, I saw the rope that held the lighting rig in place severed in two by Murdoch's shot. The top end raced rapidly upward.

As the expression on Murdoch's face dissolved from anger into confusion, the lighting rig rained down on him, crumbling him to the floor in an unnatural way. It bent him sideways with one leg in front and another in back, while the sound of breaking glass and twisting metal reverberated for what seemed like a long time.

Hours seemed to pass. I leaned back on a table next to me, and exhaled audibly. Several people, including Lionel, ran toward the stage, but I kept looking at Murdoch's broken body lying under the lighting rig. He was covered in dust and broken glass. The gun had dropped from his hand and landed several feet away.

"Cal! Are you all right?" Lionel said when he reached me. I gave a tired smile and nodded. Three men lifted the lighting rig off Murdoch. They bent down to examine him more closely, but they needn't have bothered. I knew Murdoch was dead without having to take a closer look.

The woman who'd been next to me when the shot was fired now openly wept. A couple of the others patted her shoulder and tried to comfort her. As I edged between them, they eyed me warily. The woman seemed like a nice person; ordinary, in the way most of us are. She wasn't the type to ever imagine a bullet would one day pass only a few feet from her. I looked her in the eyes and smiled gently.

"Despite what just happened, you and I were never truly in any danger. I hope one day you'll believe that." She gave me a confused look but seemed to think that I meant well. I moved back to where Lionel stood nearby.

"Bloody close call," Lionel said. "At least it looked that way from the rear."

"Felt that way. You know..." I was cut off by a series of gasps behind me. The crying woman had suddenly fainted. Her female companions eased her down to the ground. The men who had been examining Murdoch rushed over to her. One of the men bumped into me as he rushed by and uttered a vague apology. He had a crew cut and a red and black checkered jacket like Marlon Brando had worn in *On The Waterfront*. As all this was happening, I could hear sirens outside. They seemed to be getting closer to the theater.

"We have to go, Cal," Lionel said. While everyone tended to the woman, Lionel and I went to Murdoch's body. His head was turned to the rear of the stage, and his narrow eyes were fully black and opened wide in an empty stare. Blood trickled from his ears, and most of the color had already drained from his face. He still clutched the bag of money in his left hand.

Lionel and I stood on opposite sides of Murdoch. As I lifted his torso up to remove his wallet, Lionel began undoing his belt and TRI.

"What about the gun?" I asked.

"Best to leave it. It won't show up in any of the records of this time."

As Lionel finished, one of the men on the stage crew called out to us. "Hey, what're you guys doin' there?" he said, coming over to us. Neither of us looked up from what we were doing.

"Oh, he won't object," Lionel said casually.

"You can't go robbin' a guy just 'cause he's dead," the man said.

Lionel stood up. "If I were robbing him, I'd have helped myself to what's in that brown bag." The man paused to consider this. As he did, Lionel and I walked toward the rear of the stage without turning around. We found a set of stairs that led down into a dimly lit corridor. As we started down the stairs, we heard someone onstage exclaim, "Oh my God, this bag's full of money!" Lionel and I both laughed at this.

I opened a wooden door at the end of the corridor. It led to a deserted alley behind the theater. When we got outside, Lionel said, "It's times like this I hate having to keep our endeavors such a closely guarded secret." I didn't say anything. The sky was still bright and cloudless, and I could hear more sirens approaching. "I know that today and the last couple months have been... rather eventful," he continued.

"You could say that."

"You've had rather a lot to deal with, Cal. And if I may say so, you've borne it all exceedingly well."

Counting the time I'd spent in 1992, I'd lived the equivalent of two and a half months in the last few weeks. It was difficult to process. Maybe one never gets fully used to time travel. I'd been living amid different strands of time that ended as abruptly as they began. This—1959 and this theater where Murdoch died—would be another one of those strands. They formed a lopsided, cockeyed whole, but it was me through and through. It felt as though I was seeing myself reflected in different ponds, and I still wasn't sure which reflection I'd inhabit going forward.

Now, I just wanted to return to 2016. I'd done enough for a while. All I wanted was to sit by my living room window and have a toke while the sun went down and my apartment grew dark. I needed to have a good look at myself, letting time rush by while I sat still. Just for a moment.

"Cal?" Lionel said.

"Sorry, Lionel. Lost in thought."

"Yes. You're wont to do that." Lionel smiled. "When you do reflect on the last several weeks, I just hope you won't regret walking into that burning house back in September."

"That's the one thing I don't regret, Lionel." I held out my hand, and Lionel clasped it in both of his. We looked at each other seriously for a moment, both replaying memories from the last few weeks. Then Lionel let go of my hand and gave me one of the TRI belts.

"That was Murdoch's father who bumped into you on the stage, you know," he said as I looped the belt around my waist."

"Yeah. I recognized him."

"He and his wife, well, future wife, were standing next to me in the back of the theater while the two of you were on stage."

"I suppose that's one of the more unusual dramas anyone will ever witness," I said.

Lionel smiled. "After you, old man."

As I pressed the button on my belt and the familiar sensation began to envelop me, I noticed the rear door of the theater drawing open. Nineteen fifty-nine faded before I could see who emerged.

Chapter 23

Friday December 16, 2016

I BROUGHT MY prepared remarks at our fall semester colloquium to a close and opened the floor to questions. This was usually the time to get nervous. Outside of politics, you'd be hard pressed to find anyone as close-minded as an academic listening to a colleague deliver a paper at a colloquium. As expected, my nemesis Bruce Hardwick raised his hand as soon as I'd finished. He didn't even wait for me to call on him before starting in.

"You see, imagining time travelers in ethical thought experiments and such doesn't really get us anything, Cal," he lectured me condescendingly. "If anything, it makes matters worse. Your time traveler has a free hand in muddying the waters of history. Consider if a white supremacist got hold of your time machine and took some detailed schematics of an atomic device with him to 1939. Suddenly, we're all wearing swastikas and replacing the pictures of George Washington in grammar school classrooms with Adolf Hitler. There's nothing ethical about that. And for what? Just to see what would happen? It's like giving someone a free hand with gene manipulation. It's a Pandora's box only a craven fool would choose to open."

In the third row of seats in Noll Hall's small auditorium Lionel—the proverbial 'craven fool'—rolled his eyes.

"As I demonstrated at some length, Bruce, one doesn't have an utterly free hand when it comes to the past. The First Law has seen to it that the past can't be changed. About the most your white supremacist could accomplish would be having Hitler autograph a copy of *Mein Kampf*." No one seemed to get the Indiana Jones reference.

"Oh, well that's pretty arbitrary," Hardwick said. "You can't just draw a line there as a matter of convenience."

"I'm not drawing any lines. The Allies won the war. The Axis powers lost. It's merely the way things happened. No one can go back and change things, because no one *did* go back and change things. This gets to my main point. History, quite unlike things we can do in the present, is perfectly safe. It can't be changed.

"Nonetheless, ethical questions abound. Take the issue of killing versus letting die. Perhaps our time traveler goes back in time and becomes part of someone's life for a while, someone for whom," I paused a moment to gather myself. "Someone for whom he begins to care very deeply. Let's say this person is murdered, just a few months after our time traveler departs again for the present. He would have to allow her to quote-unquote die again. However, is that truly an instance of 'letting die?' This death occurred in our time traveler's relative past, long before he even became aware of it." I remembered the time Laura asked me to explain my philosophical research. I wondered how she would feel about me talking this way. "To our time traveler, it would certainly feel like *letting* her die. He'd feel her loss. Regret and self-loathing seldom fall within the boundaries of logic."

I suppose I had healed a bit during the last month. Time has a way of doing that to people. I still thought about Laura now and then. Not telling her the full truth about her fate still troubled me. Telling her wouldn't have changed anything. Yet it still felt like I owed her that much.

Then Margo raised her hand. "Well first off, Cal, I think it's pretty remarkable that you've written such a thoughtful paper in such a short time, especially with everything you've been through these last several weeks." This drew a couple knowing chuckles from the audience, including a few of my students who attended.

"To be fair, I had a great deal of this paper outlined *before* I went on the lam," I said, drawing more laughter. That was only partially true.

Shortly after we'd returned from 1959, I traveled back to 1940 and spent three weeks there writing this paper. Only 15 minutes passed in 2016 during my time away. I'd intended to write it entirely on a manual typewriter. It seemed so quaint and wonderful at first. If nothing else, I loved the sound of the typewriter. Nevertheless, it proved too cumbersome. Fortunately, I'd snuck my laptop along with me. There was no Internet in 1940, so I had no distractions. There was nothing to do but write and enjoy the past. That's what I'd done, just as I'd always intended to.

"Since this is the second of your papers that references this First Law of Time Travel," she said, "I have to ask, how do you justify your confidence in it? In fact, where is the evidence that the First Law is even manifest to begin with? I mean, your time traveler is still doing rather a lot while he's back in time, apparently shackled by this First Law."

If only she knew. "That's a good point, Margo."

"I know. That's why I made it," she said, making it sound playful and funny.

"Maybe I can put it this way. Our time traveler *could* do things that were already part of the narrative of history. For example, you could, in a sense, save someone's life. I could pull someone out of the way at the last second just before a grand piano came crashing down on top of him like in a cartoon. Even though the person I pulled out of the way would probably feel gratitude, in another way I wouldn't have truly prevented that person's death. He was never going to die on that occasion. It just so happens that our time traveler was the one to save him. That isn't changing anything. Not if it had happened that way to begin with. The only 'change' is that our time traveler learned that he was the one who pushed this person out of the way.

"The First Law is a law of logic that happens to govern time travel, just as the Square of Opposition governs logical relationships among categorical propositions." I paused before adding, "You could even take someone from the present and lead them to their death in the past, provided that was the way the narrative had unfolded in the first place." I saw Lionel smiling knowingly.

This was how we'd gotten the better of Nick Murdoch in 1959.

Our original plan had been to ensure that he was arrested for murdering Steve Millard. Once he was behind bars, we could see that Murdoch was also tried for his other crimes for which we had abundant evidence. In the process of doing some further research into Murdoch's shady background, we uncovered a story about his parents. They had once been interviewed for a newspaper article. The article was about a bizarre accident that occurred at a theater where they worked part-time. Once we saw the two photos taken around the time of the accident, the latter of which showed Murdoch and I at the theater in 1959, our plan to inform the police was moot.

Murdoch and I were destined to travel back in time, but we still had no idea when this would happen. For all we knew, this trip back in time wouldn't occur for another six months.

Even when Murdoch suddenly appeared at my office, I still didn't know if that would be the day we traveled back in time together. Photos or not, there was a great deal we didn't know about the events of this trip to 1959. We certainly didn't know about any nearby bank robbery. Even worse, we didn't know whether it was Murdoch or me who had been killed. Replaying the scene in my mind, it was hard to believe we'd actually pulled it off.

Other than the few weeks I spent alone in 1940 writing this paper, I hadn't traveled back in time since we'd returned from 1959 about a month ago. I still saw Lionel regularly, along with Roger and Jack. In fact, Jack sat in on a couple of my philosophy of time seminars. During one class, he asked a question that revealed a little too much about time and time travel, but I enjoyed having him there.

"Well Cal, you certainly are giving your time traveler some remarkable insight into the ways of time," Margo said.

"I don't know. You have to figure that any time traveler wouldn't be doing all this alone. He'd need a great deal of help from his fellow time travelers. And from his friends." I nodded at Lionel.

It was getting close to 5 o'clock, so Margo brought the colloquium to a close. I talked with her and some others as the audience filed out. It was a relatively new experience, but several of my colleagues seemed genuinely interested in my research. Lionel stood a few feet away, waiting for me to finish chatting before coming over.

"Very good stuff, Cal. And of course, I appreciated all the subtle references you made to our recent travels."

"Thanks for sitting through this."

"Wouldn't have missed it for the world," he said. "You, uh, haven't had any further trouble with the police have you?"

"Nah. The last I heard from them was a little over a week ago. I told them again, through my attorney, that until Murdoch was safely behind bars, they weren't seeing hide nor hair of any bank surveillance video."

"And they swallowed all that?" Lionel guffawed.

"My story about the cigarette butt outside Millard's apartment checked out, so they probably planned on questioning Murdoch about everything else once they picked him up. Now they'll never get the chance. Honestly, I don't think they ever believed me about the tape. As far as they're concerned, the matter's closed. For once in my life I'm glad to be written off as a flake."

We walked out the rear door of the auditorium. The air was chilly, but it wasn't windy. Some snow flurries had begun to fall in the fading daylight.

"Are you going away anywhere during the Christmas break?" Lionel asked me cautiously.

"Early next week, I'm going to visit my parents for a few days over the holiday. But other than that I'll be around."

"Ah," he said. We walked a little further in silence. I thought I saw him trying not to smile.

"Look, if you're waiting to ask me for help cooking your Christmas goose, you're out of luck. I'm not too good with roasted fowl."

"Oh no, it's nothing like that," he said, looking at me with a raised eyebrow. "And where do you get Christmas goose from? Not all of us Brits live in the middle of a Beatrix Potter story, you know."

I laughed. "Hams usually come precooked, I guess."

"Quite," he said. "As a matter of fact, I would like your assistance with something."

"Does it involve wearing bell bottoms?"

"Afraid not. But how do you feel about spats and bow ties?"

"I could be talked into it. Or the spats at any rate."

"Excellent," he said. "I knew you needed a bit of, shall we say, space. Otherwise I would've asked you sooner."

"I'm just glad you asked, period."

"I may have built the damn thing, Cal, but I think it's fair to say the time machine is yours as much as mine. It belongs to *us*, all four of us."

"Thank you, Lionel."

"My pleasure, old man," he said. We walked silently for a moment. I noticed how deserted and quiet the campus was on this winter afternoon. Most of the students had started leaving for Christmas break. We passed a man sitting on the steps nearby who was probably waiting for someone. It felt like we had the place all to ourselves. The past sometimes felt that way, too. After another moment, Lionel rubbed his hands together and began telling me about some inquiries he'd made into a rare type of cigarette lighter that I mentioned in passing a couple weeks ago. It was a Ronson touch tip table lighter, just like the kind Humphrey Bogart used in the *Maltese Falcon*.

I listened eagerly as Lionel told me about a factory in New Jersey, picturing the mid-1930s all the while.

§ § §

I shouldn't be here, I thought. At least, it shouldn't be me *here. Someone else maybe, but not me. And why did it have to be here, of all places? That wasn't up to me, of course. Someone else had decided that. The concrete step I sat on was very cold. It could have been a block of ice but for the fact that it wasn't wet. The building across the way was open and unlocked, but I didn't dare go in there. Part of me wanted to, just to see how close I could get my hand to the flame without getting burned. Old habits, I guess.*

Some people began filing out of the adjacent building. I got alarmed when three young people I recognized began veering towards me. Could I get up and leave without them seeing me? How would I explain things if they did see me? I pretended to adjust my hat and put my head down as though I was rubbing a sore neck.

"I know, right. He's pretty into that shit," I heard one of them say as they passed.

"It is kinda cool though. Not the tensed verbs and stuff, but the rest of it's all right. At least he's not a dick about it whenever you try to talk to him."

"Oh I know, right? One time I went in to talk with Laughlin about…" I heard the first one say as they faded into the distance without noticing me. That was close. Had they seen me, it might have given the game away.

I rubbed my hands together to warm them and checked my watch. It was about ten after five. Almost on cue, the doors to the adjacent building opened again and two men came out. They didn't appear in a hurry. I felt my heart rate increase in spite of myself. There was nothing to worry about. They wouldn't see me. The two men now

215

passed by me, about 25 feet away. I overheard the one man say something about a Christmas goose that drew a chuckle from the other man. I smiled too.

It was second time I had heard myself say this to Lionel.

I tried to recall the rest of that evening after the colloquium as I watched Lionel and me walking farther away. I had hoped that seeing myself here with Lionel a second time might bring back some memories of that day in December of 2016, but it hadn't.

Then the door to Noll Hall opened again. A lone man emerged. He was about my height, but with thick black hair and a gray coat. He never even glanced over at the steps where I was sitting. I suppose he had good reason not to worry whether anyone was following him.

When he got far enough ahead, I stood up from where I was sitting and followed him as he followed Lionel and me in the direction of Dancy Hall.

The Entropy of Knowledge
Mark Dellandre and Britton Learnard

We've all had moments when we felt like we were surrounded by idiots...Babylon Briggs feels that pain every day because his town, his planet, even his galaxy, is jam-packed with the most thick-headed simpletons imaginable. So when his home world is invaded by a group of equally clueless conquerors, it's up to Babylon to save the day. The only question:

Is he smart enough?

**The Adventures of
New World Dave**
Chris Cervini

In the spring of 1519, Hernán Cortés arrived at the shores of Mexico to conquer the Aztec Empire and claim its gold for Spain. That's what the history books tell us. But sometimes, right in the middle of the history we know, somebody goes and does something to change one important detail, and the world is never the same...

www.ingramcontent.com/pod-product-compliance
Lightning Source LLC
Chambersburg PA
CBHW071331250626
47159CB00004B/1565